THE
LAUNDRY BASKET

THE
LAUNDRY BASKET

G.M.C. LEWIS

BOOK ONE

OF THE MONKEY'S FIST

COLLECTION

Copyright © 2014 G.M.C. Lewis

The moral right of the author has been asserted.

Apart from any fair dealing for the purposes of research or private study, or criticism or review, as permitted under the Copyright, Designs and Patents Act 1988, this publication may only be reproduced, stored or transmitted, in any form or by any means, with the prior permission in writing of the publishers, or in the case of reprographic reproduction in accordance with the terms of licences issued by the Copyright Licensing Agency. Enquiries concerning reproduction outside those terms should be sent to the publishers.

Matador
9 Priory Business Park
Kibworth Beauchamp
Leicestershire LE8 0RX, UK
Tel: (+44) 116 279 2299
Fax: (+44) 116 279 2277
Email: books@troubador.co.uk
Web: www.troubador.co.uk/matador

https://twitter.com/GMCLEWIS

ISBN 978 1783064 489

British Library Cataloguing in Publication Data.
A catalogue record for this book is available from the British Library.

Typeset in Goudy Old Style by Troubador Publishing Ltd
Printed and bound in the UK by TJ International, Padstow, Cornwall

Matador is an imprint of Troubador Publishing Ltd

Dedicated to the members of the Sanford Housing Co-op

Part 1

Sock

Tem reaches over and switches off the alarm, remembering he'd set two to ensure he doesn't miss his flight. Her eyes are open and unsmiling, so he checks his argument log to try and recall the specifics: the roll of the waves under the clean hull, diving into the sharp spring sea, rowing to the beach to meet old friends, learning about lunar cycles, tides, sea floor topography, winds, currents and all the other elements that influence the ebb and flow. Then the developing argument; it starts about nothing, well the laundry to be precise, and escalates quickly through frustration and miscommunication, as it always does. They have been in love for a year and the elements of hell it has brought to them have defined their relationship and interaction, much more than the heaven.

The laundry. Who gives a fuck about the laundry! How he wishes he could pull back the dirty sheets and argue with the real monsters that lurk underneath, but the ancient email to an ex-lover that can never be unwritten, and its spawned child of impotence, will always sporadically limp and crawl between them. Her impenetrable eyes that will not see him through the intervening mist; eyes from a different time, nurtured by different experience, seeing very different perspectives on the world. His terrible silence that speaks a language to her that he doesn't understand. His demands that she make sacrifices for him as he has done for her - sacrifices that she never asked him to make in the first place. These creatures are insoluble. Best left under the sheets. Stick to the matter at hand. And so they grapple over the inane, until they are bored and full of hate. Then when one of them has walked away (her this time) they try to reconcile, because they love each other and can't bear to be apart and hurting the one that they love. But they've never been good at this; the resentment that they can ferment in each other is a truly powerful brew and every proffered touch and kiss is received coldly, each jest and injection of lightness is twisted into seriousness, and even if a continuation of the argument is averted, no healing occurs, just a mere stemming of blood. And so with the last. They break for a spell as they travel back to London on a train and a motorbike and reconvene in the stifling history of her room, where they manage to avoid hostilities, but also any affection, before dropping into sleep, exhausted, hurting and curled away from each other.

"You want us to be friends."

"I've been thinking about it more and more."

"Then let's be friends."

Silence, then:

"Fine."

He rises and drags on his clothes, hurriedly grabbing his possessions, considering brushing his teeth only momentarily, opting to get out as fast as possible before one of their resolves break and they collapse back in on themselves like an autumnal puffball. Dressed, he picks up his crash helmet, rucksack, laptop bag and jacket before leaning in to give her a kiss, almost toppling back into the bed as his load swings forward.

"Bye."

"I washed your t-shirt and socks – the t-shirt is on the upstairs landing with one of the socks and the other sock is on the rail downstairs."

He looks at her one last time, seemingly uncertain of what to make of this information.

"OK. Thanks. Bye."

He pulls the door to and moves quickly up the stairs, easily locating the plain beige t-shirt with blue trim and one grey sock with purple trim as she had explained. The sock had been bought in a pack of ten grey socks all with a differently coloured trim, to aid pairing. He moves back down the stairs, aware that she will be able to hear him moving through the quiet house on the other side of her door. He cannot see the missing sock among her clothes, on the long radiator in the corridor as he descends to the ground floor of the house. Into the kitchen: nothing but the stale smell of smoke, old fat and an abundance of crumbs. He spies a clothes horse through in the sitting room at the back of the house and, with a hint of unease (ten people live in the house and despite their relaxed attitude, he still dislikes the thought of being found unaccompanied this far off the path that leads out the front door), moves further into the house. He still can't see the sock, but looking through the back window into the rear garden, he sees clothes hanging on the washing line – did she say 'downstairs hanging in the garden'? He knew that he had begun to listen to her less attentively and a confirmatory click of this is unhelpfully triggered as he struggles to recall what has been said to him only three minutes ago.

He tries the door to the garden. Locked. He unlocks it and steps out. He has never been here before. He used to live ten doors down the street and the dimensions of the garden are not dissimilar, but the small differences of detail and appearance feel alien, like seeing a familiar face reflected in a mirror. The garden is the other end of the block to his, so the perspective he is used to has been reversed. Where is the decking he built? When did the vegetation take over? The garden feels darker, more solemn, enclosed, oppressive; each item of junk, every tool and piece of rubbish, feels like an impostor. For some reason when he walked into this garden he expected familiarity and the lack of it has created a strange inversion in his head. He looks down and sees that, along with his beige t-shirt, rucksack, laptop bag, crash helmet and jacket, he is still holding the grey sock with purple trim.

He can smell tulips.

He thinks of the plane leaving as he stands in this strangely familiar garden.

Cycling Shorts

The clock says 10.46am. The timer flips to 1 hour 00 minutes and a hint of panic becomes audible within the room. Barbara is out getting a coffee at the moment, but if she gets back and sees that the clock has cleared the hour, she will rage, no ifs, buts or maybes – there will be immediate, extravagant, wobbling rage and nobody wants that. Tanya looks across the office at Donnie. He's currently pulling his quiff so hard that his cheeks are shaking and his face appears to be on the verge of bisecting between the eyeballs and brows, which indicates that he's probably got snagged on a SPRAT or a 'Small Print Reader Anus Tight'. A SPRAT is one of those rare breeds of customer that is capable of absorbing and understanding the indecipherable jargon that is crammed into the bottom of practically every action that can be perceived as having contractual obligation between two parties, and using that information as a way of saving tiny amounts of money (compare with a SPRAY, or 'Small Print Reader Anus Yawning' who absorbs the same information, but uses it to shit all over you). This at least means that there's no immediate threat of a 'Donnie Vertical Suplex' and they have a small chance of clearing the backlog before things kick off.

Barbara is the office assistant manager and she is a monster. (Tanya has never seen the actual office manager, but she assumes that he/she is Lucifer, or someone of equivalent demonic standing.) Barbara is a huge, irrational, quick-tempered, firecracker of a woman, with a greasy flop of red curls atop her primitive-looking head. Dr Stone – swoon – would have described the head as brachycephalic and exhibiting enhanced prognathism, but then the only reason she could think of for her unbelievably handsome and foppish old physical anthropology lecturer to be anywhere near the offices of ISIS would be to conduct a study on the regression and retardation of the human mind in the contemporary work environment. The thought that her involvement in such a study would be as part of the subject group, not as part of the observers, fills her with no small amount of shame.

Still nothing from the workshop, so she flicks back over to the ever patient Mrs Andrews:

"I'm so sorry to keep you waiting Mrs Andrews."

"That's OK, my dear."

"They're very busy in the workshop today, but I know they're doing their best to have a look at your computer this morning and they promised to let me know the situation as soon as possible."

"Don't you worry my love, I can wait."

"If you like I can give you a call straight back as soon as they've given me an answer, to save you waiting."

"Oh no dear, that's what the gentleman said yesterday. I made sure to stay near the phone all day - my hearing isn't what it used to be, you see - but he didn't call back and when I tried to call back later, I kept getting cut off. I'm happy to hold if that's OK."

"Of course, that's absolutely fine Mrs Andrews and I'm very sorry again about your problems yesterday - we've been having a few technical issues with the phone lines, but hopefully they've all been sorted today. I'll put you back on hold then."

"OK, bye then."

It made her blood boil to think of Mrs Andrews waiting next to the phone all day, probably not even daring to go to the loo, in case she missed the call back from that spineless, lying git, Donnie, which obviously never came. Donnie is one of Barbara's minions. She has six of these sub-demons that make up her permanent staff; most of them have become so desensitised to their surroundings that they no longer exhibit any signs of human emotion and have a sort of glazed appearance, like giant monotonal toffee apples. But wrestling-mad,

Elvis aficionado Donnie actually seems to get some sort of perverse pleasure from working in this hellish call centre. The rest of the office is composed of what appears to be a constant flow of shell-shocked temps that desperately try to deal with the combination of mind-numbing boredom and roaring mental abuse that typify Barbara's regime. They cling to their jobs like shipwrecked mariners on an upturned hull, floating in a sea that knows only doldrums and tsunamis.

ISIS (IT Security and Insurance Solutions) is a computer insurance and claims company. If a customer has an insured computer that happens to be damaged, ISIS arrange collection of the injured unit, assess it, and then repair or, if necessary, replace with a new computer, on a 'like-for-like' basis. This 'like-for-like' phrase in the small print is crucial – ISIS buy cheap desktops, laptops and handhelds in bulk and their interpretation of 'like-for-like' is identical in terms of specification, but not necessarily build quality. So customers claiming for damage to their top-of-the-range Mac would, often as not, have their unit replaced with a top-of-the-range cheap Chinese import. The worst part of it is that ISIS are making such a considerable amount of money by selling second-hand, very expensive repaired computers, through their sister company 2PC, that the workshop pretty much writes off any nice-looking piece of hardware that comes their way, regardless of the issue. Combine this with the marathon periods customers tend to spend on hold (listening to a never-ending loop of Pachelbel, broken up by a deeply sincere, sexy female voice telling them how important their call is to ISIS) and you can pretty much guarantee that spending a day working at ISIS will lead to exposure to emotions such as simmering rage, hysterical laughter, abject despair and utter apathy. It is bathed in the light of this particular emotional spectrum that Donnie seems to shine.

The clock says 10.51am. This is the slowest that time has ever been. This is like watching paint dry, through the heightened mental acuity of a car accident. She has been temping at ISIS for almost two weeks and cannot afford to walk out of another job. The rain grows in intensity for a moment against the windowpanes that look out over the damp streets leading towards Monument, the swollen Thames and the newly completed Shard. Beyond that, the puddled, potholed streets, their gasping drains struggling to swallow London's rapid runoff, lead past Southwark Park and finally to home and sanity, where the majority of her housemates are doubtless still curled up asleep in their warm pits. She looks at her Lycra cycling shorts, still dripping on the radiator behind her workstation. They are black with an indigo stripe and have a padded cushion sewn into the lining of the crotch for extra comfort. Her desire to tear off her hideous uniform – an orange shirt with a little Egyptian-style 'ISIS' logo and a brown skirt – pull on her clammy damp cycling gear and leave is almost irresistible.

She checks her phone; still no text from Tem. Did he say he had meetings this morning? His job seems to be becoming increasingly demanding and the work trips overseas that are looming on the horizon are casting an even bigger shadow on their already troubled relationship.

The timer flips to 1 hour and 03 minutes. This is bad. The timer on the big screens monitors the average waiting time that customers who have phoned up ISIS have been kept on hold. When it reaches the 1 hour mark, one of two bad things is likely to happen: if Barbara notices, she will go apoplectic, unleashing the full force of her fury on the already beleaguered temps; if Donnie notices, he will employ his 'Vertical Suplex' move, whereby he answers and hangs up on the longest waiting clients so quickly that his fingers almost blur, until the average waiting time gets down to about twenty minutes, sowing the seeds of wrath in a block of their clients, who were doubtless already seething. Either way, when that timer hits the hour mark, people start sweating.

The clock says 10.55am. It hadn't been a particularly bad argument last night, by their standards, but there was something about Tem's reaction to her accusations that was more worrying than his anger. He just seemed to go limp, like there was no fight left in him. She'd never seen him look so tired and sad. Maybe she should text him.

"WHAT?"

"Oh hi, I've got Mrs Andrews on the line, ref: 230001476, who was hoping for an update on her damaged desktop, which –"

"MAKE?"

"It's a Dell."

"MODEL?"

"She's not sure. Her cat knocked a glass of water –"

"IT'S FUCKED."

"OK, shall I tell her that we'll be replacing –"

"NOT MY DEPARTMENT."

The line goes dead. As a temp, she's not authorised to issue replacements so, according to the company rules, she now has to wait until one of the permanent staff is free and pass the customer over to them. At that very moment she sees Donnie finish his call, check the board, check Barbara's empty desk and, without a moment's hesitation, answer and hang up on 32 callers in less than 30 seconds. He stands up and, sweeping his hair back, he cries:

"This ain't no garden party, brother; this is wrestling, where only the strongest survive. Wooooo."

She takes off her headset and nips over to his desk, putting on her best dizzy blond attitude.

"Donnie, you are so crazy!"

"That's how we roll, sweet cheeks."

"Great. Um, Donnie, I've got a massive favour to ask."

"Ask away."

"I've got this nice old lady on the line whose unit's a write off and she just needs a replacement issuing. Shouldn't take a second and I'm not authorised to do it, so I was wondering..."

"...Whether the Donster could accommodate?"

"Um, yes."

He looks her up and down in a thoroughly unambiguous manner that sets her skin crawling and then, quietly, almost whispering, as if this is a deeply intimate moment, he says:

"Put her through."

"Thanks Donnie, you're a star." She pops back to the desk, feeling the weight of his eyes on her rear.

"Mrs Andrews?"

"Hello?"

"Thanks so much for waiting. I'm afraid we're not going to be able to repair your old computer, but you'll be pleased to hear we'll be issuing you with a replacement right away. I'm going to put you through to Donnie, who is one of our team leaders, and he'll be organising your replacement for you."

"Oh thank you for all your help, Tanya dear."

"My pleasure Mrs Andrews, putting you through now..."

She sees Donnie answer the call and, without a word, he hangs up on Mrs Andrews, picks up his cigarettes and walks out of the office.

Unbelievable, you absolute complete asshole. She's about to stand up and follow Donnie out but at that moment, Barbara totters back into the office and Tanya realises her phone is ringing as the next call is being directed to her now free line.

What's left of the morning passes in further painful slow motion. She takes early lunch, resisting the urge to insult Donnie on her way out. She picks up a reduced calorie (and price) coronation chicken sandwich on brown from Sainsbury's and then sits alone in the grimy, strip-lit staff kitchen and texts Tem with a: "How are you, sorry about last night and did you pick up the waterproofs for the boat trip this weekend?" It all sounds half-hearted and insubstantial. She knows that he would have normally texted her by now.

Why couldn't they make things work? It didn't seem to matter what the problems were, it was just the intensity with which they loved and conversely hated each other that seemed to be the issue. She thinks about their first date. They'd gone to see Gogol Bordello and ended up walking through Hyde Park at 3am. At first she'd thought he was an attractive moron; good for a snog maybe, but probably not much else. She soon realised that his buffooning carapace shielded an intelligence that was warm, humorous and razor-edged. She opened up to him like she'd never opened up to anyone before and it was an intense, liberating freedom to be able to genuinely communicate with someone (not just to listen to a sensitive, articulate mind, but to feel that emotional intelligence unlocking and drawing out her own deepest thoughts and secrets).

"You want me to tell you what it signifies, Mr Temujin... what is your surname?"

"It's not important right now," said Tem, "what's of fundamental importance is the significance of the arch. Jesus Christ, tell me about the arch quick!"

"This is all pretty ancient mystical stuff though. I'm not sure if your modern brain can appreciate the wisdom I'm about to hand you."

"I can do ancient - look, I'll eat that stick," Tem proceeded to pick up a stick and begin gnawing the end of it like a dog.

"That is so strange. OK, I'll tell you. Stop eating the stick. So most of what we know of the Valdivian culture is what has been deduced from the cosmograms that they left behind. Essentially the cosmograms were the Valdivians form of writing - stone blocks, carved in various shapes with etchings on them to signify the various elements of their world, both spiritual and corporeal. The two main types of cosmogram that have been found were either square in shape or round and it is thought that square stones contained messages relating to earthly phenomena and the round ones related to the celestial or godly. Are you with me?"

Tem had slowed down a little and then grabbed her from behind, whispering in her ear:

"You are particularly attractive when you use big words."

She'd shrugged him off, continuing:

"There was also a more unusual third type of cosmogram, which was rounded on one edge and square on the other, and it was this which was thought to have signified the link between the earthly and the celestial."

"*Highway to Heaven.*"

"If you like. The significance of these ancient 'writings' was not... What is that?"

"It's the music from *Highway to Heaven*. Didn't you ever watch *Highway to Heaven?*" he said. He was turning on the spot like a rain dancing chief, humming a tune.

"Nope. Are you listening to the ancient wisdom I'm imparting?"

"Yes, the roundy, squarey stones represent a conduit between heaven and earth."

"Good boy. Now look at the Marble Arch."

He'd stopped and looked:

"Ooooh, roundy, squarey stones."

"This is why kings and generals, or scientists and explorers, would be marched through the Marble Arch or the Arc de Triomphe after some momentous triumph, because they were deemed to have bridged the gap into immortality and their achievements would echo through history forever."

"Nice. So, if I were to piggyback you under that nice little arch over there, our love for each other would piggyback its way up through the stratosphere and echo for eternity in that great pigsty among the stars?"

"What was that word you just used?"

"Ummm, piggy?" said Tem smiling.

"No, no, one of the other ones."

"You mean the sloppy one?"

"Yes, with the prefix 'our'."

"Oh, I see. Presumptuous, would you say?" he'd said, his smile fading.

"Well, this is our first date."

He'd given her a long look and then said:

"Gardener."

"What?"

"My surname is Gardener."

The jovial mask was gone. The moment was broken. The evening had still been good, but the perfection had slipped and sobering gravity was upon them.

It had been like that ever since; they'd be steaming along together, through these uniquely special moments, when all of a sudden, a seemingly innocuous element of their interaction would become highlighted and distort everything that followed. As soon as he'd started talking about love, she'd immediately tensed up. Was it some internal mechanism that was unable to separate happiness from grief, so as soon as the one showed up, the other's presence was assumed to be just around the corner? If so, why doesn't it work the other way? Her misery is not often accompanied with delight. He'd told her that he didn't think she believed her relationships could work and because of that she'd always be looking for the faults that would confirm her beliefs – it was like a self-fulfilling prophecy. She doesn't want this to be true. She does believe in their relationship. She has to. She loves him. She just needs time to change. Things are going to be different from now on.

Suddenly she needs to see him desperately – a deep physical need. She picks up her phone and calls his number – straight to answerphone, the voice warm and empty. Where is he? What's he doing? Who is he with? Why is his phone off?

She gets back to her desk early and, before she opens her line, she finds Mrs Andrew's file and calls the number. No answer. She'll try again later.

She feels the enormous presence next to her before she sees it.

"Urghhh, what is this?" She turns to see the brachycephalic head inspecting her Lycra cycling shorts on the radiator, prognathic enhancements at their inspective maximum.

"My cycling shorts – I got a bit wet on the way in this morning."

"Well kindly keep them out of sight, will you?"

"Of course, please accept my apologies."

"Don't you take that tone with me, young lady. Now, we've had some complaints this morning about people getting hung up on after waiting on hold for considerable periods of time to have their claim dealt with. This is not what I call good customer service." Barbara appears to be waiting.

"Um, no."

"Can you imagine how it will make our customers feel to spend up to an hour on hold, then finally get through to one of our service agents, only for them to be hung up on?"

"Not very pleased?"

"That's right, not very pleased. Now I know you're new and it can take a bit of getting used to the phone system, but our goal is to provide our customers with excellent service. Hanging up on them after they've been on hold for an hour is NOT VERY GOOD CUSTOMER SERVICE!"

Barbara paces slowly next to Tanya's desk, allowing her explosive outburst to resonate around the office.

"Do you know what a SMART target is?"

"Is it a Specific, Measurable, Achievable, Relevant, Time bound target?"

"Oh, who's a clever clogs? That's right: Specific - start giving our customers a decent level of service and stop hanging up on them; Measurable - by the number of customers I get screaming in my ear that they've been hung up on, i.e. zero, i.e. this needs to be; Achievable - I don't know, are you suited to working in a call centre if this is not achievable? Relevant - I'd say so, this is why we pay you; Time bound - one more complaint today and you can find yourself another job. Is that clear enough for you SMARTY pants?" Barbara holds the hand she has been using to count out her five SMART points in Tanya's face. There is a small, slightly smudged smiley face in blue biro in the centre of the sweaty palm.

"Clear."

Barbara's brachycephalic head looks out of the window at the rain for a long moment with an almost rueful expression, as if wondering what distant wrong turn in her past had led her to this regretful impasse. Then, slowly, her head turns at the exact same rate as the rest of her huge trunk and she rolls away like some fused, bloated floral robot. It's pointless trying to grass up Donnie - he brown noses better than a panto cow's back legs. She imagines them as a wrestling tag team in fluorescent pink leotards. She then tries not to.

The clock says 1.16pm. Thank God it's Friday. 4 hours and 44 minutes to go. Then it'll be out of here, home, shower, and off to see Tem's band play tonight. Tomorrow they'll be off down to Brighton for three whole days and nights with Tem and her friends sailing on The Captain's old boat and the forecast says that the rain might even stop for ten minutes at some point...

But right now she's still in ISIS and the weekend seems a million miles away. She experiences a moment of doubt; how can she possibly make it through the rest of today? She has to: she's skint, there's a recession on so she's lucky to have a job (even a really crap one) and deep down she knows if she ends up back on the dole again it's going to be even harder next time to get off it.

"WHAT?"
"Ref: 230001491."
"MAKE?"
"Mac Book Pro MD311LL/A."
"IT'S FUCKED!"
She switches back to the customer.
"Mr Kent?"
"Yes, hello."
"I'm afraid the workshop says that a repair won't be possible, but we will be able to organise a replacement unit –"
"What?"
"I'm sorry, but the workshop "
"It's got a small crack in the screen."
"Oh... Maybe they found some other faults..."
"What a joke. OK, I just want my cracked computer back. Unbelievable, I've had to take two days off work to get this picked up in the first place because you ballsed up the collection, then I wait on hold for an hour to be hung up on and when I finally manage to speak to someone you tell me you can't even fix a cracked screen. I can't believe that you have the cheek to charge people for this so-called 'service'."

"Unfortunately we won't be able to return the damaged unit, but we'll get you a like-for-like replacement –"

"What? What replacement?"

"I believe it would be very similar –"

"WHAT? This is a joke, this has to be a joke. You have to be fucking joking?"

"Mr Kent, I realise you're upset and I'm sorry to be the bearer of bad tidings, but this is, unfortunately, ISIS company policy."

"This isn't company policy, this is fucking theft! You're stealing my property! I want my computer back! Are you all mad?"

"Please, Mr Kent –"

"What's your name?"

"Tanya."

"Listen to me, Tanya. My line of work connects me with people who – how can I put this – iron out problems –"

"Tanya!" Barbara's back.

"Putting you on hold, Mr Kent. Yes, Barbara?"

"I've just had a call from a very distressed old lady called Mrs Andrews and do you know what she told me? She told me that she's been trying to call this office for two days now and when she finally managed to speak to someone, she got cut off. Can you guess who she was speaking to?"

"Mr Kent? Thanks for holding. Unfortunately I'm resigning from this shit job now, but I'm going to hand you over to my moron of a boss. Her name is Barbara Letz and she is partially responsible for developing the ISIS company policy, which is, as you've correctly guessed, criminal..."

Barbara is grabbing for Tanya's headphones, but Tanya holds her at arm's length.

"... In that they intend to sell your computer second hand once they've repaired the cracked screen and send you a replacement worth roughly one tenth the value of your old computer." Barbara goes limp. Tanya presses on. "In regard to your work connections who 'iron out problems', perhaps I can signpost you in the direction of my colleague, Donnie Rogers, who hung up on you earlier, as someone who might benefit from their attention."

"Tanya?"

"Yes, Mr Kent?"

"Good luck to you, girl."

"Thank you Mr Kent, and good luck to you too – passing you over to Barbara now."

Tanya stands and wraps the headphones around Barbara's brachycephalic head. The impact of her enhanced prognathism has been minimised by the extension of her lower jaw, which is hanging loose amidst her neck fat. Tanya now unbuttons her orange ISIS shirt with the stylised little Egyptian motif, kicks off her slip-on shoes, unzips her brown skirt, which drops to the floor with a wiggle of the hips, and elegantly steps around the moribund looking Barbara in just her bra and knickers. She takes her Lycra cycling shorts with the indigo stripe and padded cushion for extra comfort from the radiator and slides them up her long slender legs.

They are warm and dry.

Suspenders

Sammy is sitting in front of his laptop. He is wearing boxers and smoking rollies. He has three chat windows open, two of which are periodically flashing to indicate a new chat message. He is currently devoting the bulk of his divided attention to a website called 'Get Saucy', where he is chatting to 'Daddy's Girl 86', a 26-year-old, slim, very cute, Caucasian dark-haired girl from Hackney (looks a bit like Alanis Morrisette) with a father-daughter fixation:

> > Then he's going to slowly take off those naughty clothes his daughter's been wearing
> > gasps – they are nice clothes
> > Hmmm, they're naughty and you've been a naughty girl. Daddy's shaky stick is getting really big and angry isn't it? It's gone all purple in the face, it's so angry. Maybe someone needs to give it a kiss to make it feel better? Maybe if you're a good girl and make Daddy's shaky stick feel nice, Daddy will make your butterfly feel nice too

In-between whiles, Sammy is on 'Guardian Soulmates' chatting to 'Autumn Fire': a 29-year-old pale, flame-haired girl, who is seeking an articulate man with more to offer than just genitalia:

> > May I enquire as to the manner of charitable function in which you are employed?
> > Alas, my current remuneration is earned in a manner of

considerably less manifest allure than your financial exploits; I minister to those good souls of the capital on whom life's sorrows have weighed too heavily, resulting in melancholy of the spirit.

Sammy keeps flicking back to the third window, even though he knows it will flash at him should the user sign back in. He reads the short stretch of conversation from earlier today again.

> Hey hun, are you there? X
> Hello sailor, what you up to?
> Sitting here fantasising about you...
> Cheesemonger, I'm perfectly aware that you're far more likely to be sat in front of the TV watching Songs of Praise with your grandmother than floating in a bath of sexual lubricant, gently enticing your enormous member to pinnacles of delight as you imagine me loosening my oh so tight corset...
> You got me (and granny) – what are YOU up to?
> This and that... To be honest I've no idea why I bother with this nonsense at all, anyway – I'm not looking for anything casual and I've already met someone who I sort of like, but I guess I find this whole internet dating world intriguing and repelling in equal measure.
> It is a rather odd manifestation of animal reproductive behaviour.
> For sure – the hardware is so alien! A mouse is without doubt the most bizarre example of a sexual appendage, in any animal species I can think of...
> I know, it's weird isn't it – sometimes I think about how the West views the whole Muslim system of arranged marriages with such disdain, and yet we're more than happy to hand the responsibility of life partner selection to a bunch of nerds pissing about with computer logarithms! I mean, did you really put sufficient effort into your personality profile

questionnaire for you to think your computer will understand you better than the family that raised and nurtured you for 20 years? It is the strangest mechanism for connecting with potential mates, but then I guess people find a freedom on here that they wouldn't dare to entertain in reality...
> Hey, you still there?
> Oi, Fleurs?

But 'Les Fleurs Du Mal' had disappeared again. Shit, why does he have to get so randomly boring and meek and agreeable whenever he chats with her? She always responds to his chat requests but she also always manages to keep him at arm's length, maintaining an aura of mystery, whilst being perfectly frank ('I've already met someone who I sort of like' did not go unnoticed). He doesn't even know what she looks like. What a mess.

The other two chat windows are flashing:

> closes my eyes and kisses it lightly
> Now kiss it properly my girl – I want to see Daddy's shaky stick going right into your mouth
> opens my mouth a lil and sticks it in my mouth
> Hmmm, that's right my girl, just like a lollipop. Now Daddy's going to be nice and play with your butterfly. Does that feel nice?
> nods a lil

> Would it be impertinent of me to suggest a rendezvous, in order to engage in dialogue, should we be able to find a mutually convenient time and location?
> It would be fascinating to encounter in person such a seasoned traveller of the four corners; I am presently lodged in the fair borough of Southwark and would venture to advocate a meeting within its confines. Should that prove convenient to your esteemed self? Perhaps a beverage at one of its plenteous

hostelries this Sunday afternoon, if fate should decree that the emerald shores of England can retain you from your economic tendings for sufficient duration?

> Now I think it's time these two made friends. Why don't you lean back and I'll give your butterfly some kisses and then we'll see if your butterfly can help Mr Shaky Stick calm down. Mr Shaky Stick really likes Butterfly doesn't he – looks like he wants to go inside. Ooooh, it's very squeezy isn't it? Daddy's going to push it all the way in nice and slow – does that feel nice?
> it hurts

This response triggers a switch in Sammy's head. Is this just fun or is this profoundly wrong? Who exactly gets off on fantasies about incest and abuse? Alanis? Does he? His fingers tap the laptop like a guitarist warming up as he debates whether he wants to take this to its conclusion. Well, in for a penny, in for a pound:

> Oh, but you're being such a good girl for Daddy. And you're making Mr Shaky Stick feel so much better. He really loves sliding into your butterfly...
> Excuse me!!!???

Oh shit, shit, shit! Sammy's laughing as he shuts down the window he'd accidentally flicked over to, with the anti-cockcentric 'Autumn Fire'.

"Boring anyway," he mutters.

> Oh, but you're being such a good girl. And you're making Mr Shaky Stick feel so much better. He really loves your butterfly.
> nods
> Daddy's really proud of his little girl, she's been so good. Now shall we play a bouncing game? Daddy's going to roll

onto his back and his little Cutie Pie's going to climb on top, like the bouncy castle. That'll be a nice time won't it?
> nods
> Hmmm, such a good girl, up and down, up and down. Oooh, does it still hurt a bit baby?
> yes
> Well Daddy's going to go nice and slow. Oh look what Daddy's found on top of Cutie Pie's butterfly – her secret button. Shall we give that a gentle rub – does that feel nice now? Is that a bit better? Hmmm and Daddy loves his girl very much, from the tip of her nose (kisses) to the tips of her toes (kisses)
> mmm daddy
> Is my baby girl starting to feel all warm in her tummy tum? Hmmm, and all tingly in her butterfly? Mr Shaky Stick's going really fast now, isn't he? Oh baby girl, kiss Daddy now. Hmmm Daddy loves his girl
> kisses u
> Ooooh, you need to be quiet my girl, we don't want anyone to hear about our secret game. Daddy's got to cover your mouth. Ooooooh. Quiet baby, quiet
> screams into your hand
> Oh my girl, such a good girl, Daddy loves his girl, oh my baby. Now we have to remember that this is our special secret, OK?
> nods

Sammy is staring hard at the screen. He is not so foolish as to try and over extend an obvious conclusion, so he closes the chat window and sits thinking for a moment. *That was weird. That was so weird.* Sammy gives this particular exchange very low odds at ever leading to a physical encounter, but still, something happened just there that was strangely, curiously and perversely exhilarating.

Sammy's been perfecting his internet dating technique for well over a year now. He still cringes at the memory of his first pitiful forays into cyber-dating: it was hopeless, like being dropped into a foreign country without any of the necessary linguistic abilities, but, though he was not what you'd call ambitious or driven in terms of a career, he was extremely persistent when it came to pleasurable pursuits. Through painfully slow trial and error, he'd moved from site to site, perfecting his approaches and studying his marks, talking dumb to the LOLs, spouting filth to nymphos, feigning sincerity to the lovers, failing again and again, until finally a result (reached more through mutual pity than attraction), shortly followed by another, then a gap and then he snared (or was snared) by a real veteran, a teacher, a linguist. She lifted the veil, showed him how to take the initiative, how to not care, how to keep filling his leaky cup of confidence so that he might stay in control. She gave her willing and eager student the seductive power he yearned for and suddenly everything clicked.

Now the moves were no longer conscious; like a skilled chess player, he merely studied the flow, guiding it to his advantage, allowing his opponents to open up to him before scything through their defences.

He leans back and stretches, then drags his hands down his tired face – how long has he been sat like this? His back aches from T3 to T9 and he's got Cayenne eyeballs. He listens to the sounds of the house around him: occasional pans are clattering downstairs in the kitchen, accompanied by Elsa's off-key singing; next door Billy is watching *Countdown*; somewhere across the hall someone is stringing a guitar; and above him he can hear Ben and Anna chatting and occasionally bursting into fits of hysterical laughter as Tom Waits drawls along in the background. Ben is the newbie in the house and it's pretty hard not to like him: incredibly bright and witty, generous to a fault, an absolute party animal, sweet and sensitive just when you need it. Secretly, Sammy hates him a little, but never for long and certainly not when he's in the same room. Definitely hard not to like.

Another burst of hysterics from upstairs. Ben's ultimate gift to the house seems to be the effect he has had on Anna. Up until 3 months ago, when Ben moved in, she had made no attempt to disguise her morbid depression, which she indulgently dragged from room to room. Sammy was not alone in considering mechanisms for evicting her. Pedro had casually offered to hit her over the head and bury her in the garden with the same shovel. Sammy had actually felt it necessary to turn this offer down – you just never knew with Pedro.

He rolls another smoke. A new chat window has flashed up on his laptop. He views the profile: 'Chloe 69' is a fit youngish-looking MILF, who is clearly not on this website for the chat. She is definitely attractive, but there is something about her photo which makes him feel slightly uncomfortable – maybe the red suspenders?

> Hiiii how r u?? r u free this weekend for a quick fuck??
> Hi there, I'm good thanks. That could be possible – when are you available?
> Wat bout u?? R u ok anytime? How about 2night or Saturday night?
> Tonight 9-11pm, Saturday 12-3pm or 10-late
> 2night looks perfect…
> Shall I come to you? Where would you like to meet?
> I willarrage for a place… My friends out 4 the weekend so can take her pace near Clapham… so 9pm 2night? My pussy will b waiting for u
> Can't wait – my number 07*********
> Soo 2night after 9 right? How long can u stay?? Need to tell my friend? R u ok going back late night??? Or any limitations
> Should be able to get to Clapham for about 9.30 – can stay all night or head back late if you prefer
> Perfect… Heading back will be better… If it was my own apart would love to stay bak all night but… :(… Next time will arrange at in my own place.
> No problem – really looking forward to getting my tongue inside you x
> Cant wait – texting adress now. Door will be open x

Seconds later, Sammy's phone pings. Even an easy roller like this still gets his adrenaline pumping at the moment of capitulation. He looks at the profile picture again – still a hint of discomfort. Those suspenders are really standing out now. What is it with the suspenders? Suddenly he thinks of his mother.

"Woah, what's going on in there?" he mutters to himself as he starts digging around in his bag, trying not to think about what he's thinking about, but controlling this flow of neural activity is like a skydiver falling from a plane in a car and trying to push the brakes.

He wet himself during Dhuhr. All the other kids got up and started making their way to the next class whilst he remained in humble, clammy genuflection on the dark area on his prayer mat. Ten minutes later he was walking home from the Ecole Anwal in Menara district, drying fast in the early afternoon sun. It was eerily quiet: no birds, few people, no breeze, just the oppressive heat emanating from every surface. He slipped quietly into the cool of his house, just off the Rue El Jaouze, using the side door and sneaking up the back stairs. He got to the first floor landing safely unseen and was about to climb the second flight of stairs to his bedroom when he heard his mother talking oddly to Hanif, who was answering in muffled monosyllables down the corridor. He crept towards the voices. His parent's bedroom door was open and, reflected in the cracked glass of their wardrobe mirror was his mother, stood with one leg on the bedside chair, wearing black stockings and suspenders and a white bra. Hanif was on his knees, with his head nodding in between her legs. Sammy could see a splash of blue, pink and yellow in Hanif's right hand, bunched on the cool white marble – the omnipresent multi-coloured feather duster that cleans mantelpieces and tickles naughty boys.

Sammy is still looking for his pills. He is looking in places that he has already looked and he is also looking in places that they cannot feasibly be.

His parents never spoke about their separation. He remembers being questioned briefly about where he had been that afternoon, after the school informed his parents about the incident at prayer time. He recalls his mother's face as she listened to his honest but undetailed answer: serene as ever, with just that delicate finger at the corner of her mouth, her body angled slightly away from his father, towards the window, trees, sky.

They've escaped! Somehow they must've fallen out of the bag, or the wallet, or the pocket, or the whatever, and ended up somewhere that isn't in the pages of this book, which was found in the strange little space above the door, where they cannot possibly be! Not even in a world where people genuinely fall off ladders and accidentally impale themselves on cucumbers whilst they were fixing the curtains naked would the pills end up here. Not even there!

He had never been punished for wetting himself. They never punished him for anything again.

This is bad. Pedro is away till tomorrow, so there's no way he can get more from him. Kal in 6 is reputed to stock such things, but without guaranteed discretion this is unthinkable. To go without is to risk more holes in the cup of confidence and the red suspenders have raised the stakes beyond any reasonable level. He looks at his phone; he should be leaving. He should be leaving 5 minutes ago.

Suddenly his phone buzzes into life in his hand, making him jump. It's an image file from 'Chloe 69'. He opens it and looks at it, expressionless for a moment, then, finally, he sags into his chair and rolls another cigarette.

Snood

Anna had bought the guppies because she thought they looked like little gypsy dancers, with their multi-coloured velvety tails flowing out behind them: three males (which turned out to be the more attractive sex) – a marbled dark blue version, a powder blue lyre-tailed one (her favourite) and a crimson one – and a female, which looked rather bulky and drab in comparison. Now she looks through the algae green glass in disgust at the teeming mass of fish that seethes at the surface of her small aquarium. They are almost exclusively hybrids of the dark blue and crimson varieties (it turns out the lyre-tail isn't a very competitive design) at every stage of life, from the clouds of fry to the half-eaten, white-fleshed skeletons that patrol the sediment at the bottom of the tank. Weird mutant hunchbacks had started to evolve as the tiny little gene pool had become increasingly inbred and all the other fish (excepting one mud-coloured, sturdy sucker catfish, which she rarely saw) – the neon tetras, the marbled hatchet fish, the chocolate gouramies – had long since died.

Her father had given Anna the tank as a gift. He'd said it was the gift of life and that it would do her good to get closer to nature. Initially she'd been enchanted by the tiny little microcosm at the end of her bed, but slowly her sense of wonder had turned to distaste as she watched the male guppies' relentless rape of the female and the ensuing death of the other fish, which seemed unable to compete with the increasingly numerous guppies for food. No matter how much she feeds them, nothing seemed to get past the gluttonous little fish. And here is another thing to worry about: someone had told her that if you keep feeding the fish, they keep eating until they burst, so when are you meant to stop? Gradually the accumulation of shit and algal blooms had slowed the filter down and the tank had stagnated. If this is the gift of life, she can do without it.

She lifts the little feeding hatch, watching as the guppies' efforts to get in front of each other intensify. It is always at this moment that she hates them the most; her stomach coils as she watches them fight with each other to get on top. She opens the blue tub of flakes – green, red, brown and amber like fishy autumnal leaves – and drops a pinch through the feeding hatch, which is coated with a thick layer of both crusted and soggy deciduous mush, then sniffs her fingers, cringes and goes to the sink to wash her hands. By the time she returns to the tank, the flakes have disappeared, so she repeats the process, this time with even more displeasure as some of the flakes stick to her slightly damp fingers.

She makes one last check of Facebook, Hotmail and MySpace before logging off her computer, then picks up her mobile, car keys, purse and green snood (a very snug tubular scarf), locks her room and goes downstairs.

Sammy is in the kitchen smoking a cigarette and flicking disinterestedly through a magazine that has been on the kitchen table for so long, it has become attached to it.

"Hey."

"Alright," he says.

"How are you doing?"

"Alright."

"Have you seen Ben today?"

"Nope."

"It's just that he was meant to be coming with me to Oxford – I've got this bloody Speed Awareness Course and we were going to go out after..."

Sammy is looking at her with unfeigned boredom.

"What are you up to today?"

"Oh, you know...." Sammy doesn't elaborate.

"Can I pinch a rollie?" Anna doesn't actually want one, but she knows it will irritate Sammy and the miserable git deserves it.

"D'you think you'll ever buy your own?" he says, handing her the pack.

"Thanks mate."

She rolls quickly and efficiently, helps herself to Sammy's lighter, and with the cigarette hanging out of the corner of her mouth, she picks up her things and says:

"Listen, if you see Ben, can you tell him I've had to go without him, but I'll be back later – and can you tell him to turn his phone on once in a while? Oh, and thanks for the smoke. Right gotta go, see ya later, have a good one –"

"Anna."

"Yes mate?"

"My lighter."

"Whoops, sorry, here ya go." She throws it towards Sammy more forcefully than he'd expected. He fumbles and it goes clattering to the floor. "Ooh sorry, bye."

The air is cool, but the sun has momentarily shown itself through the grey and Anna is humming something as she smokes her way to her car. She is one of the few residents of the housing co-op who owns a car, as most cycle, but she wouldn't be able to get all of her juggling clubs, hula hoops, poi, stilts, etc., that she needs to run her circus skills classes in schools and festivals and so on without her Lean, Green, Juggling Machine – a new shape VW Beetle that her parents gave her. When she gets to the car, she finds her passenger side wing mirror has been fractured. No note, no apology; just another serving of anonymous London blight that has become a regular feature of her life in New Cross.

Despite the cracked wing mirror and the fact that she has to drive a considerable distance to pay penance for a speeding offence, Anna is in particularly fine spirits. She can't bring herself to be pissed off about the speeding ticket, because every time she thinks of it, the context makes her smile.

It was about a month ago: she'd been to the cinema with Ben and they were having dinner and discussing what to do next. At this point in time, Anna was getting concerned that they were going to end up caught in the friendship trap. Everything was so natural and fabulously easy between them that they had become incredibly close in a very short space of time. What if they decided that they were too important to each other to risk spoiling it? And of course, there was the unspoken rule that you should never date anyone else on the street, not that anyone paid any attention to that – the street was littered with broken hearts from previous heedless couplings.

"Let's climb Snowdon."

"Ben, Snowdon is in Wales."

"I know, it'll be great – my dad used to take me and my sister when we were kids. He'd wake us up in the middle of the night and throw us in the car and then we'd climb the Watkin path in the dark. Every twenty minutes, Dad would stop and read some of Wordsworth's poetry from *The Prelude*. I remember getting to the top on one occasion and Dad reading a passage about the mountains poking up through the clouds and it was exactly as described, with 'A hundred hills their dusky backs upheaved'. Honestly Anna, it's a magical place – you'll love it."

"Ben, it's 10pm – we'll be driving all night."

"I'll drive, I don't mind. Hey, think about it; it's Wednesday tomorrow – what better way to see in Wednesday than at the top of Snowdon?"

She couldn't really argue with that kind of weird logic, so they loaded up with snacks and hit the road.

They got to the car park at just after 3am. The night was cloudy, but their eyes adjusted to the dark quickly as they made their way along the forest track at the foot of the mountain. Anna was terrified: she was most definitely a city girl, and walking around in the middle of nowhere in the middle of the night was about the most ridiculous thing she could imagine. Anybody could be out here – what if they were set upon by some mad, axe-wielding sheep farmer? Who the hell would be there to help them out here? She kept going – she absolutely would not show Ben that she was scared. They came out of the forest and the mountain opened up before them. Ben kept stopping and reading out passages of the poem from his iPhone and Anna would stand there smiling and say "How lovely" or whatever, deep down wishing that she could get the fuck off this mountain.

As they climbed higher, they began to encounter patches of slushy ice and snow. Before long, the path was inundated with wet slipperiness. They slithered on, their trainers and jeans soaked and cold. The path became steeper – what Ben described as 'the belly and chest of the mountain' – and Anna was now seriously scared. She could no longer make out any path at all and had no idea how Ben was navigating over the snowscape. Suddenly the ground lit up around them and, upon turning, they saw the full moon finding a gap through the clouds and burnishing the snow-clad corrie with thousands of refracted stars. Neither of them spoke. All of her fears disappeared in that moment.

As quickly as it had appeared, the moon was shielded once more behind the gilt-edged cloud and then darkness returned.

By the time they reached the 'shoulder' of the mountain, the conditions were deteriorating rapidly: the wind up here was fierce, a sleety rain was beginning to fall and even Ben was finding it hard to keep to the path somewhere buried beneath the snow. He turned to her and, bringing his head close to her hoodie, said:

"Not today – we need to turn back. Getting to the top is optional; getting back down in one piece is compulsory." He looked at her face, pulled the green snood that he always wore over his head and, pulling back her hoodie, quickly pulled it over hers. It was warm and smelled of him. They turned back and no sooner were they off the shoulder than things became easier again. They slid back down the mountain, talking of dry feet, car heaters, hot baths and thick duvets as dawn announced its damp grey arrival.

When they got back to the car, she changed in the back seat while he drove. He had a spare hoodie and some tracksuit bottoms in his bag, which she put on, ditching everything else but the snood. She'd climbed back into the front seat and dozed off almost immediately. She woke as the car emerged from the Blackwall Tunnel back into South London.

"Good morning, sleepy." He looked tired, but he was smiling.

"Oh my god, we're here! You should have woken me up, I could've driven a bit."

"It's fine - you looked too cute to disturb. Ummm, I might have some bad news..."

"Oh?"

"I think I might've got flashed."

"Oh dear." Anna stared ahead for a moment, then turned in her seat to face him and slowly unzipped the front of his hoodie and slid it off her left shoulder. "Well did you, or didn't you?" she asked, looking directly at him with her head cocked to the side. He glanced over and she zipped herself back up.

"I don't know. It's hard to tell. It all happened so fast."

The car rumbled quietly off the A102 and onto the A2, towards Blackheath.

"I think I might've got flashed."

"Oh dear." Anna turned to him again and once more slowly unzipped the top, this time sliding it off her right shoulder. "Well did you, or didn't you?" This time when Ben glanced over, Anna was dragging her right index finger along her lower lip as her left hand zipped the top back up. Ben swallowed. He looked over again - Anna was looking down at his trousers with an eyebrow raised.

"Well hello."

Back at the house, they'd managed to sneak upstairs without being noticed. They opted for her place. She let him have all his clothes back - except the snood, which stayed on for the duration.

The M25 is painfully slow and by the time she gets to the M40, she's running considerably late. She laughs at the irony as she pushes the Lean, Green, Juggling Machine to 100mph to ensure she isn't late for her speed awareness course. She makes it, just, though she almost disembowels her car on the huge speed ramps that litter the centre, like great concrete tasters of what is to come.

The course is run by a tall, clean-shaven, grey-haired man, clad in tweed. He looks and behaves more like an ex-policeman than any other ex-policeman she has ever encountered. The course facilitator is severe with attendees on arrival, but once he has laid down the ground rules and established his natural authority over each of them, he allows them to see his gentler, more humorous side. The message is simple: 'Play by my rules and this whole experience needn't be too painful – you might even learn something – but woe betide the guilty speeder who attempts to ruin this experience for the rest of the class. Justice will be swift for anyone who does not follow the rules; their card will be marked with non-attendance, they will lose the money they spent on coming to the course, they will gain the points they had hoped to divert from their license and this whole journey will have been for nothing.'

She looks around the room. Apart from a couple of boy racers, the majority of people on the course appear to be pensioners and they look either intimidated, entertained or bored. She wonders whether the high percentage of older people is due to a slowing down in reaction time to the big yellow boxes by the side of the road, or if there is a secret sect of pensioner petrol heads tearing up the highways and byways, in a race against time to get their bucket lists ticked.

The old man next to her is awkwardly hobbling about around his all-in-one desk chair, looking at the floor and muttering.

"Have you lost something?" she says. The old man doesn't respond to her, but keeps looking and muttering.

"Excuse me, have you lost something?" she repeats a little louder.

"Oh hello, yes, my hearing aid – I can't find my hearing aid," he shouts back at her. She stands up and helps with the search, but there is clearly nothing to be seen on the floor in his vicinity.

"I'm sorry, I don't think it's here," she says.

"I must've left it in the car," he shouts, "thanks for your help, anyway."

Mr Tweed begins to deliver his tedious wealth of knowledge,

warming the class up with mortality rates in car accidents at different speeds, then tests their sense of injustice by moving on to the rise of the speed camera. He pauses once in a while to ask questions that no-one will know the answer to, or, in all likelihood, will remember once their penance has been served.

"How many speed cameras are there in the Thames Valley area?"

"Where do most car accidents happen?"

As is the way in such situations, a few participants are eager to please, enthusiastically answering, and then offering enlightened yips of surprise when Mr Tweed supplies the correct answer. Some even manage to dredge up a supplementary question to drag out the moment.

With the arrival of the multiple choice question slides and informative graphs, it becomes apparent that her desk neighbour, whose name is Ted, is not only aurally challenged, but also visually impaired to boot. Anna does her best to relay the questions and information on the screen to Ted by bellowing them into his ear. Ted periodically grunts his appreciation and writes down notes that seem to have no bearing on what she is saying – it seems more like a shopping list: milk, eggs, oil...

Half an hour in, the class is divided into groups in order to discuss reasons why people might 'turn to speed'. Mr Tweed is attending to a group principally composed of eager beavers at the far end of the room when the classroom door opens and a young suited woman enters and, seeing a spare chair, sits down with Anna's group of three.

"Hi guys, I'm Grace," she says, interrupting a rounded woman called Beryl, who had been allowed to warble on about the state of the canal towpaths in Oxford because Anna didn't care and Ted couldn't hear. "Sorry I'm late," whispers Grace conspiratorially to the group as she hangs her coat onto her chair, then, seemingly identifying Anna as an ally in the group, says to her, "what have I missed?"

"Well," says Anna, "the man in tweed has asked us to discuss the reasons why people might 'turn to speed', as in drive rapidly, so Beryl here was just telling us about how, with all the rain that we've been having, St Edmunds towpath has got awfully mucky."

Grace nods her head and says, "I see."

"Apparently it's got so bad," continues Anna, "that you can't walk along there unless you wear some stout walking boots or wellies – isn't that right, Beryl?"

"What's going on?" says Ted.

"That's right," says Beryl.

"We were just talking about canal towpaths and why people drive too fast, Ted," Anna bellows in Ted's ear.

"Going too bloody fast," says Ted and chuckles.

"That's right," says Anna, "that's right."

Grace smiles sympathetically, then says:

"Well I know why I 'turned to speed' – because it's bloody great fun! I'm sure there's plenty of people who'll say they were late for work, or didn't realise that the speed limit had changed, but deep down we all love to press that accelerator harder than we should, to feel the thrill of defiance pushing us back in our seats. In these small ways, people are able to cope with the mundanity of their ordered existences."

"I'm Anna," says Anna, holding out her hand, "it's nice to meet you, Grace."

At that moment, Mr Tweed walks past their group and does a quick double take when he sees Grace. A look of intense irritation sweeps across his face and, moving himself directly in front of Grace, he says aggressively:

"How did you get in?"

"Hi", says Grace smiling sweetly, "I'm ever so sorry I was a little late – the traffic was terrible – but the door was open, so I just came and joined in. I hope I haven't missed anything too important –"

"The door was not open – how did you get in?" Mr Tweed remains immoveable as old cobblestones.

"Oh, someone was coming out as I came in. I didn't realise I couldn't enter. I'm very sorry I was late – I came all the way from London –"

"Get out," says Tweed.

"But I've said I'm sorry. The traffic was terrible. It wasn't my fault –"

"Get out of my class," he says again, pointing at the door.

"Please, if I don't do this course, I'll lose my job," says Grace, making a last-ditch plea for mercy.

"You can come back and do the course again when you've learned the value of punctuality. Now, get out."

"Very well." Grace's demeanour seems to change and now, in a voice devoid of emotion, she says, "May I have your name?"

"Erwyn Jones," says Tweed, still pointing at the door. Without another word, Grace picks up her bag and takes her coat from her chair. Giving Anna a little wave goodbye, she walks out.

"Some people," says Tweed, shaking his head and still looking mean. He then smiles and says, "OK, I'd like a volunteer from each group to come up and feedback your answers to the class."

Anna looks out of the window at the grey afternoon, listening distractedly to Beryl attempting to communicate with Ted, and sees Grace walking back to her car – an olive green vintage sports car – waving one arm angrily, the other holding a mobile to her ear. What a shame.

Finally, the course finishes. It is getting dark and a steady deluge of rain is pouring down outside. Anna watches bemused as sensorily challenged Ted locates his vehicle, gets in and drives off; no doubt to go shopping. She gets in her car and checks her phone – still nothing from Ben. She calls his number – straight to answer. "Hello gorgeous, well, that was absolutely mind-numbing – you owe me big time Mister, I shall expect recompense for my 4 hours of utter boredom in the format of you buying me an unnecessarily expensive dinner, then taking me to see some ballet, or other visual arts I would otherwise not ordinarily be watching, then I want my back scrubbing in the bath, followed by a full body massage and then, and then.... and then I want snood time. Hmmm, I've missed you today. Where are you? Turn your phone on. I'm extremely annoyed."

The rain continues to fall all the way back to London and then, as per usual, the traffic slows to a crawl on the M25 – an accident ahead.

The signs are directing all traffic onto the hard shoulder. The jostling for position begins: indicators on, looking for gaps, watching the assholes racing down the emptying outside lane to get to the front. No kind souls today. She pushes; horns blare behind, she raises her finger and suddenly she thinks of the coiling mass of guppies, the frantic, single-minded primordial brew of selfish individuals; the desire to eat and eat until your stomach splits, whilst those around you starve...

The accident is a big one: she curses the rubberneckers in front of her, all the while inspecting the carnage from the corner of her eye as she creeps past. Three cars involved; it looks like a truck has ploughed through the middle. One car has come off much worse than the others; fire crews are trying to cut someone out of the crushed metal, plastic and glass. It must be a small person.

She accelerates away, glad to put the everyday horror behind her, pushing through the darkness towards home, her friends, Ben. As if summoned, her phone rings. She answers, switches it to speakerphone and balances it on her leg.

"Hello," she says.

"Anna, it's Hendo. Listen Anna, something's happened – where are you?" He sounds strange, bunged up, like he has a cold.

"I'm just driving. I'm on the M25. Where's Ben?"

"Anna, can you get off the motorway and call me back as soon as you've stopped?"

"Hendo, what's going on? Is Ben OK?"

"Just call me back, will you?"

"OK, OK, I'll call you in a minute."

The line goes dead.

Numb.

The car passes over a rough patch of tarmac, momentarily changing the sound of the car's motion before returning to smoothness. Headlight fractals appear behind in her cracked wing mirror. She pulls the snood up over her nose and breathes.

Shirt

Grace can feel her phone buzzing by her side which, in a way, is helpful, as it is distracting her from the intense pain in her head. She needs to answer it, but this clearly isn't going to be possible with two people's hands in her mouth. Why can't they just rip your teeth out and replace them with something indestructible, like Kevlar or something, save all this unnecessary pain and suffering and time? Christ, the time that gets wasted! Good idea - mental note: *Tell Jessie to have a look into the possibility of Kevlar teeth. Save some time.*

She wonders if this will be one of those times when attempts to save time end up costing you more time, which reminds her that she's got that bloody speed awareness course to attend on Monday next week - and if she doesn't go this time, that's her license gone. She remembers the moment again - that stupid old woman! Old people should have their licenses revoked as soon as they begin to show signs of creeping. It really wasn't her fault this time. She'd been stuck behind this old bat doing 25mph in a 30 zone, flashing her lights and making it patently clear that she was in a hurry and needed to get past, but the crone just kept creeping. When she finally turned off - probably to pull over and die - giving Grace the opportunity to put her foot down, there was a camera waiting for her. It clearly wasn't her fault, but nevertheless, she was the one who was going to have to pay the price. Christ, she would do anything to not have to go and listen to those patronising assholes tell her why going just five miles an hour faster than the speed limit can increase the risk of fatality for a pedestrian more than fifty per cent. Maybe if you're driving a piece-of-shit Korean import, but not for the driver of an Audi R8 Spyder that delivers over 500bhp; they should have different driving rules for people who can afford decent cars, because they perform differently.

Jesus, that's fucking painful. She's pretty sure that's way over a seven on the Wong Baker scale or whatever you call it – apparently you can measure pain, whereby two is annoying, four is uncomfortable, six is horrible, eight is dreadful and ten is agonising. Well this tops a seven, easy. Maybe it wasn't such a good idea to tell the dentist to skip the anaesthetic, but there was no way she was going to go in front of the board at ten with droopy lips and a dozy tongue. She will bear this. She will grip the armrests and list *The Simpsons* characters on the poster on the ceiling and she will bear this.

Stupid old woman! She wishes she could remember the number plate. She could trace that motor in a second, then send in the boys to put her out of her misery. Apparently the speed awareness course takes four hours. Four hours! She'll need to sedate herself before she goes in; there's no way she'll be able to keep her opinions to herself for four hours. She needs to get cameras attached to the front of the Audi (and the Jag) in case this happens again, then at least she'll have the satisfaction of knowing that the person responsible for inflicting suffering on her will be reaping tenfold the suffering in return.

Her phone's vibrating against her leg again. Damn, that hurts! This dentist was meant to be good – why the hell does he have to jam that sharp metal point into her teeth so relentlessly? Whether or not she had any dental issues before she came in here, she's going to have plenty by the time she leaves. What the hell is he doing – digging holes into her teeth so he can charge her for wedging them up with fillings? Dentists are a shadowy bunch. The whole water fluoridation controversy has got nothing to do with communists and sapping bodily fluids. Dentists simply invested heavily in an element, then claimed that adding it to water supplies would be invaluable in keeping the population's teeth healthy, when in truth it probably crumbles your gnashers over time. Then all they had to do was put their feet up and wait for the profits and patients to come pouring in, as the gullible governments jumped double-quick to obey the word of the men in white coats. Funny how people trust men in white coats slightly more than men in suits. At the end of the day, they're still only men. Until the entire upper echelons of suits and white coats have a majority population of women inside them, the developing world will continue to eat itself as it spins down ever-decreasing circles of economic chaos.

That's a nerve. What the hell is the point of nerve endings in teeth? "Aaarrgghh," she yells.

What a week! Mr Gulliver had actually called her this morning to find out what the fuck was going on. He said for him a deadline was a deadline and he was extremely uncomfortable about requests for extensions. Did she know how much money was resting on this? Course she fucking knew! There was a cool six hundred grand for her alone if she could get the papers through by the end of the week. Obviously she didn't say that: Seagull Industries, for which Mr Gulliver was the elusive CEO, were about the most ruthless property development outfit in the world. The company's main talent was winning major building contracts – most frequently from corruptible government officials who were more concerned about lining their own pockets than they were about provisioning the people they were meant to serve with safe living environments that were built to last. Once a contract had been bribed into Seagull's control, they were frequently then subcontracted out to the lowest bidder or highest briber in the locale and Seagull would then step aside, ensuring that construction would be carried out to the lowest standards for the highest possible premium. There were tenement buildings the world over waiting like steel-sprung teeth for the next minor quake or major breeze to trigger their fall.

For circumstances where bribery wasn't effective, Seagull had a well-stocked reservoir of personnel that were able to employ other methods for winning contracts for the company. These specialists were able to apply a considerable amount of leverage to remove the obstacles that inherently litter the path of the unscrupulous property developer.

It is Grace's job as a resolution manager to navigate a project around or sometimes through these obstacles, and these obstacles often tend to be people – obstinate people. Some people are more obstinate than others, which is precisely why she'd been required to call on the services of James Kent – one of Seagull's specialist staff from somewhere near the bottom of the reservoir. Most people will do pretty much anything you want them to if you threaten to show their partner photos of them screwing high-class prostitutes or post them photos of their loved ones through the crosshairs of a sniper rifle, however there is a small minority of people who don't have loved ones and, unlike the rest, these people can sometimes be *galvanised* by pressure. It's these people that just won't give in while they're still breathing.

Gary is one of these people.

In order for Seagull Industries to secure the multi-million pound contract to redevelop New Covent Garden Flower Market into luxury accommodation, they require the approval of local government officials, but they also need agreement to relocate from the current tenants. Few would disagree that Gary is the glue that binds the flower market community together: he chairs the stall holder committee, sits on an array of steering groups within the wider community and works tirelessly to ensure the flower market is strongly represented as part of the local authority agenda. His endorsement of the redevelopment plans carries the weight of the disparate majority and unfortunately he is not keen to see his beloved market turned into 'condominiums for posh cunts'.

James sent in the heavies on Monday and they were under strict instructions to not take no for an answer. Bernard, to be fair, is just brawn, but Ig's a professional; he's got real skills. They worked him for over two hours and came away with nothing. Nothing! Well, they took one of his ribs: disgusting. The guy must be indestructible – they should make teeth out of him! "He's just a market stall holder," she'd told James. Admittedly the background check included time spent in the armed forces over in Northern Ireland when he was younger, but that's going to be the best part of two hours at a Wong Baker ten. Imagine that, watching someone cutting into your torso and breaking off one of your ribs! Apparently Ig was fetching the blender when a police patrol had started circling a little too close to the lock up for comfort and they had been obliged to beat a hasty retreat. They say that it's not enough to just cut pieces off a person; to really take away a person's hope, you need to make them watch the bits of them that you've trimmed off get liquidised, so they don't start thinking about getting a John Bobbitt. It really is awful work.

Still, six hundred grand is a lot.

Ow, ow, ow! That drill is going right into the nerve. There's really nothing like a drill penetrating the bone in your head to remind you of what you're made of.

"Please, Miss Evans, you must try to keep still – I really strongly recommend that you let us give you the anaesthetic; the temporary facial palsy will last for no more than two hours." The dentist and his assistant have taken their hands and instruments out of her mouth.

"Under absolutely no circumstances will you be putting your needle in my mouth this morning," she says as she sits up and spits into the little sink by the chair. "No way, Jose. When I was thirteen, there was this lad called Joe in my school who once tried to give a speech in front of the whole year after a visit to the dentist and he made a right pig's ear of it – couldn't get the words out properly – and people were pissing themselves at the spectacle. He was ridiculed for days afterwards and picked up something of a nickname – can you guess?" She takes the opportunity to rinse her mouth as the dentist and assistant look at her in bemusement. "Strokin' Joe Frazier – you know, like the boxer? He picked up a speech impediment after that, started to stutter and – last I heard – he was committed to a mental institute after he tried to hang himself with his little sister's skipping rope. D'you see the point? You cannot open the door for one second and let those fuckers get under your armour, because once they're in, they'll eat you alive. Look at this shirt and tie – this is my armour. I used to go to board meetings with a blouse and skirt and heels, but I quickly realised that men don't give a shit what you say if they see you as a woman. You have to look the part, you have to blend in, because in conformity is strength. If you look different, the enemy will see you as being the weak link in the chain and try to exploit you. Hang on." She takes her phone out of her trouser pocket and answers it, raising her hand as she does so in response to the dentist looking like he might want to say something. "What? Oh shit! Give the sharks some coffee and tell him I'll be there in twenty minutes and tell James that if he doesn't have a signature from Gary by close of play today, I'm going to make sure that Mr Gulliver understands that it was him who has blown the deal. And Jessie, tell James that Pluto doesn't like loose ends. I don't know, just tell him."

She hangs up, gets out of the dentist's chair and takes her coat from the hanger in the corner.

"Miss Evans?" says the dentist.

She raises her hand again and says, "I'll be back."

"But, Miss Evans –"

"Don't worry, my assistant will make another appointment." She slams the door behind her and strides off down the corridor.

She'd heard some bits and pieces about Pluto – enough to know that she didn't want him on her case. He was Mr Gulliver's bodyguard and personal enforcer and by all accounts he'd make Kent and his team look like the cast of *Rainbow*. The resolution management section were all aware that Pluto had enabled Seagull Industries to branch out into some quite lucrative sidelines, such as narcotics and people trafficking. This had been facilitated by displacing the leadership of the competition – a task that had been accomplished single-handedly. These were some large, seriously influential well-protected organisations with big budgets and fingers in lots of pies. In most instances, Pluto was instructed to leave the fingers – particularly if they were felt to be malleable and of some use – but the head and vital organs could always be replaced with a Seagull-approved transplant.

James Kent, with his family connections in government, was thought to be one of these fingers, but at the end of the day, if he couldn't be trusted to complete the most basic of tasks, the finger would need to be removed from the pie. If finger and pie were too closely intertwined to be separated, then Pluto would eat the bloody lot.

She arrives back at the office. As she rides up in the lift to the fifteenth floor, where she is due to meet the planning board and update them on the final agreements of local councillors and market sellers on moving the vegetable and flower market to a site somewhere beyond Leytonstone, she receives a call from the man of the moment.

"Hello James," she says warmly.

"Alright Grace? Listen, the lads have been on the sniff for the greengrocer all morning – he's called in sick at work and he's not at his house either."

"Oh James, perhaps that's because your boys pulled one of his ribs off – he must be feeling under the weather." James Kent is not stupid enough to say anything. "What I suggest you do is employ some of your local knowledge and expertise to find that man and get him to sign the necessary paperwork and get it to me by 5pm today, or I will be losing out on a considerable amount of money and you will be needing to find an army to protect yourself from a man called Pluto."

"Grace, he's gone to ground – we're never going to find him."

"Well, all I can say is I hope your lovely wife Chloe and your son Karl aren't about when Pluto finds time to slot you into his busy schedule, because he doesn't like to leave loose ends lying around." She holds her hand up to Jessie who is coming round her desk to intercept her as she heads towards the boardroom. "So James, please, for both our sakes, put some thought into it. He's an average cockney bloke and if he's not in the hospital getting his broken rib looked at, he'll be in the pub, or watching football or down the bookies. Call me when you find him." She hangs up, says "Not now" to Jessie over her shoulder and strides into the boardroom.

"Gentlemen, thank you all so much for getting here early. Everything is moving ahead according to schedule: a majority of members have now approved the move of the market to the new location in Leytonstone and the contract for subsequent redevelopment of the site going to Seagull Industries is now a mere formality. We have held three resident consultation events across the borough and, though attendance was quite low, the leader has agreed that we have satisfied the necessary consultation criteria in order to proceed. Apart from a small number of stall holders, who we will be completing final negotiations with today, all businesses have signed over agreements to relinquish their right to trade at the market, so we should be ready to move to stage three next week."

Silence. She is being watched very carefully. She imagines twelve sets of gills, pulsing, drawing the water across highly tuned sensory organs evolved to identify any trace of panic in every show of confidence. They taste the water for prey.

"I believe that we had agreed to make the handover at close of play today. However, I'd like to ensure that we have no loose ends so that a smooth transition can be made between the consultation team and the implementation team. In consideration of the probability that these final negotiations can be rather long, drawn-out tedious affairs, and in light of the fact that we will not be able to begin implementation until Monday of next week, I wondered if it might make sense to make the handover first thing Monday morning, if that is acceptable to the board?"

Silence again, as they taste the water once more. She looks out at the huge panoramic vista of London sprawling before her and imagines that standing in this room in this silence, surrounded by these sharks, is the most normal thing in the world. She will bear this.

Finally, Bell speaks:

"Miss Evans," he says slowly, indulgently, "you appear to have something on your shirt."

She looks down and sees a thin trickle of globular dental blood running parallel to her tie.

Six hundred grand is a lot.

Slanket

When she wakes up, Mark has gone. She still has a tingling sensation in her ears from the gig last night. She considers the possibility that she is getting too old for punk gigs, but then she decides that if that is the case, she might as well quit now, move to Castle Greysulk and pull up the drawbridge.

Mr Buttons jumps up onto her bed and begins purring in earnest as he pushes his head into her face. The cat is fiercely cross-eyed and has a very small head in relation to its body. Mark calls him Mr Muttons.

"Hello Buttons, at least somebody loves me, eh?" She pushes the cat away, as she is getting quite a bit of cat hair in her mouth, and climbs out of bed. She goes to the bathroom, brushes her teeth and then walks to the window by her bed and looks out over Borough Market. Rain is falling heavily once again, but the market is still a bustle of intermingling multi-coloured umbrellas. She can smell Goan fish curry dominating various other delicious aromas drifting up from the huge steel pans of food bubbling away below.

"Hmmm, yes Buttons, we're hungry aren't we?" she says to the feline coiling round her legs and looking up beseechingly at her (and out of the window at the same time). She goes into the tiny kitchen section of her studio flat and looks in the cupboards. There is one dainty-looking pouch of gourmet cat food, an array of sticky-topped condiment bottles, a jar of instant coffee and one onion covered in tiny blue polka dots.

"OK, here's the plan Buttons," she says, taking the cat food pouch from the cupboard and putting it in the pink cat bowl, "today we're going to have a slanket day – you're going to eat this and I'm going to have some coffee, yes that's right, hmmm, coffee, who knows – I might lose some weight. Then I'm going to get the slanket and we're going to curl up on the couch in front of the TV and look for something worthy to watch, then give up and watch *Downton Abbey* instead, until 6pm, when Grace is going to take me out for dinner, somewhere expensive, and I will fill a doggy bag full of enough goodies to see us through Sunday. Then on Monday, with any luck, one of my clients will decide to pay me and then we'll be able to pay the rent and the bank won't repossess the flat and...." The cat has finished wolfing down its deluxe breakfast and no sooner has the last morsel disappeared than it bolts out of the cat flap. "Where are you going? This concerns you too! Muttons, you little shit!"

She sighs and puts the kettle on.

Her mind skims over the details of her life, like a skater on thin ice: the issues of her debt; her inability to sustain a meaningful, long term relationship; her steadily ticking biological clock; her work as a psychotherapist that seems to drain her emotionally, whilst giving very little in financial return; her deep sense of isolation and loneliness; her awareness that she has gained a considerable amount of weight in the last couple of years. All these things are boiling away like angry welts on the bottom of her frozen river, weakening the ice and drawing her ever nearer to the moment when she will fall through into that sullen, gloomy darkness and join the growing ranks of those that her local PCT describes as 'languishing with long-term mental health problems'.

She sometimes wonders whether she is like one of the latter-day saints who went to live in leper colonies and eventually succumbed to the disease that they had originally gone to cure. If she spends the entirety of her time with depressed, anxious, angry, paranoid, insecure people, surely it is only natural that their discontent will rub off onto her in time.

Maybe she should drop out completely like her younger sister Elsa and go and live in a hippy commune, before it's too late. Elsa seems happier there than she has at any time since Scott's death. She had never been particularly close to her sister, as there was quite an age gap between them, but they had seen a little more of each other since the tragedy; how could she not empathise? Contrary to what she had expected, the hippy commune has turned out to be the best thing that could've happened to Elsa and she's made some really close friends – funny coincidence to see Tanya last night at the gig, and her boyfriend, who was playing bass in the band, seemed nice too, though a bit moody.

She makes the coffee, gets into her slanket and goes straight to the recorded episodes of *Downton Abbey*, pulling the warm covers around her grumbling belly.

Grace finally picks her up at 7.30pm in her green vintage Jaguar, though she doesn't actually speak to her in the car as Grace is having a conversation with a Mr Bell's secretary and expressing her gratitude for the extended deadline. When she hangs up, she immediately raises her hand to indicate she wishes for silence from her friend and then makes another call to a man called James, who Grace informs of the deadline extension and then tells him in no uncertain terms that they have to acquire the final deeds by first thing Monday morning or they will both be up shit creek and he will be without a paddle. She knew Grace's work was tough and demanding, but even she is surprised to hear how aggressive Grace sounds, particularly since she can hear a considerable amount of restraint in her voice.

They pull up outside Nemo's and Grace hands the keys to a valet. She immediately feels underdressed as they walk up the steps and into the lobby; Grace's suit clearly cost considerably more than she has earned this quarter. Grace is welcomed by name and they are smoothly guided to her 'usual' table. The restaurant is fitted out like the inside of an old submarine, with huge riveted bolts around every seam and corner. Each of the doors leading to the kitchen and rest rooms is a rounded hatch with brass wheels like those that submarines have to make the pressure seals. At each end of the restaurant is a very large, circular window looking into what appear to be two enormous tanks, one of which houses a formidable-looking Great White Shark and the other a very large squid. Their table is the epitomy of Victorian nautical opulence, with a subtly lit teak wood table and green leather armchairs. Hanging above their heads is a periscope which glides weightlessly down and displays a menu when she places her eye to the lens.

"This place is amazing! Is that shark real?" she says. A waiter approaches dressed in navy trousers and a white roll neck jumper. Without a word, he opens a bottle of Meursault and pours a small amount into Grace's glass, who gently moves the glass in small circles on the table then lifts it to her nose, inhales, sips a little, rinses the wine over her tongue and finally nods to the waiter, who then pours for them both.

"So how have you been, Emma?" says Grace.

"OK, I suppose. Sounds like things are as hectic and complicated as ever in the world of Miss Grace Evans," she replies.

"Ah, well yes, but without complications I don't suppose many of us would have anything to do."

"Well, as long as you're happy. You know I still don't really know what you do..." she says enquiringly.

"Oh, it's really boring to be honest. So, I hope you're in the mood for some seafood...?"

The food is sensational and they manage two bottles of the Meursault with the attentive but unobtrusive waiter regularly filling their glasses, though Em isn't too sure that Grace's glass gets filled as much as hers.

"So what about Mark?" says Grace.

"Oh nothing, I still see him once in a while. In fact, I saw him last night, but it's the same old thing; he's the nicest, funniest, most amenable guy you could wish to meet, right up until the sex, and then he doesn't want to know. It's ridiculous! Ejaculation, then mute! At least he's got his post-coital weeping under control. Sometimes I think it would be better if he just pissed off back to his wife and kids in New Zealand. What about you – anything serious on the cards?"

"Of course not; men are only good for one thing, though I hear some of them are learning how to cook and clean, which is promising. You have to assume that all men are rats and treat them accordingly."

"Oh, speaking of which, get this – I was on the *Guardian* dating website yesterday and chatting away with this guy who actually sounded quite nice. It was all very civilised, you know, 'Perhaps we might take the opportunity to enjoy a beverage this weekend', and so on, when all of a sudden he launches into 'Who's your daddy – I'm gonna shove my shaky stick up your butterfly'!"

"What?!"

"Honestly! He was clearly having several conversations at once, some of which were considerably different in tone to the one we were having. Either that, or he was a complete schizophrenic and there was a change of driver at the wheel!"

"You should've gone with it."

"I thought that after, but he dropped our conversation as soon as he realised."

"Shame, that sounds like it could've been interesting," says Grace.

"You know, I think I might've thought of a way to sort the wheat from the chaff when it comes to men."

"Oh, I'd like to hear this." Grace leans in and makes a pinnacle of her index fingers under her nose.

"Well, you know my sister has moved into this hippy commune in New Cross?"

"Yes."

"Well, I was out at Purgatory last night watching this gypsy punk band –"

"That sounds like a cross between hip and sad."

"Favour the latter. Anyway, one of Elsa's housemates was there and she's actually really nice. She studied anthropology and one of her areas of expertise was primatology – she reckoned that when it came to apes, you could tell a society's sexuality by the size of the male's testicles."

"I'm listening," says Grace.

"Apparently, gorillas have extremely small testicles in relation to their body size and this is because they live in polygynous societies, where one silverback rules the roost and expects to mate with all the females. Because he is the only sexually active male around, he doesn't need to produce masses of sperm; he is merely topping up his ladies every time. Therefore, tiny nads. Compare this with chimpanzees that live in polygynandrous societies –"

"Polygy-what?"

"Polygynandrous – where everybody is screwing everybody. Male chimpanzees have very large testicles in relation to their body size because when they copulate with a female, they know that Uncle Bob has probably only just finished there himself, so they need to be making gallons of baby gravy for their sperm to stand a chance of pushing to the front of the queue. Hence, whopping nuts."

"OK, what about humans?" says Grace, intrigued.

"According to Tanya, the situation with humans – and bonobos, whatever they might be..."

"Oh they're pygmy chimps – very cute."

"... Is medium-sized testicles..."

"Oh." Grace looks disappointed.

"Which means that humans are somewhere in between; it could swing either way, so to speak."

"Right, so what's your new strategy for men then?"

"Well, Tanya pointed out that there's a great deal of size range hidden away out there when it comes to human testicles."

"Granted," says Grace, nodding.

"So bag yourself a man with tiny spuds and you're in business," she says.

"Hang on a minute," says Grace, "you said small testicles were to be found in societies where one male gets to have sex with lots of females who only have sex with him. That doesn't sound like a very good deal to me."

"Ah no, but the point is, all men are going to be unfaithful regardless of their testicle size..."

"All men are rats," agrees Grace, nodding.

"Exactly - they believe it to be their divine apish right - but *if* you find yourself a man with small testicles, he will always assume that you are faithful to *him*," she concludes triumphantly.

"Oh, I see, yes, very clever."

"And then, after Tanya had finished her little lecture, she patted her boyfriend on the shoulder and said what lovely small balls he'd got. He did not look pleased. Really liked her..."

They both lean back in their chairs in satisfaction and look around at the other diners in the submarine restaurant. Emma is feeling a bit drunk and suddenly a wave of melancholy and nostalgia sweeps over her.

"I've been thinking about the past a lot; sometimes I wonder if our best days are behind us. Remember when we were in India? I don't know if it's rose-tinted glasses, but I feel like I was so much happier then. D'you remember us sitting on that mountain near Pushkar with our heads full of bhang and watching the sunrise over the desert? Those beautiful green and turquoise bee-eaters flying all around us, and the only sounds were the peacocks crying in the village down below. I remember thinking that everything just seemed so simple and perfect and defined. I feel like I'm becoming more blurred as I get older."

"Em, darling, we wanted to see the world as a black and white place because the mind wants to simplify what it sees. We didn't have the experience of real living that brings with it the realisation that the world is a grey place."

"Maybe," she says.

"Shall we get dessert?" suggests Grace.

"I might just have a brandy."

"Being careful, are we?"

"What d'you mean?"

"Oh nothing, I was just saying -"

"That I'm fat."

"Em, you do tend to eat a lot when you're a bit low."

"Oh great, so I'm fat AND depressed now!"

"Oh Em, I didn't mean that." Grace looks around and a waiter appears almost instantaneously, "We'd like an Armagnac –"

"A large one," Emma says.

"Yes, a large one and I'll have the pomegranate sorbet with white chocolate and chili ice cream."

"Yes madam," says the waiter.

"Jesus, he spoke," she says to nobody in particular. Grace looks at her with a neutral face.

"So come on," she says, as if it's costing her a huge effort, "I want to know about this company you work for."

"There's not much to say..."

"Oh come on, I want to hear about all the wonderful things your company does."

"Well, it's just a property development company; they build places for people to live."

"No, really?" Her sarcasm is gaining strength. Their orders arrive. She downs her Armagnac in one and says, "Come on Grace, I figure you're working at a higher level than 'they build places for people to live' considering the amount of money you are obviously earning. I'm sure I'm not that stupid that I can't handle a slightly more technical description of what your company does. With all the massive profits that you're making, it must give you *such* a good opportunity to put something back into the community."

"Seagull has been buying considerable tracts of land in Africa and planting forests to offset their carbon emissions."

"Oh this is too good to be true. Where?"

"Uganda."

"What an amazing coincidence. So Tanya's boyfriend, whose name was Tem, is an aid worker and he just happens to be going out to Uganda on Tuesday to try and help raise the profile of displaced people out there who have had their homes and their land sold by the government to companies who are buying it for carbon offsetting. Apparently subsistence farmers who have lived and worked the land for generations are being violently removed in order to make way for these wonderful western environmentalists."

"It's not as black and white as that, Em."

"People are being shot and killed, women are being raped."

"I'm just saying that our company is buying land out there in good faith; it's not our fault if the Ugandan government doesn't accept these people's claims to the land."

"Never your fault, is it Grace? As long as the world is grey, you don't have to take responsibility for anything. You can just keep grabbing money."

"There's nothing wrong with making money."

"I'll tell you what's wrong with making money; it's an unnatural desire that can never be satisfied. You can never be full with money, so you just keep taking and taking until there isn't enough for anybody else."

"Fine, if money's so unimportant to you, you can go halves on the bill, can't you?" says Grace.

There is a long pause.

"OK, fine," says Em.

Grace offers her a lift, but she doesn't take it. It takes her three hours to walk home in the steadily falling rain. When she gets to her flat, Mr Buttons is waiting for her by the door. He immediately begins purring around her legs. She has not brought a doggy bag.

"Fuck off Muttons," she says, kicking the cat up the arse.

The lights in the flat do not work. Using her mobile phone for light, she checks the fuse box. There is nothing amiss.

She gets into her slanket and sits on the couch in front of the empty TV screen. She pulls her slanket around her and sits in the darkness of her cut-off flat.

Strip

"Your strip is like your battle dress, man." Pedro takes a long drag on the joint and continues, "It's like the highlander's kilt, the red Indian's war paint, or the SAS with the black jumper. When I put this Millwall shirt on, I'm ready to face the enemy. I have made my mental preparations and I accept the possibility of death, man I welcome death with open arms, because this is the only noble death left open to a warrior man like myself in the modern world. The modern world, 'e want to take away my purpose, my fighting spirit, 'e want to cut my *cojones*." He grabs his crotch and squints as if he is staring into the sun. "'E want to take my power and domesticate me, like, how you say, the neutral dog."

"A neutered dog," enunciates Hendo very carefully in his Glaswegian twang. He is sitting in his usual chair at the end of the kitchen table, wearing Pedro's sombrero and drinking Special Brew.

"Exactly. The newder dog, that's what the modern world wants us to be: we placid, we smile, we nice to be left with the babies, we shit in the box. No more howl at the moon, no more running with the pack. 'E want us to suppress our very nature, 'e want to take away the specific ingredients that make us a man. But not Pedro, huh. I know the score and it ain't no conspiracy, man; they ain't no-one hiding in the shadows pulling the strings like a puppet; all the planes flying over don't got no chemical sprays to deposit on the population and make us docile. This is evolution, man. But we got too good, we take the natural out of the natural selection. We so good at making the order from the chaos that there ain't no chaos left. But we need 'im; too much equilibrium don't make an equilibrium. So I put on my shirt and I stand up to put the balance back in the balance. I put a little chaos back in the mix. 'E benefit everybody when Pedro go *loco*, huh."

He sings to the melody of 'We Are Sailing':

"No-one likes us, no-one likes us,
No-one likes us, we don't care,
We are Millwall, super Millwall,
We are Millwall, from the Den."

Elsa comes out of her room.

"Guys, can you keep it down just a little bit, please – I've got to work tonight and I could do with just a couple of hours' more sleep."

"Eh, beautiful, I so sorry – these cun's got no respect for they housemates, huh. Pedro keep them quiet for you, OK?"

"Sorry Elsa," says Ben, as he pours water from the kettle onto his dried noodle breakfast, "we'll put a muffler on him."

"Thanks guys, later," says Elsa as she shuffles back to bed.

"You can get these things now for dogs," says Billy, putting aside his newspaper for a moment, "that fit to a dog's collar, and if the dog barks or makes a loud noise, it squirts it with a jet of water. That Japanese girl I was seeing, Kira, she had this nasty little dog, a Spitz, that would bark all day. Her neighbour was a taxi driver who worked nights, so he needed to sleep in the day. Well this dog made this guy so crazy, he'd come round and complain and I'd tell him, y'know, sorry, but what are you gonna do? Anyway, he could see he wasn't gonna be able to do anything by shouting at me so he came up with a better solution – brought Kira one of these electro-squirty-collars one day and that was it. I put the thing on it, took him about 20 minutes to get used to it, running round barking and yelping, and after that I never heard a squeak from the little fucker again."

"You ain't putting no electric squirty collar on Pedro, man – you don't even wanna try. I'll be kicking your ass so hard, you be buying groceries with your mother for a month."

"OK Peds, easy buddy, easy." Ben puts aside his bowl of noodles and holds his hands up with eyes wide in mock fear. "That sounds real nasty and look, you're scaring Billy – he's gone pale and everything. For Billy's sake, keep it down a notch will you?"

"OK Ben, since you ask so nicely and because Billy scared," Billy is still nonchalantly reading the sports pages, "I make myself *Senor Tranquilo* till we leave the house, but listen guys, today is an important day, this is the big one. I cannot stress the importance of your first trip to the Den. This is the once-in-the-blue-moon opportunity for the forces of chaos to rise up and shake the foundations of our society. Not too much, but just enough for the people to remember why they are alive. Tonight we will run with the pack boys; we will howl at the blue moon and shake our *cojones*," he grabs his crotch and squints as if he's looking at the sun, "at the world, the *hijo de putas*..." He tails off into a stream of Spanish curses.

"Is Sammy coming to the match?" says Billy to Ben.

"Nah, he hates football," says Billy, folding the paper and tossing it into the recycling.

"Shame, we almost had all the boys out on a school trip together."

"Well there's Pete, too."

"True, but y'know, I don't count Pete. It's funny, I sort of expected to get to know Pete a bit more since he offered to help me with my training, but he clams up whenever we talk about anything but boxing. I mean, he comes alive when he's on the job and he knows everything about the sport, and I mean everything: who won what when, how they trained, the tactics, what they ate! It's unbelievable. He's a great trainer."

"You might not notice the difference," says Ben, "but I think this thing you two have got has made a real difference to him; he's way more sociable than he was when I first moved in. He never used to come out of his room at all, apart from to eat and to shit. He sat down here the other night with me and Anna and Hendo and smoked his pipe for a good few hours. Granted he didn't say much, but he seemed happy enough to just sit there with us and enjoy the company."

"Maybe you're right. It's amazing to think that he's been living here for almost thirty years."

"One of the founding fathers."

"Yeah, and he just seems to have become a part of the furniture."

"I guess it must be weird for him. He must've seen hundreds of housemates come and go over the years. You must get tired of making friends with people and then they move on and you have to start all over again. It must be wearing. You can understand him being aloof."

"But what does he do? I mean, where does he get his money from? He doesn't claim dole, he doesn't work - well certainly not in any conventional sense that I can see - and he doesn't seem to have any friends, I mean apart from us. He just lives in that dark room - what does he do all day? Smoke his pipe? Watch films? Play online poker? Spank his monkey? The monkey gets tired."

"Depends on the monkey, Billy. Anyway, I know what you're saying, but I really think Pete's good. Life kicks everyone up the arse once in a while: we all get our hearts broken, we all get let down by the people we love, we all make mistakes, but some people take it hard, they aren't so thick-skinned and they take it to heart and they find it's hard to pick themselves up again and they don't like to feel like that. Maybe some people decide that the best course of action is to limit the risk of further damage and close off the exposure to the outside world as much as possible. It's like the difference between a cavefish and a fish in the sea - they're no better or worse off than each other, they're just suited to different environments. It's no wonder Pete's been here so long - this house allows him to be a recluse without completely isolating himself from the rest of the world. It's perfect for him, really."

"I know you're right, I just can't help superimposing myself into his shoes and feeling thoroughly depressed by the experience."

Pedro listens to Billy and Ben talking with interest as he rolls another joint.

"Hey lads, we should make a move fairly soon, aye?" says Hendo. "Give us time to sink a couple of pints on the way."

"Sounds good," says Ben.

"One for the road, eh boys? *Vamos!*" Pedro says as he puts the joint behind his ear and pulls his beret over his head.

"What's going on, lads?" Pete is coming down the stairs.

"Just off to the football, Pete," says Billy.

"What about training?" says Pete.

"What happened to Sunday being the day of rest?"

"What happened to Saturday being the day of training and abstinence?"

"Hmmm, it was just a couple of beers, Pete…"

"It's a long road, Billy. If we walk it together you need to be 100%."

"OK, OK," Billy turns back to Pedro, Hendo and Ben. "Guys, I'm gonna give it a miss, I'll catch you later." With his back to Pete, he squeezes his balls and pulls a face for them like he is staring at the sun.

They step out of the house onto the street. Lorenza is walking towards them.

"*Hola bonita*," Pedro says.

"*Hola Pedro, que tal?*" she says. She nods at the rest of them.

"*Muy bien*," he says. "Hey, what are you doing tomorrow evening, huh? You like I can make a space in my diary and we can go for a drink?"

"Hmmm thanks Peds, but I'll be spending tomorrow night with Professor Quiggin." She taps the front of one of the books she's holding.

He squints, "*Zombie Economics*, huh? 'E explain how people pay their death tax, is it?"

Lorenza smiles, "Nice try, but no – it's about the resilience of economic ideas around market liberalism in the aftermath of the global financial crisis." Pedro shows off his best vacant smile. "Basically, he argues that deregulated markets and policies designed to make the rich better off will rise up from the dead again, unless we can come up with credible alternatives to fill the void they have left in people's heads."

"You know what Lorenza, I have no clue about what you just said. Some words came out, I hear them and now they gone."

"OK, well it's nice to see you Pedro. I better get going."

"OK, maybe see you next week for that drink, huh…"

"No, I'm busy. Bye Pedro," she calls over her shoulder as she walks away.

"... And maybe after the drink, we have a little nice time with Pedro's *julo*, huh," he whispers under his breath as he watches Lorenza disappear into her house.

He runs to catch up with the rest of the lads who have walked on ahead.

"Eh, sorry guys – I think Lorenza is in love with me, huh. She always wants to talk with me and she looking at me like I'm the coolest guy."

"Peds, what are you waiting for, man?" says Ben. "Lorenza is a hottie."

"Pedro like to take his time," he says as he lights the joint. "Like the cat playing with the mouse, I pat her this way, then I touch that way, and then, when I'm ready, I eat her up."

Coldblow Lane swallows them whole as they cut through the tunnel, under the tracks into the area the Millwall loyal call 'open country'. None of them have had what could be described as sleep for over thirty hours.

There are a few Millwall fans in the pub on the way to the ground but then, as they get nearer to kick off, the Millwall shirts just seem to appear out of nowhere and suddenly they are in it – a great herd of black and white shirts, thousands strong, that seem to have displaced all the other formats of human that are to be found on a typical London street. The noise levels increase at a seemingly logarithmic rate as voices join in unison. Pedro feels the freedom and joy as he releases himself into the mob. He looks at the other two: Ben swept along with the tide, shouting and singing with the rest; Hendo seemingly quiet and thoughtful beneath the sombrero, but still here experiencing this moment with him, his brothers, his family.

He spots a group of Bushwhackers, members of the Millwall firm, rolling out of The Alfred. There is a palpable tension in the atmosphere now, an underlying violence seeping onto the street as more of them leave the pub, like gas from a broken pipe. They are out in force. Up ahead a small pocket of away fans are in the wrong place at the wrong time. Or are they? He watches them as, hands in pockets, they nonchalantly watch the growing group of Bushwhackers behind them. Playing it cool or planning an assault? They've got some balls if it's the latter. Ben is unaware of the developing situation, laughing with a tall Indian dude next to them who is carrying his son on his shoulders. Hendo is watchful, but seemingly uninterested in the away fans. Pedro returns his attention to this small group and feels his adrenaline spike as they suddenly move closer to each other, shielding the body of one of their number from sight, a shaven-headed, heavily-built short guy who can just be seen focusing his attention on whatever is in his hands. Pedro wolf whistles and immediately his two friends stop what they are doing and begin moving towards him. He catches Ben's eye and nods imperceptibly towards the away fans. At this moment, the group of away fans break apart; through the sea of bodies, fire is visible. Flames suddenly fly into the air and for a split second the entire street seems to catch its breath as the two petrol bombs hang at the top of their arc before plummeting into the heart of the Bushwhackers and lighting them up like dancing, screaming Guys on November the 5th.

The chaos is short-lived. Fans near the flames try to push away from them, some of those further away try to get nearer to help, some Bushwhackers try to push through the crowd to give chase to the offenders, who end up being the only people who move anywhere, disappearing off down a side alley. The flames are out in less than a minute and although a few guys' legs are burnt, they feign disinterest in their injuries and the procession continues to march towards the stadium as though nothing has changed. But everything has changed.

The game is uneventful and at times it feels as though it is the players on the pitch who are spectating as the Bushwhackers whip the home crowd into a frenzy of chants. The final whistle blows and the crowd pours out of the stadium, bloodthirsty and ready to inflict damage. They manage to get out of the doors together but there is a riot outside; bottles flying, fires everywhere, people running, mounted police wading into the affray. Pedro sees an away fan lying unconscious on the floor with three Bushwhackers stamping on his body: head, torso, legs. He sees a mounted policeman pulled from his horse and fall into a jerking mass of fighting – his baton swings briefly and then he disappears. He sees a Bushwhacker run up to the riderless horse and punch it in the eye; it rears up in surprise and seems to stagger backwards on its hind legs before rolling onto the road, where it is set upon by more men, some of them swinging bollards and rubbish bins. He sees the shaven-headed away fan who threw the petrol bombs earlier staggering down the road, laughing, with blood pouring from his head. He sees a skinny young Millwall fan, wearing a woolly hat and scarf, run up behind the bloodied man and batter him round the head with what looks like a crowbar. The man drops like a sack of butcher's meat.

"Peds, c'mon matey, let's get the fuck out of here," says Ben. "C'mon, I can see Hendo waiting over there." He follows Ben wordlessly. He sees Hendo up ahead, standing alone and slightly to the side of the street, still wearing the sombrero. Suddenly a man steps out of nowhere and punches him hard in the face. Hendo buckles and the man starts in with the boot. He sees Ben shout and start running forwards, bursting out of the crowd, running low and catching the man side on in his mid-section, lifting him clear off the ground and dumping him on the pavement. Pedro sees Ben's shoulders working briefly over the man on the floor, before he turns and squats down next to Hendo. Pedro reaches the scene and sees Hendo holding his nose, with blood streaming through his fingers. Ben is talking calmly to Hendo, seemingly heedless of their surroundings and Ben even seems to laugh at one point. He cannot hear them and they seem distant to him. He steps away from them and in a moment he is in the flow of people moving away from the chaos. Momentarily he holds himself, turns and sees Ben looking around for him, then he turns again and stumbles away. Calmness begins to return to him as he puts corners between himself and the noise of the riot. Within ten minutes, Pedro is back home on the street, but suddenly he is overcome with shame at leaving his friends. He knows they will be close behind him, so he decides to hide out in the garden and wait a while until after they return, before making his entry along with a reasonable explanation for his losing them.

He sits on one of the benches a little way down the street from his own house and rolls a joint. His hands are shaking, but he calms immediately once he begins to smoke. He looks at the houses in the street; squares of multi-coloured lights ignite the windows and laughter rolls down the street from house eight's kitchen. The street is blissfully unaware of the carnage only three blocks away. Distant sirens are the only reminder that what he just experienced was real at all.

Lorenza is sitting at her desk by her window on the first floor of house six, reading. She has a strand of hair in her mouth. There is something about her, the way she seems to fly above the shit of the world untainted, working hard and making something of herself. She has an innocence and a braveness that he envies.

He can hear footsteps, then Hendo's voice cursing as he looks for his keys outside their door, and finally the door unlocking.

He thinks of the cavefish and the fish in the sea. He thinks of the sleepy little village of Herrera del Duque in Estremadura, where his parents would take him as a child to see his grandparents. He remembers the cold stone walls inside their house in the midday sun. He remembers the men drinking at the *taverna*, the one small block of light in the cool, damp, early morning darkness, before going to work for the day, pink hams hanging in the smoke from the bar behind them. He remembers Uncle Alfredo riding to work on his horse Goliath, laughing and saying "Late again," as he patted Goliath's neck, who had stopped to chew the roadside grass.

He looks down at his shirt, the black and white of his strip.

He looks at Lorenza's window again, but the light has gone out.

Sable

Ig switches the light on and goes straight over to fill the kettle. "Man, these English folks is serious bout their football, huh?" Ig waits for an answer from Bernard and when none is forthcoming, he carries on. "I mean, don't get me wrong, fans at an American football game will happily kick crap out of the away fans just like most other sports, but that was something else this evening, you know 'm sayin'?"

Bernard looks at Ig, then wordlessly rests his enormous bulk into a chair, takes his gun out of his coat and begins to automatically check it over.

"You want a coffee, Burns?" says Ig.

"Yes."

"You got football fans like that in Lichtenstein, Burns?"

"I am not from Lichtenstein," he says.

"Where you from then, brother?" says Ig.

"It does not matter. And we are not brothers."

"Alright, alright, I hear ya. Man, I'm just tryin' to be friendly. If we gots to work together we might as well try to get along OK, don't ya think?"

"It is not professional to make friends in this business." He has taken his gun apart and is looking disinterestedly at Ig down the length of the barrel.

Ig thinks this over for a minute and then finally says:

"OK, well how bout talkin' to pass the time? I promise not to try and befriend you."

"The violence after the game was evidence of a healthy community. If people are not given an outlet to express their anger and frustration, they begin to boil like your kettle."

"OK, OK, that's an in'restin' perspective."

Ig turns the gas off, pours the boiling water into a cafetiere and brings it to the table with two cups. "How 'bout those innocent folks who gets hurt in the violence, huh? Ain't so healthy for them now, is it?"

Ig finishes plunging the cafetiere and pours. He hands Bernard a cup and takes a seat opposite.

"Imagine it is like the forest fire. People understand that if there is a forest fire every couple of years, it turns forest litter to ash, which is good for the soil. It burns at a level that doesn't kill trees and the animals can hide in their burrows or outrun the flames. There are even some trees that rely on fire to germinate their seeds. But if you do not have regular small fires, the leaf litter builds up and then when the fire finally starts, it burns with too much intensity, fast and deep into the earth, and everything dies: the trees, the seeds, the animals. What we have seen this evening is a little forest fire."

"That's a nice analogy. So you's sayin', that even though innocent folks is gettin' hurt, it's for their own good, cos if they don't get a little bit of regular hurt, they's goan end up gettin' some real nasty hurt somewhere further down the line?"

"This is inevitable. In Srebrenica, this is what happened."

"That where you're from Burns? Zebraneeta?"

"It does not matter where I am from."

"Unnerstood. So in summary, a little violence keeps a community healthy."

"Correct. Organisations such as ours are like park rangers, who are sometimes required to go and shower some sparks around if a fire has not started naturally, in order to maintain the healthy forest."

"Showerin' sparks, huh. You'd be referring to your Glock, I'm a guessin'", says Ig, between sips of his coffee.

"You are very perceptive for an American."

"I try."

"Look at this," Burns says as he takes a bullet from the magazine of the gun and holds it up for Ig to see. "What do you see?"

"A bullet," says Ig.

"More precisely, this is a hollow point round, encased in a 19mm Parabellum cartridge. Parabellum means 'prepare for war', from the saying, *si vis pacem, para bellum*. 'If you seek peace, prepare for war.' The arms producers of today understand the philosophy I am describing as well as the ancient Romans."

"Holy shit, that is some deep shit man! I mean I ain't so sure those Roman dudes was talkin' bout zactly what you is talkin' bout, but you sure is animals from the same farmyard."

"No, you do not understand because you are American. You have no sense of history." Bernard is rapidly reassembling the gun.

"Man, we all come from the same place. We all got history, an' mostly, it's the same one."

"No, you do not understand. When European settlers and African slaves colonised the Americas, they wiped the slate clean, they forgot their own history, destroyed the indigenous people's history and started a history of their own."

"Well maybe. Hey, what d'you think's takin' the guv so long?"

No sooner has he said the words than the door to the office opens and Mr Kent walks in. He sees the coffee.

"Oooh, is that coffee fresh?"

"Sure is, Mr Kent," says Ig.

"Lovely jubbly." He grabs a mug from the kitchen cupboard and pours himself a brew, then goes to the fridge. "No milk. Black it is." He takes a seat at the head of the table, takes a swig of the coffee, grimaces and then begins.

"Alright lads, we are running short on time. I've got eyes all over town looking for the grocer, but I need you lads to close off the options for him as quick as you can. We need to smoke him out. Ig, Burns and me will deal with the junk from the match, meanwhile I want you to check with your man on the force and see if he can come up with anything – the grocer's going to be in a lot of pain after your last visit and I'm thinking if he ain't gone to hospital for treatment, then he's going DIY, which means he might've needed to break in to a pharmacy or a clinic for morphine. In fact, just sweep the whole area for B+Es and robberies since Wednesday – the cozzers are bound to know something. Soon as you're done, you can take the junk back to his cage and then I want the grocer's pad turned upside down; if we can't find the paperwork, we need some leverage and fast. OK?"

"No problem, Mr Kent," says Ig.

"Good. We can still come out of this shining. OK, Ig, anything we need to know about the junk?"

"No Sir, name's Connor Henderson. He jus' got himself 3G in arrears and then skipped his deadline after a personal visit from yours truly. He needin' a little lesson in punctuality is all."

"Fine, Bernard, you go fetch him from the car and take him down to the basement – use the back door." Bernard responds instantly, rising from the table and putting his gun away as Mr Kent issues further instructions. "Ig, you better use the office and make some calls – give us a shout when you're done."

The night is silent and black as Bernard walks around the side of the house and then crosses over the roundabout with the small Japanese maple at its centre around the front. The security light triggers as he walks by the little tree, intensifying the dark beyond its range. He crunches over the gravel into the black void, to where he knows the cars are parked in front of the garages. He dislikes the dark intensely. Every expanse of darkness opens up a window to the past and, if it's dark enough, he falls through that window, landing in Potocari on that one night in July 1995 when he was just twelve years old.

His mother and father and older brother had fled to the UN-declared 'safe zone' of Srebrenica in Bosnia and Herzegovina as General Mladic's troops, known as the VRS, and other Serbian paramilitary forces called the Scorpions, spread into the region encircling the safe zone. With nothing but the clothes on their backs, they had fled to Potocari, hungry, fearful and exhausted, as the VRS moved into Srebrenica with UN forces offering little resistance. A UN force of four hundred Dutch peacekeepers was stationed at Potocari and Bosniaks in their thousands descended on the area, seeking protection from the approaching storm. Over the course of just a few days, the Serbian forces proceeded to massacre eight thousand Bosniaks, mostly men and boys, under the very noses of the Dutch peacekeepers. His father and brother were shot. His mother had dressed him in girl's clothes and they had eventually escaped on a bus to Kladanj.

Whenever he recalled the horrors that he had witnessed during that period, it always seemed to be condensed into a single moment. Not the endless trail of men, both young and old, who were taken behind the white house to the accompanying staccato of gunfire. Not when a young mother was told to silence her baby and, when she could not, it was taken from her and its throat was cut. Not the little boy's head paraded on a Serbian knife, with the screaming mother behind holding his headless corpse. Not the unborn baby torn from its mother's belly and dashed on the tarmac. It was his mother in her sable fur coat, that always made her look like she was on her way to the opera, running to the side of her neighbour's daughter Jasmina, who had been surrounded by Serbian soldiers, and begging them to leave her alone. Then he had watched her run to a Dutch soldier, who stood nearby with headphones on, and begged him to intercede, while Jasmina was lifted from the ground by three of the soldiers and raped by the fourth.

He did not remember any sound, as if he had worn the headphones and they had played emptiness, whilst his mother lay at the feet of the Dutchman, silently screaming in her sable coat.

He unlocks the car with the remote and walks to the boot. No sooner has he opened the latch than the boot flies open, almost catching him in the face, and a pair of tied-together legs kick out at him violently. He steps back, takes the Glock out of his jacket, then catches the feet with one of his enormous hands and points the gun into the boot, right at the junk's face. The struggling stops immediately. He lets go of the feet and, with the gun still pointing into the boot, he raises his left index finger and shakes it in silent admonishment. He puts the hood back on the junk's head, pulling the strings around the neck. He puts the gun away, grabs the junk's ankles with both hands and pulls him out of the boot in one swift lifting motion that ensures his hands, which are tied behind his back, do not catch on the edge of the boot. Lowering the junk's covered head to the floor, he gently lays him out flat on his back. He checks the boot and, once satisfied that there are no stains or damp patches, he closes and locks it. He picks up the junk under the arms and flings him over his shoulder, walks round to the back of the house, past the swimming pool and, ducking slightly to get his huge frame – plus body on shoulder – under the veranda, he opens the access door to the basement, where Mr Kent is sitting on a wooden chair waiting for him. He puts the junk on the chair in front of Mr Kent and then, in response to Mr Kent's nod, removes the hood.

"Cigarette?" says Mr Kent, "No? Mind if I do? I'm trying to quit, but you know... Have you ever been scuba diving? No? Can't say it ever appealed to my tastes in particular either, but it's my daughter you see, she got me into it. She's an adventurous one that one; must get it from her mother, I suppose. It certainly doesn't come from me, anyway; I'm more of a creature comforts man myself. Can't see the point in trekking off to all these God-forsaken places to see what's right under your nose. But her: started out with the Brownies, then it was the Guides, then she was off on the Duke of Edinburgh Award – have you heard of that? Probably originated in Scotland, judging from the name. Anyway, in case you're not in the know, it's a sort of outdoor pursuits scheme, y'know orienteering and so on. Then after that it was Operation Raleigh. She did a selection weekend up in the Malverns and this wasn't just a camping weekend, let me tell you, this was proper SAS shit: skinning rabbits, swimming across half-frozen lakes, eating termites, you name it. So anyway, she's one of the two percent who get selected to go on to the next stage and the following year she is sent off to Borneo to build tracks in the jungle and monitor sea slug populations on the reef and so on. Well, whilst she was out there, me and the missus happened to be in the vicinity, so we dropped in to see how she was getting on and that's when she convinced me to sample the life aquatic. There's a tiny little island off the east coast of Borneo called Sipadan – it's meant to be the best dive site in the world. It's basically a column of rock rising 400m from the sea floor, with a tiny little desert island on the top. You drop into the sea and then drift down the sea wall and let the currents carry you along and oh my God, it is amazing." Mr Kent leans forward excitedly. "Virgin reef, turtles everywhere, huge shoals of fish every colour of the rainbow – triggers, jacks, groupers, barracuda, parrot fish, moray eels, stingrays, you name it; but the ones which interested me the most were the sharks and, let me tell you, there was thousands of 'em. The main ones that you see are the reef sharks – black tips and white tips. Generally, close to the reef, they tend to be small, four or five feet at the most. Sharks of this size have a certain look about the face. They're very smooth and streamlined, and reminiscent of their little cousins, the dogfish. They're not particularly scary. I mean, don't get me wrong, I wouldn't offer them a bleeding finger – little dogs can still bite – but you don't fear for your life when these guys are swimming around. It's when you drift away from the reef and out into the blue that you start to see the bigger sharks – six, seven, eight feet long – and these are the ones you don't turn your back on. When they get to this size, something in the shark's face changes; they lose that smooth innocence of youth and take on a bulky, more angular appearance. The jaws seem to take on a life of their own and, instead of that neat rounded line on the underside of the head, the rows of teeth that keep marching out over the years leave that mouth hanging open more often than not, twitching like toned muscle. But it's the change in the eyes that really gets your heart pumping that little bit harder. They say that the eyes are the windows to the soul and there is a darkness to a big shark's eyes, as if the accumulation of death that it metes out over the years has blackened its soul."

"Look at me, Mr Henderson." The junk starts to wriggle and cry out muffled shouts through his gag at the mention of his name. "Hold him. Look into my eyes, Mr Henderson, and tell me, how dark do these eyes look, because I'm beginning to wonder if the same thing will happen to a human as happens to the shark."

The internal door to the basement opens and Ig walks quietly in. He stands very still for a moment surveying the scene.

"Mr Kent?" Mr Kent turns and Ig beckons him over with a finger. They huddle for a moment and then Mr Kent can be audibly heard to say, "Run that by me one more time Ig, there's a good lad." Ig leans in and whispers to him again. Mr Kent turns and looks at the junk for a moment, then raises a finger and with a reassuring smile says:

"Be right with you."

Mr Kent turns and looks at Bernard. The smile has gone. He says, "Got a second for me, Bernard?" He walks over.

"When Ig told you to go and grab the guy in the hat after the match, what sort of hat was the guy that you grabbed wearing?" says Mr Kent quietly.

"A big Mexican hat," says Bernard.

"You're absolutely certain?"

"Is there a problem, Mr Kent?"

"Yes, there's a big fucking problem my friend. You've got the wrong guy!"

Bernard flashes pale and red as blood rushes from and to different parts of his face. Someone else must have made a mistake. He doesn't make mistakes.

"I promise that was the guy wearing the Mexican hat. Honestly..."

Mr Kent looks at him for a long moment.

"Where's the hat, Bernard?"

He struggles to control his anger.

"It fell off when I grabbed him, I swear Mr Kent..." he says, hating every obsequious intonation in his voice.

"Enough, we don't have time for this. Bag 'im and dump 'im, then you and Ig best get crackin' and find me my grocer." The fact that Mr

Kent keeps his temper, stays calm, even though he is clearly very angry, makes Bernard's humiliation worse. He is boiling with the injustice of the situation. He wants to say something else, but what can he say? He turns and walks back towards the junk, who is looking at him and smiling under the gag.

"What are you smiling at?" he says and launches his fist into the junk's face. His head snaps back with a sickening crack.

A silence follows the noise. Bernard's back remains turned to Mr Kent and Ig, but even so he knows that they can see the light playing across the contours of his face reflected in the sable-black glass of the small window that looks across the pool. He sees the fear and surprise in their faces. The muscles in his face contract against his will beneath the naked bulb.

Bernard stands in silence and the dark window yawns.

Scarf

Ted's face contorts for a moment as he hears the coins he is inserting into the ticket machine dispensing beneath as fast as he can load them. He takes out his handkerchief and mops his brow. Deep breaths; his doctor had told him he must try to take deep breaths when he feels himself getting tense. This essentially means he needs to try and take deep breaths from the moment he wakes up to the moment he goes to sleep, possibly whilst he's sleeping too. He certainly didn't get much rest at night over the weekend – there's something very odd about the house at the moment, to say the least. He's probably just worrying about Connie; Lord knows where she's got to. She must've gone to stay with her friend Daisy in Cornwall and taken their grandson, Paul, and the dog with her. Strange of her not to leave a note or return his call and let him know what's going on, but he'd been under so much pressure over the weekend that he'd barely set foot in his own house – these bloody community engagement events were a real bind.

He could not see the point; you can't leave the general populace to decide how they should be managed, it would be utter chaos. Besides, it was the same old handful of griping moaners showing up at every single event, no matter where it was held, with one sole purpose in mind; to complain. To complain about the bin men breaking the lid of their wheelie bin and how it won't close and the foxes get in and it's a God-awful mess every morning and who has to clean it up? That's right, poor old griper. Or to complain about why have they changed the number 32 bus back to a number 3 bus; there's already a number

3 bus running from Tottenham Swale to Pall Mall, did he not know? What could possibly be the point? Think of all the bus stops they'll need to amend, who is going to pay for that? Let me guess... That's right, poor old griper. And with fuel prices climbing through the roof, who is going to freeze to death when the nights close in? That's right, poor old griper. And what's the council doing about it? Not a bloody thing, that's what. Poor old griper doesn't know why she loyally votes for his party election after election. Ted smiles, he feigns concern, he reassures on topics of which he has no understanding and he imagines his fingers tightening around the poor old griper's throat and silencing her complaints for good.

Finally the machine swallows some of his coins and spits out a travel card.

"Finally," he says. He picks up his ticket and the small hillock of coins he's made in the steel trough and turns towards the barriers, thinking as he does so that someone should do something about those hopeless machines. What on earth was wrong with human beings vending the tickets?

He gets to the ticket barrier and inserts his card, puffing all the while. His ticket pops up and taking it he walks forward into the barrier. A small red sign says 'Seek assistance'. He tries the ticket again, with the same result.

"Oh bloody hell," he mutters. Deep breaths. People are tutting behind him. OK! It was hardly his fault, was it? He reverses and then cuts across the flow of human traffic, generating additional tuts, towards the spotty young scrote who is casually leaning on the disabled manual barrier.

"I only just bought the bloody thing," he says, shoving it in the young man's face.

"OK Sir, deep breaths," says the young man, opening the barrier.

Deep breaths! Everyone's bloody at it! He should turn round and let the whippersnapper know who he is.

The bloody escalator is being renovated, so he is forced to use the hard, steep central steps. Somebody should do something about this level of service, considering the price you pay. He looks at the name proudly inscribed on the boards of the company responsible for servicing the escalators – 'GERYON – for life's little ups and downs'. Oh yes, hilarious. He half expects the boards to tell him to take deep breaths.

Ted gets to the platform puffing heavily and, after mopping his brow with his handkerchief, he picks up his train of thought. Essentially, most individuals are unfit to make the important decisions about society; they are too small-minded and unable to see how their own issues and observations interact and fit into the big picture. Even small groups of people lack the required scope to make informed, balanced decisions on matters of national and international importance. Of course, governments still have a role to play in steering society along, but even they are guilty of making short-term decisions to gain credibility with the voters. The real visionaries in this day and age are the huge multinational corporations; only they have the resources, strength, market sensitivity and independence to guide the human race into the future. The council had long taken the view that local government should forge strong links with businesses and work in partnership wherever possible to galvanize projects in the public interest. It is only natural, in his eyes, that if he is working with large multinationals to assist them in building better housing for his ward, then he is entitled to a little compensation in view of the huge profits that they will generate from such developments. After all, somebody has to police the movers and the shakers and it isn't going to be done by standing back and tossing around the odd withering comment at a council meeting. Someone needs to roll up their sleeves and get their hands dirty. This is what it means to be one of the elite, this is the secret; understanding that rules are established to keep the general populace of simple-minded Luddites and gripers on the straight and narrow where they belong, thus enabling the elite to soar above the ordered ranks, unrestricted and free, to allow their superior intellects to do the best for all.

He looks fondly at the black, white and mauve stripes of his scarf, the colours of Balliol College – what heady days. Fragrant cloves wafting through the first cold nights of autumn, soaking up glass after glass of mulled wine and bellowing 'The Gordouli' at the gates of their rivals at Trinity. The feasting and the dancing and the drinking down of the world's knowledge, for after all:

"There's no knowledge but I know it.
I am Master of this College,
What I don't know isn't knowledge."

He could do anything in those days: from seducing young maids in a punt on the Thames to dazzling his cronies during the holidays, with speeches delivered stood on a table in the beer garden in the 'Tolly'. He would pander to the influential, knowing that he would be returning one day to take up his rightful position in politics. By the time he'd graduated, he could get away with murder and nobody would turn a hair.

He is slowly being edged down the platform as more commuters swell the numbers waiting for the next train. He should've taken the overland to London Bridge. Bloody DLR. A young woman in a black pencil skirt, white blouse, black jacket and heels is stood nearby. She looks pale and vulnerable. He imagines what it would be like to have a gadget that could freeze time, allowing him to freely move around whilst others remained static and unaware. He would definitely be pushing the button right now. He would squeeze his way through the crowd until he was next to her and then slowly unbutton her blouse. With one hand massaging her breasts, he would leisurely take out his member and proceed to sing a limerick or two in front of all these miserable morning commuters whilst massaging himself between the legs. He looks along the platform - there are probably a few others he'd be conducting some physical examinations on. Then finally, once he'd sung his heart out, he'd button everything back up and calmly make his way back to the exact position he'd been standing in - very important, this - and push the button to return to real time.

Good lord, what is he thinking? He hears the train approaching from down the tunnel and begins to manoeuvre himself parallel to where he believes the doors will stop. The train squeals to a stop in the exact perfect position. He psyches himself up for the big squeeze. There is a pause. He hears tutting from behind him. Every momentary delay adds to the tension, seconds passing like elephants on tightropes. Then the lights flash on the door buttons, the doors hiss and beep, and as soon as there is a space big enough to fit him, he shoves himself onto the train. There are a few noises of disapproval from the other passengers as some of them edge around him in order to get off the train, and then the wave plunges into the gap.

"Can you move down please?" come the voices from the doors. He tries to maintain a space around him. He can hear the honking of disease-ridden noses, venting their contents into used tissues.

"Please can passengers move down the carriage to allow as many passengers to board as possible," says the conductor on the overhead tannoy. He is bracing himself to hold off more pressure when he sees the black jacket and pencil skirt crushed into a space nearby. He turns slightly and yields to the pressure a little and, as if by magic, the young girl is pushed into his belly. A couple more people cram themselves into the tube before the sliding doors begin to beep. Everyone breathes in and they are sealed off from the still-growing crowd of frustration on the platform.

The train groans into life and then, gradually picking up speed, it plunges into the darkness of the tunnel, swaying from left to right as it makes its way under the river. The girl cannot reach any of the handholds and is unable to prevent herself from leaning into his belly as the carriage lurches from side to side. She looks up at him:

"Sorry," she says, with an apologetic smile on her face.

"Quite alright," he says ignominiously and then, reaching into his pocket, he takes out his handkerchief and mops his brow.

The train worms its way along the Isle of Dogs, dropping few passengers and leaving steadily growing clumps of humanity at each station. He luxuriates in the girl's inadvertent proximity and this special moment of unplanned intimacy they are sharing. He feels himself thickening under the shadow of his ponderous belly. The train terminates at Bank and the contents of the train spews forth, filtering down the side tunnels and leaving him in their wake, staring ruefully after that delightful slender behind and blond hair that half runs, half skips through the crowd away from him. Rushing to some anonymous desk and computer, leaving a gently thinning spindle of memory between her and himself. There was a connection there. There was something. Something had definitely passed between them.

As he makes his way through the labyrinthine passageways towards the Circle Line, he hears a thick gravelly voice singing up ahead. Oh no, that's all he needs; some bloody scrounging musician and him having dropped behind the main pack, solitary and vulnerable. He reaches the top of the escalators and sees the busker. The man is big and his voice is powerful and intimidating. He tries to increase speed, but his legs protest. He glances at the busker again and finds the man is looking directly into his eyes. His face looks bloody and bruised and his nose appears to be broken. They are staring at each other and the man's words are pouring into him, though he cannot understand them and he suddenly feels naked and terrified. He tries to walk by, but he cannot; this man has seen into the very depths of his soul and this man knows what he hides there. He turns back around and, reaching into his pocket, he pulls out a note. Smiling desperately, he drops the money into the big Mexican hat that rests on the floor in front of the man. The man's lips are moving, but he does not hear him.

He turns away, praying that he will be allowed to walk on unmolested, and doesn't look back again.

Ted doesn't realise that his phone is missing until after the steering group meeting that is supposed to be looking at the redevelopment of New Covent Garden Market. He needs to call Grace and find out what the hell is going on. He almost ended up with a considerable-sized omelette on his face when the chief planner for Wandsworth had informed the meeting that Seagull Industries had not managed to garner the full support of the market traders and there was, in fact, considerable resistance to the proposed move of the market to the new site in Leytonstone, which basically translated as meaning that somebody had made an almighty fuck-up. Either which way, it certainly hadn't been him, and the payments that he had received in exchange for his assistance in steering the steering group in a direction that would be beneficial to Seagull Industries were non-refundable. Grace knew he had that group in the palm of his hand. What the hell had gone wrong with her end of the deal?

And where the fuck is his phone? He needs to get back home and make some calls from his study urgently.

Connie's Skoda is still missing when he arrives back at Apple Tree House. His family have lived in this house for generations but, as he stands there in the drive looking at the empty spot where Connie's car should be, he suddenly feels strange and out of place, as if he has walked up the wrong drive. He feels as if the house is looking at him more than he is looking at the house. He takes out his handkerchief and mops his brow, then puffs his way to the door.

He doesn't call out when he walks through the front door. He senses that nobody has been here since he left this morning. He makes his way through to the study. On his desk, next to his computer is Connie's 'World's Greatest Granny' mug. He picks it up and sees that the small amount of tea she had left in the mug has dried to a walnut stain at its bottom.

Connie never comes in his study. It is an unspoken rule that they have.

More than ever now, he feels as if he is being watched and he suddenly feels compelled to look over his shoulder behind him. Just the bookcase. He is aware that he is desperately trying to suppress an overwhelming feeling of alarm. Where the hell is Connie? Deep breaths: one... two... three... and relax. Suddenly all the anxiety leaches out of him. What good is it to chase around trying to get hold of Connie, or Grace, or anyone? Sometimes the best thing to do is to sit back and wait a little and see what happens. There's nothing to be done about Grace and Seagull now, and Connie will be home soon enough and then he'll treat her to a home-cooked meal, his speciality – beef bourguignon with dauphinoise potatoes. They'll open a bottle of the St Julien and catch up with each other;

it seems so long since they have spoken to each other. Seems like years.

He climbs the stairs, pulling off his scarf as he does so, which he hangs over the banisters on the landing, walks into the bathroom and starts running the bath. He begins to whistle a tune, then realises that he doesn't recognise the sounds coming forth from his throat and laughs at his own foolishness. He goes into the bedroom, takes off his coat and hangs it in his wardrobe. He sits on the bed and removes his shoes, then – puffing – he goes back to the wardrobe and places them in the bottom. Next, he checks his pockets before removing his suit, tie and shirt, which he neatly lays on the bed for Connie to deal with. Then, in his underpants and vest, he goes back into the bathroom. The bath is nearly full. He turns off the tap, removes his underwear and steps in. It takes him just a fraction too long to respond to the intense heat, as he had already begun to shift his bodyweight off his other foot. His scalded foot jumps out of the water and he suppresses a scream; the bath is the temperature of boiling pitch. He tries to get his foot up to the sink to get it under cold water but fails, so hops into the shower and, standing to the side, points the head down towards his outstretched foot and twists the dial. For a moment, nothing happens, but then the shower head sprays forth what feels like white hot liquid. He does not suppress the scream this time as he blindly grabs the shower dial and twists it desperately and, failing to do so, falls out of the shower onto the hard bathroom floor to get his body out of the intensely hot spray.

Ted lies on the cool stone tiles, taking deep breaths. Most of the front of his body – face, neck, chest, belly, arms and, of course, his left foot – are throbbing in preparation for a pain that has not yet been fully realised. He stays completely still and listens to the shower as it generates steam behind the shower curtain.

A door closes downstairs. Thank goodness; Connie's home. He bites his lip as, using the toilet for support, he pulls himself to his feet. He takes a towel and wraps it around his waist and steps out onto the landing.

"Connie!" he shouts. There is no reply. He hobbles across to the banisters and looks down into the reception hall. There is nobody there. His scarf is curled in disarray on the polished stone floor where it has fallen from the banisters.

Taking a firm hold of the stair rail, he gingerly makes his way downstairs, using his other hand to hold his towel.

"Connie!" he shouts again. Still nothing, or did he hear a noise through in the kitchen? He opens the kitchen door and steps through; there is nobody there. There are some old newspapers lying on the kitchen windowsill and his eye is drawn to a small green tin that sits next to them. He walks closer and, as he makes out the familiar writing on the tin, the lingering sense of anxiety and fear that he has been holding at bay for days wades back into every fibre of his being with a dread knowing of certainty.

He doesn't bother to pick up the tin. Ted turns and, like a man in a dream, he walks to the archway that leads to the lower ground floor and descends the stairs.

Sombrero

The sombrero hat contains £3.87. He's played for two and a half hours and earned £3.87. Hendo throws the coins back in. Clearly the recently broken nose and associated swelling is not helping his case, either aesthetically or vocally. He hates busking. He hates busking, but not as much as the monkey. He needs at least a tenner to feed the monkey. Just another half an hour; he'll catch the start of the lunchtime rush and then bust a move. He picks up the guitar and, fingers protesting, plays the opening sequence for *Green Grass*. A young couple pause as he huskily sings the opening line. Perfect; if you can make one person stop in England, you're halfway to a queue. People only want what other people want in this country. He sinks into the words and Ben is there with him, showing him the chords, teaching him the simple finger picking and strumming.

"Lay your head where my heart used to be,
Hold the earth above me,
Lay in the green grass,
Remember when you loved me."

He can't believe he'd made such an unbelievable (yet, admittedly, less serious than the previous nights) social transgression and all he'd managed to come away with was a small baggie of weed, an even smaller baggie of speed and that damned sombrero hat. Not exactly the Pink Panther, but what could you do? Everyone's but Pedro's room was locked or occupied, Pedro having passed out on the couch in the living room. Still, the sombrero gave him an idea, so he banged down the speed, grabbed his guitar and headed for the Underground. At least if he was busking, he wouldn't need to be thinking about what had happened to Ben. He'd raise enough money for a dose of smack and lay low at the squat for a few days. By the time he got back, Ben would have calmed down and Pedro probably wouldn't have even noticed the missing gear and hat. Well, he could bring the hat back. Or could he? That would confirm that he'd been in the room. Whatever, he could work that out later.

Jesus, but he is feeling the cold. There must be some kind of air-con or fan blowing nearby to ventilate the tunnels. He shudders, but keeps playing. Another tube has pulled in and the next wave of passengers swarms up the escalators and bustles past, towering above his cross-legged position like giants. It's the same shudder he felt when he saw the American guy as they were leaving the Millwall game yesterday. What were the odds? He'd never even been to a football game before. Quite an experience, he had to admit.

Two months ago, he'd not only run out of credit from his dealer, Barny; he'd also generated sufficient ill will to warrant a visit from this same said American guy called Ig. He had to admit, he was pretty predictable in his visiting hours at Barny's, so he shouldn't have been particularly surprised to find Ig waiting for him. He'd met some pretty hard nuts in his time, but this Ig guy was the worst kind: hard, obviously, but not just in muscle and build and quickness of movement: he had hard eyes, almost dead eyes – no trace of emotion behind them at all. When the Ig had inferred that he would kill him if he had not come up with payment in full of the amount owing within the next week, he'd said it like he was an adult addressing an errant child. Hendo was left in no doubt that administering the punishment would generate no more feeling than the same adult sending the child to bed without any supper for reoffending – probably less.

He'd promised to have the money ready, got the hell out of there and kept a very low profile since; there was no way that he was going to come up with three grand in a week with the habits he was fostering. He had to admit that after a month with his head buried in the sand, he'd begun to feel a little less cautious. Maybe Ig wasn't quite the threat he'd imagined. Maybe his imagination had gotten away with him; he was, after all, feeling pretty needy at the time. He'd kept Pedro signing on and collecting his necessaries for him (Pedro was the only one who knew about his smack habit) but started to hang out in the garden on the street, for brief periods; always watchful, but gaining in confidence every time. The football game had been an unnecessary risk, but Peds had been so excited and when Billy pulled out after Pete applied the pressure, he couldn't really drop out too.

A few coins this time (definitely at least one pound coin) and finally, at the end of the crowd, a pink-headed balding fat man goes past, looking harassed and distracted. He finishes the song giving the fat man his full attention:

"Don't say goodbye to me,
Describe the sky to me,
And if the sky should fall,
Mark my words we'll catch mocking birds."

The man stops in his tracks, turns round and walks back to him, pulls out a fiver from his wallet and, smiling uncomfortably, drops it in the sombrero, puffing all the while.

"God bless you, Sir," Hendo says to the man, who looks faintly displeased with this comment, then turns and puffs away. He counts the money - £10.74 - perfect. And, if he can flog the travel card, he might even get something to eat. He picks up the sombrero, feeling like the thing has saved his bacon for the second time in less than twenty-four hours.

He'd been wearing the hat during the game and the surrounding fans had got a kick out of it, calling him 'Sombrero' and giving him the thumbs-up. The tension in the air had been unbelievable, almost palpable. Us and them: never had the distinction been so clear to him. The petrol bomb had got the Millwall fans really fired up, but he was on their side; they were his comrades. These men around him would die for each other, as long as it was in battle against the opposing fans. It was like a carnival atmosphere as they headed for the gates. They were almost through when he turned to look at the fans following them out, some of them singing the Millwall chant and saw, not thirty yards away, Ig, dressed completely in black, making his way forward along with the throng. Behind Ig was a black-suited man-mountain and Hendo could just make out a shorter grey-suited man sandwiched between the two; Ig and the hulk were clearly his protection. He froze for just a second too long and Ig's eyes panned round and fixed on his, instantly registering recognition. That was the shudder moment. He turned and began to push hard. Seconds later they were through the gates and immersed into a scene that was something like what he imagined hell to be: the street on fire and people being beaten and tortured everywhere he looked. He tried to move along quickly, but most of the people exiting the stadium were crammed along the walls, trying to get out of harm's way. He managed to get ahead of Pedro and Ben and finally, getting into a bit of space, he'd turned to see if he was being pursued. He couldn't see them – it was clearly slow-going getting through the bottleneck. He spotted Ben and then a hand was on his shoulder and a moment later he was lying on the deck, holding his face. He almost laughed, despite the kicking he was getting, to see the football shirt on the man delivering it. He could hear Ben shouting incoherently before his assailant just disappeared and he was left lying on the pavement, still holding his face. Moments later, Ben was by his side.

"You OK, Hendo? Let's have a look mate," says Ben. He can see Pedro standing behind Ben looking like a lost puppy. Ben pulls his hands away.

"Ah mate, that is beautiful – you look like a Jackson Pollock."

Ben's smiling at him, like they're sitting in the kitchen discussing art. "Probably not the best place to linger, though. Here, hold it here…" Ben puts Hendo's fingers either side of the bridge of the nose, "… and keep pressure on it."

He helps him stand up. Pedro has disappeared. They have walked unsteadily for ten paces when Ben says, "Hang on, we've forgotten something. Stay here."

He watches Ben jog back into the chaos and bend down. Moments later, Ben stands with the sombrero on his head and turns to face him and smiles. Hendo senses the movement of something huge to their right, something big pushing through the sea of bodies like they're just so much long grass. Ben is moving slowly back towards him and he wants to shout out a warning, the cry is hanging in his throat, but he is stunned and terrified by the speed with which the force is bearing down on Ben and what will happen to him if he does cry out and then it's too late. Ben turns at the last moment and raises a defensive arm that might as well have been a twig. The black-suited man bats him with a huge shovel-like hand and then, in a smooth movement, picks Ben's now prone body off the floor, slings it over his shoulder, turns and stalks off in the direction from which he'd come.

Hendo is still holding his nose. He feels like laughing; this is all too preposterous.

Someone is nudging his hand:

"Eh Sombrero, your hat mate." The sombrero has been returned to him.

The tube train rushes him through the tunnels as he holds the hat between his legs and concentrates on the thought of that great big mind-numbing needle in the vein.

Cass and Bruce are back at the squat on Asylum Road. He gives Cass the cash, and he scuttles off to get the goodies.

"Haven't seen you around for a good while, Mr Henderson," says Bruce.

"Aye, I've been a busy boy," he says.

"Busy getting your face broken, by the look."

"Oh aye, you should see the other guy an' all that. Seriously Bruce, me and me mates went to the Millwall game yesterday and it was utter chaos."

"Holy crap, I saw about that on the telly."

"Was like a walk through hell. Fire and brimstone an' everythin' – the only thing missing was Ian Paisley!"

"Holy crap," says Bruce.

"Precisely. So anyways, what's new round here?"

"Oh not much y'know. Old Tom passed a few months back."

"Bruce, old Tom died over two years ago. I'm guessing from the fact that Tom's expiration has only recently registered in your addled brain that there is not a great deal of current news to report, then. You and Cass still thick as thieves, I see: you're in danger of becoming co-dependent, you two."

"Co-dependent? What's that when it's at home?"

"I'd never heard of it either but apparently it's a recognised condition, which manifested itself in the case of Laura, my ex-wife – through her incredibly low sense of self-esteem – as a deferral of responsibility of all her problems onto those that she loved. Now, one would have thought that this would make her the ideal partner for an inverted narcissist, which I apparently am, this being defined as an individual who is intensely attuned to others' needs, but only insofar as it relates to others performing requisite sacrifices for the aforementioned individual. An inverted narcissist ensures that, with compulsive care giving, supplies of gratitude, love and attention will always be readily available."

"You lost me," says Bruce.

"Suffice to say, Bruce, she wanted me to take responsibility for her problems and I wanted to unburden her of her problems as much as that's possible to do, in return for her love. Sounds like a match made in heaven, but unfortunately it didn't work out and we spent ten years ripping each other to pieces, trying to work out what had gone wrong."

"Well I'm sorry to hear that, Hendo."

"Well we live and learn, do we not? What about Lara? She still about?"

"Yeah, she's still around."

"She still hooked up with Jake?"

"Not really – not seen him about."

They hear the back door slam and then the sound of high-heeled shoes on the stairs.

"Speak of the devil," says Bruce.

Lara walks into the room wearing a smart black coat, white blouse, black pencil skirt and white heels. She has blond hair and blue eyes and he has to admit that she would be very pretty if she weren't so gaunt.

"Is Cass getting gear?" says Lara.

"Aye, but I don't know if there'll be enough for the whole house," he says.

"Don't worry big boy, I've got money." She pulls out some notes from her pocket.

"Busy at the shops today," says Bruce.

"Yes, and I got you this." She pulls an inconceivably large book from her coat.

"Is it the fourth one?" says Bruce excitedly.

"Yes mate – *Goblet of Fire*, as requested."

"Oh sweetheart, you are good to me," says Bruce, caressing the cover.

Lara isn't done and suddenly pens, pieces of fruit, items of underwear, bits of wire, two mobile phones, five miniature bottles of spirits and four packets of cigarettes appear on the floor, all seemingly magically produced from her coat and tiny handbag.

"Apples and bananas?" says Bruce. "Couldn't you have got some pies and burgers?"

"They're good for your health, Brucey boy, me old muckah, so get 'em down ya."

"Can I trouble you for one of those fine cigarillos?" says Hendo.

"Sure," says Lara and throws him a pack of cigarettes.

"Ta." He opens them quickly and takes one out, then slips the rest in his pocket.

"Ah, ah. One comes free, but the packet costs four quid," she says.

"Oh sorry love, I thought we were sharing out my gear when it gets here."

"Whatever. I'm getting changed." Lara walks out. Hendo looks at Bruce and they both smile, thinking the same thing: *What a woman, what a nutter!* He's starting to feel better, but then the memory of last night claws back round to the front of his head. He's not heard from Ben and he should really try and do something before he drops off the planet.

"Lara," he shouts, "is there any credit on these phones?"

"They need unlocking," comes the voice from next door. "But you can use this," she says as she walks back in, wearing a shell suit and trainers, and tosses him her phone.

"Thanks hun." He walks downstairs, still smoking the cigarette, and finds Anna's number from his phone and calls it. She answers, says she's driving, so he says to call her as soon as she's stopped. She says she'll pull over right away, so he waits. It's dark; another day gone without sunlight. Birds are singing somewhere. His phone rings and he realises he doesn't know what he's going to say. Three times, four times.

"Hi Anna, thanks for calling back," he says.

"What's going on?" Her voice sounds shaky.

"It's Ben. I'm just a bit worried. We went to the game last night and there was a bit of trouble and we got separated and he didn't come home. I've been calling his mobile, but he's not answering."

"Yeah, me too. Oh God, I was so worried for a second there. Have you any idea what might have happened?"

"I don't know. He's probably just been arrested and spent the night in the lock-up – there was quite a bit of trouble. I just thought I should let you know – I'm not going to be about for a few days, so I thought I should just let you know what's going on."

"Hey thanks, Hendo, I really appreciate it. I'm sure he's fine, he probably just went to stay with some mates and forgot his charger."

"I'm sure that's it," he says. He's actually starting to feel a lot better about the situation himself too.

"Well thanks again, mate," she says.

"Yeah, seeya hun." He hangs up, drops his cigarette and extinguishes it underfoot.

Returning upstairs, he finds Cass has arrived and preparations are being carried out in earnest.

"Ah, wonderful Cass," he says. "First-class tickets to nirvana all round and don't spare the horse."

"Very good Sir," says Cass as he heats his spoon, "very good."

"What's with the hat?" says Lara.

Several hours have passed and Lara has moulded herself to

Hendo's side on the couch. Cass and Bruce have sunk into armchairs so low that only the tops of their heads are showing. They have not spoken for a long time.

"It's a sombrero, from the Spanish *sombra*, meaning shadow. A sombrero is a shadow maker," he says. After a long pause she says:
"Yeah, but what's with it?"
"Oh, I was doing a spot of busking."
"Are you going to play me a tune, then?"
"Are you going to pay me?"
"No, but I promise I won't steal anything off you. How's that?"
"You're a hard bargainer. OK." He drags himself forwards and gets the guitar, unzips it from its case, then, holding the instrument awkwardly in front of him, begins to play. The guitar is out of tune, so he stops and fiddles with it a while, then starts again. It's still out but he presses on this time. He's singing the inescapable Tom Waits again. He gets to the end of the first verse of 'Sins of my Father':
"Night is falling like a bloody axe
Lies and rumours and the wind at my back
Hand on the wheel gravel on the road
Will the pawn shop sell me back what I sold?"
And then he breaks. He can't get the chorus out. He begins to sob and his fingers scratch down the strings and stop.
"Oh," says Lara. She pats him on the shoulder and then pulls herself up from the couch. He grabs her hand and, with tears streaming down his face, says:
"Don't leave me."
"I'm going to bed."
"Can I come with you?"
"No," she says flatly. She takes his hand gently from hers, then reaches down and picks up the shadow maker and puts it on his head.
"Goodnight," she says as she walks to her room, closes the door and twists the key in the lock.

Part 2

Shell Suit

The fat man draws Lara near to him. She'd seen him checking her out on the platform and positioned herself in the carriage within firing range of his mucky paws. *Don't look for work if the work will come to you*, she'd often told herself.

She'd got his Blackberry within two seconds of bouncing into his rounded belly, but the only other pocket she could get access to contained a solitary, slightly damp handkerchief. She was satisfied with the phone, though; despite its grubbiness, it was a fairly new model and it would ensure that she wouldn't go without tonight. There was also a middle-aged Indian woman directly behind her who got off at Canary Wharf minus her iPhone and three pound coins. So, by the time Lara got off at Bank, she was off to a flyer. She changed to the Central Line and headed to St Paul's, which was a new foraging area for her. She would not be going near to Oxford Street for some time now; that great big security guard's hand on her shoulder had given her the fear something terrible last week and there was no way she'd run the risk of bumping into him again. She never had to run. If you were running, you were doing something badly. But she'd run like hell last week and the bastard had chased her for a long time. Lara had the jump on him but the security guard had got the stamina on her, and she'd thought her lungs were going to explode when she finally lost him by stepping into a doorway, then stepping back out and walking towards the sprinting hulk in a nonchalant window-shopping manner. It was a gamble but it paid off and he ran straight past her full pelt. Sometimes, on a busy street like Oxford Street, a change of rhythm can be as effective as a change of appearance in giving someone the slip.

Lara tries Dorothy Perkins first; Dotty P's are usually pretty soft touches. She wanders round the shop, browsing the various items but specifically looking for something from their new range that is expensive. Finally, after a long search, she goes to the changing rooms. The shop assistant outside the curtained cubicles says:

"Good morning, how many items would you like to try on?"

"Three," she says, showing the assistant the three jumpers. The assistant gives her a large plastic tag with the number three imprinted on it. As soon as she is in the cubicle, she puts the three jumpers and the tag she is holding on the small bench and takes out a fourth jumper she has tucked neatly into her coat. She strips it of price tags and labels and then, having located the elongated electronic security tag, she uses a small penknife in her bag to get in the gap and jimmy it open. The tag is old and tired and offers little resistance. She removes her black coat and blouse and puts the jumper on, then puts the blouse and coat back on over the top, picks up the other three jumpers and the tag and steps back out of the cubicle.

"Well, what did you think?" says the assistant amiably.

"I really like this one, but I'm not sure if it's a good fit for me – I mean, I like the design, but it's not that comfortable round the neck. You've got to be comfortable," she says.

"Oh, that's quite right Miss, it's the most important thing," says the assistant supportively.

"I think I'll get it, but I'm just going to have another little look around," says Lara. She wanders round the shop a little, slides the electronic security tag under a pile of jeans and then, when a few more customers have walked in, steps back out onto Cheapside. She crosses at a pedestrian crossing and enters a coffee shop directly opposite Dotty P's. Using the three pounds she stole from the Indian lady on the tube, she buys herself a latte and installs herself in a window seat. She asks the man behind the counter if he'd mind watching her things, then goes to the rest room and removes her coat, blouse and new jumper. She puts her blouse and coat back on and, with new jumper in hand, returns to her coffee.

At exactly 10.15am, the girl on the till at Dotty P's goes for a tea break and is replaced by the changing room assistant. Lara crosses at the pedestrian crossing and re-enters the shop.

"Hello again," she says to the amiable young girl. "I'm so sorry about this, but I bought this jumper earlier today - I really liked the design - and I got back to the office and put it straight on and I'd been wearing it for maybe ten minutes..." Lara is making a show of scratching at her neck.

"... And it wasn't quite comfortable?" completes the girl, smiling.

"Exactly," Lara smiles with relief. "I just liked the design so much and... so stupid of me..." she says, shaking her head.

"Not at all, Miss - it's the most important thing," says the shop assistant, as she raises her eyebrows at Lara knowingly. "If you can just give me the receipt and I'll sort out a refund for you."

"Oh no," Lara looks momentarily crestfallen. She looks in her handbag and says, "I think I had it in the carrier bag and the cleaner was emptying our bins and I think he must've just tossed the bag in with the rest because I can't... seem... to..." she trails off. "Oh dear, so stupid," she says. "Oh well, nothing to be done," says Lara, as she looks back up into the sympathetic face of the shop assistant.

"Listen, I'm not supposed to give refunds without a receipt but I can see this is an honest mistake. Hang on a second," says the shop assistant as she walks towards the back of the shop. Lara holds her breath. When she sees she is just checking the price of the jumper, Lara surreptitiously pops a security tag from a pair of knickers she had subconsciously picked up and drops them in her bag. The tag falls in with the other knickers and moments later the penknife is back in her pocket.

"You are so kind, thank you so much," says Lara to the assistant as she comes back to the till.

"That's fine," says the shop assistant magnanimously. "It's forty-nine pounds." She punches the 'No Sale' button on the till and counts out forty-nine pounds. "Here you go."

"Thank you so much, that's so very kind," says Lara and begins to walk out of the shop.

"Miss?" says the shop assistant.

"Yes?" says Lara.

"The jumper."

"Oh dear me, so stupid, so stupid," she says, putting the jumper back on the counter and walking back out of the door with a final thank you and goodbye.

Lara buys a pack of cigarettes and smokes one in the shadow of St Paul's Cathedral, then carries on with her work. She runs the strategy again over the lunchtime period but the next shop assistant will only allow her to exchange the goods, so she immediately goes to the sportswear section and gets herself a new shell suit. If she didn't have to work, she would wear nothing but shell suits day in, day out. They are undoubtedly the most comfortable clothes you can buy. She steals her lunch using a Tesco self-service machine (great inventions) and then remembers she needs to pick up a book for Bruce, so pops into Waterstones at London Wall to do the necessary. She decides that if the next Harry Potter is physically bigger than this one, Bruce will have to go to the library for it.

Lara picks up another phone on the way home and goes for a pint of Guinness at the Hobgoblin while she waits for Abdul to crack it and the other two phones she'd picked up earlier. The pub is quiet and on the television is a programme where city people with extraordinary sums of money at their disposal look at houses in the country that they might move to. She follows the couple around the screen as they look at various beautiful mansions: one mirrored by the edge of a lake, one concealed deep within an oak forest, another perched on the soft contours of a rolling hill. She realises how out of place she would look in her shell suit, stood next to this man in his Barbour jacket and green wellingtons. She also realises that, after thirty years in London, she wants nothing more now than to go back to Devon; the place where she was born, but has never really lived.

Lara decides that if she cannot find a man in a Barbour jacket and green wellies to go with her, she will take her shell suits and go on her own.

Abdul has cracked the phones, no problem. He says:

"Lara, I couldn't help but notice, your 'uncle' has got some seriously fucked up stuff on that phone – I'd wipe the contents before you sell it, I mean, give it back to him."

"OK, I'll take a look."

"If you want, I can wipe it for you now."

"That's OK, Ab, I'll make sure there's nothing important on there that my uncle would want to keep and then I'll wipe it myself. Hey Ab, you ever thought about movin' to the country?"

"No darlin', no jobs there, innit."

"I guess, not sure the Barbour would suit you anyway."

"Eh?"

"Ignore me, I've been thinking."

"Drink plenty of water darling, you hear me, plenty of water!"

"You're crazy, Abs!" she says, laughing. "*Hasta la vista*, baby!"

When Lara gets back to the squat, she finds Cass is out and Hendo is there with Bruce. Bruce loves his new book. Soon enough, Cass shows up with the horse and not long after that they're all lined up and feeling fine. Cass and Bruce pass out, but Hendo is full of talking. He gets out some grass and he and Lara smoke a joint. He keeps going on about how 'the brown and the green will keep you serene' and it makes her want to laugh and think about the countryside at the same time, so she goes to the toilet to get her head straight. As soon as she closes the door, she feels exhausted and a bit sick. She squats down in front of the sink. Lara thinks about how the brown and the green will make you serene and she laughs a little. She puts her hand in front of her mouth as if to catch it and then she bursts into hysterical laughter, with one hand on the sink and one hand in front of her mouth. She laughs so hard she thinks she might pass out, but finally, thankfully Lara calms down.

She takes a couple of deep breaths and thinks all of a sudden that she likes Hendo. He seems solid. Maybe she could feel comfortable with him in the countryside. Comfortable, like she was wearing a shell suit.

She stands up, walks out of the toilet and goes over to Hendo, who is lying on the couch and curls up next to his side.

"What's with the hat?" she says.

Suits

The nausea seems to be passing. He rises slowly, careful not to set his head spinning again, using his arms as levers against the sink as well as his legs. A square in the centre of the mirror is heated from behind and stays mist-free. He used to love these little details that delicately intimated the luxury he had managed to afford for himself and his family: the fridge that makes two kinds of ice, the garage door that opens automatically when his car approaches, the voice-activated entertainment system, the roundabout at the front of the house with the little maple tree in the middle. But, as he looks into his half-shaven face in the small heated square of mirror, he feels unease within himself that he has allowed a collection of frivolous crap to become his trophies, to emulate his worth, to validate his life.

"Jim, I'm going now," Chloe's voice echoes up from the hall, "I'm out with the girls tonight, so you need to collect Carl from football, OK?"

"Bye, Dad."

He stares silently into his own eyes, listening to his wife and son downstairs as they pick up bags, coats, scarves, hats, keys, listening for a response from him, and finally, after a moment of quiet, there is the slam of the front door. He is aware of the noise from the extractor fan, which is activated by the bathroom light, so he reaches over and pulls the cord and then stands in the silent darkness, listening to his own breathing.

He thinks about light and the absence of light. He thinks about the cover of Pink Floyd's *Dark Side of the Moon* album, with the beam of light refracting through a prism. He remembers buying the album when he was twelve, with his paper round savings, the day his father had taken him to watch his first football match. It had been an amazing day: he'd bought the album from W H Smith in Islington, then they'd watched West Ham beating Everton 4-3; and – on the way home – they'd seen an amazing rainbow. A supernumerary, his dad had told him and then, in his typical physics teacher voice, he'd explained the wave nature of light, the importance of the droplet sizes and distance travelled through the raindrop, thinking that young James wouldn't understand as usual. But, instead of sitting silently in the passenger seat, he'd taken the album from the W H Smith bag and said, in the most offhand way he could muster, despite his reddening cheeks:

"Like this."

His father had actually laughed.

"Why yes, almost..."

It was the only time he could recall his father laughing with him.

He wonders if his father had had a mid-life crisis, had been brought to his knees on a Monday morning in the middle of his morning shave, sick with the horror of his own weakness, his own pathetic submission to a reality that had constantly pulled away from his will, his dreams, his control, leaving him emptied and drifting in a vacuum, with nothing but his material trophies to gauge his rank. Probably not. Doubtless his father had had mountains to climb: the loss of his wife, his inability to reconcile his science and his faith, his disappointment in his son for not sharing his academic zeal, but his father had never seemed to doubt *himself*. Maybe that was the burden of his generation. He thought of his son and Chloe's constant assertions that Carl was autistic, or had Asperger's, or SAD, or was hyperactive. Carl just seemed to enjoy the company of his computer more than people, as far as he could tell but, either way, whether he was an introvert or had a disorder, there was plenty of latitude for him to blossom into a fully dysfunctional and disaffected adult, standing in a darkened bathroom on a Monday morning, just like his old man.

He hears that cracking sound again in his head (or was it?) and quickly reaches out into the darkness to turn the light back on. He jumps to see himself now in the fully cleared mirror.

"Come on big boy, snap out of it." He takes three deep breaths, splashes the residual shaving gel from his face, reapplies more and finishes shaving. He looks at the various bottles of facial moisturisers and aftershave balms that Chloe has bought for him and then opts for a splash of 'Old Spice' (his father's preferred cologne) which Chloe says is cheap and nasty and detestable.

He steps out of the en suite, walks through the bedroom and into his walk-in wardrobe. Someone had once told him that Einstein (or someone equally famed for their intelligence) had only multiple copies of the same clothes in his wardrobe, believing that spending time deciding what to wear in the mornings was a waste of valuable mental energy. It was a philosophy that he had taken to heart, but he now looked at the rows of dry-cleaned, grey suits with little enthusiasm. What he needed was change. He rummaged in a box of his old clothes at the back of the wardrobe and found a West Ham shirt he had not worn since the 1990s that had somehow escaped Chloe's charity shop clearouts, but no alternative to grey suit trousers.

He makes his way downstairs and pops a decaffeinated 'Nespresso' pod into the coffee maker and then takes the muesli out of the larder and pours some into a bowl. He goes to his expensive fridge and pours skimmed milk on top. He eyes his breakfast distastefully. Dusty rubbish was how he'd once described muesli to Chloe and now he ate it every day. He takes the bowl to the bin and pours the contents in, then puts the bowl in the sink. He goes to the coffee machine and takes his freshly prepared decaf and pours that down the sink. Next he rummages through the cupboards, eventually surfacing with a stovetop coffee maker and a coffee bean grinder. He locates some real Javan coffee beans at the back of the freezer and, once he's got a fully caffeinated brew going on the AGA, he turns his attention to edibles. He is not surprised to find nothing in the way of sausage or bacon in the fridge but settles for a portobello mushroom, prosciutto, sundried tomato and Camembert omelette served with heavily buttered toast, brown sauce and ketchup.

His mood has improved considerably by the time he has finished his breakfast and, after putting another brew of coffee on, he goes to his office and there, concealed behind a copy of Paul Mckenna's *Stop Smoking for Good*, is a pack of Marlboro Reds and a lighter. As he removes a cigarette from the pack, he sees one of Chloe's hairclips on his desk. He envisages her taking it out as she flirts on the phone. With him? With someone else? He couldn't blame her. More than twenty-five years of marriage had made them acutely aware of each other's behavioural traits, both conscious and subconscious, an awareness that had slowly consolidated the fact that they were completely unlike each other in terms of their desires and what they had to give.

Chloe had always seemed so certain about her sexuality and was always very vocal about what she wanted and, because he was unable to reciprocate in this way, he had spent a long time believing that perhaps he wasn't sexual; that maybe he had a low sex drive. Whenever he'd tried to take command of their sexual direction, as she constantly instructed him to do, he felt like a fraud. His doctor, his priest, his teacher, his domineering sadist, his pervy office manager, his hostage taking terrorist; every stereotypical sexual fantasy he could think of had felt contrived and, no matter how enthusiastically they played their parts, underneath the costumes and catchphrases, the performances were wooden.

He'd spent a long time trying to analyse what actually turned him on, but there just didn't seem to be any pattern to it. His entire sexual history, both before and during his marriage, seemed to be a random scattergraph of events, the only predictable element of which seemed to be their apparent decrease in frequency.

He puts the hair clip back down on the desk. There is an email waiting to be read in his work inbox. It can wait. He goes back to the kitchen where the coffee is bubbling on the hot plate. He removes it from the heat before it runs dry, as his mother had once shown him, rinses his cup and fills it again. He opens the patio door and walks past the pool and the sauna, down to the large decked veranda that looks down over the small wooded area at the end of the garden and on to the Thames, which lies concealed in a thick mist. In the distance the Queen Elizabeth Bridge stands to the west, jutting above the river fog and beyond the city towers marking the edge of the horizon where the next queue of rainclouds rolling off the Atlantic are edging nearer.

He looks at the lawn stretching out below him and sees it for what it is: a rectangular expanse of green. He then thinks about what it also could be: he could walk down there and lie down on the grass, feel the cool dew beneath his fingers; he could look between the blades and see a microcosm of life, the smartly uniformed soldier bugs, the segmented detail of millipedes, coiling worm casts, the apple white lichens and emerald soft sphagnum moss; he could smell the dank sweetness of decomposing humus from the nearby woods; taste the citric sap of a dandelion leaf. The lawn is still the lawn.

He feels that he is approaching a pivotal moment; something of fundamental importance is nearby, and if he can just keep thinking clearly, he will be able to reach in the bag and pull out the album.

He takes a sip of coffee, lights his cigarette and blows cumulus clouds into the verdant misty morning.

He thinks of the scattergraph and he thinks of the lawn and he understands that his nature is chaotic: the things he finds funny, the things he finds sexy, the things he finds beautiful, are in a constant state of flux. He understands that his emotional response will be diminished whenever anyone tries to establish order over this natural chaos: he is not amused by stand-up comics and punch lines; he does not find strip teases sexy; he does not see beauty in mascara, lipstick and foundation. He suddenly understands that the seemingly random mechanics of his desire will always be drawn to that which is naturally impressive, to those individuals and elements that are without conceit and undemanding of attention.

He considers his life: his decaffeinated coffee, his fridge that produces two types of ice, his priest's costume and anal beads, his steady job, Friday night at 'Jongleurs', his dusty fucking rubbish. The truth is, he is a mere spectator in Chloe's world and living in the carefully planned structure of her world so deeply contradicts his integral nature, it is killing him.

He finishes his coffee and resolutely stubs out his cigarette. He walks back into his office and leaves the Marlboro Reds and lighter unhidden on the desk. There are now two unread messages in his inbox. Unusual. He opens the window and looks at the first:

> Deadline expired

He opens the second:

> Pluto en route

"Oh shit."

The doorbell rings.

"Oh fucking shit!"

He looks around frantically, then pulls out a copy of Sun Tzu's *The Art of War* from his bookcase and removes a key attached to the inner cover. The doorbell rings again. He unlocks and opens his bottom left desk drawer and takes out a Beretta PX4 Storm 9mm pistol, which he then tucks into the back of his grey suit trousers. He walks awkwardly out of the office and approaches the front door, jumping as the bell goes again.

He opens it. A DHL woman is standing there with a van behind her.

"Mr Kent?"

"Yes?"

"Special delivery of a laptop?"

"Oh yes, uh, hang on a minute."

He closes the door and breathes deeply, then takes the gun out of the back of his trousers and puts it on the hallway sideboard. He opens the door again and says to the courier:

"Sorry about that."

"No problem. If you could just sign here..."

He hears that cracking sound in his head again and feels nausea creeping up his throat.

"What?" says Mr Kent.

"I said, it's a lovely place you've got here. Are you OK, Sir?"

"Fine, here."

"OK and here's your receipt."

"Thanks."

"Have a good one," says the courier, turning back towards her van.

Mr Kent walks back into his house and closes the front door slowly behind him. He picks up the gun and runs up the stairs two at a time. He enters the bedroom and walks straight into the walk-in wardrobe and, standing in front of his row of grey, he pulls off his West Ham shirt and takes a random suit from its hanger.

Skirt

Friday night gigs in the city centre are a lottery. It's the moment when the city changes outfits, when the suits hand over the baton to the weekend crew and, if your timing is out just a beat, you can end up playing to a crowd of arseholed bankers, or, worst of all, you can fall between the two and play to no-one.

Audience is crucial. Plenty of these gigs are prepared to pay you, but only based on the number of punters you can bring along, so leftover suits and randoms don't count. To drop a coin in your hat, customers have to tell the door they came to see you specifically. It adds a certain amount of pressure to the evening. Most of the time you're not thinking about the music; you're thinking about which of your friends are going to show and who of their friends they might bring along. When the inevitable stream of texts come rolling in at the last minute to say, 'Sorry but...' you tell yourself it doesn't matter and you don't care, and it doesn't make a difference to your friendship. But deep down, you know different. A card has been marked and one day there will be a day of reckoning: when you're sat in the life raft with limited space and the sharks are circling; when the lottery numbers roll in and you're picking your friends to come along on an all-expenses paid trip to everywhere; when you headline at Glastonbury and you're inviting people backstage for an after show party with all the other living legends – on that day, these cards will be checked, the loyal supporters will be richly rewarded and those that said yes when they meant no will be eaten, left behind and excluded. Usually, for gigs like tonight – Friday @ The Purgatory Club – we do not expect to get paid.

Another problem with Fridays is that you've all got to be at the venue early to have time for a decent sound check. Some places will actually specify times for bands to do their sound check, and if you miss your slot, tough shit, but at most of the gigs we're playing it's first come, first served, so everyone's trying to get off work as early as possible to get ahead of the rush hour, get a decent sound check and then chill for a few hours before going on stage. Often as not, particularly with a big band like ours, you're always missing at least one person, so the rest of you all just sit around getting tense: watching the other bands sound check; the drinkers drinking too much; the smokers smoking too much; the ones on the wagon wondering whether they should eat something to settle their nerves, then worrying that maybe this will leave them feeling bloated, so instead they fiddle around with their phones, leaving messages for people who are clearly underground, crammed next to disgruntled commuters who begrudge them the extra space their instrument cases are taking up. Eventually the sound engineer will usually say it's now or never, because he wants to get some food from anywhere but this bar, so you sound check as best you can without bass, or drums, or lead guitar, or something else of equal fundamental importance. Usually your sound check doesn't sound good because you're missing something and because you were in the middle of eating when you were called up, which only added to the nerves.

I am beginning to think that London is not the place for us to make a breakthrough into the music scene – London is where you go to play gigs once you've made it. London doesn't give a fuck – the city is saturated with music, and people are immune to anything they don't recognise, picking out the familiar from the constant barrage of sound that emanates from buskers in the tube, a radio in a greasy spoon, a muezzin in a minaret, a 90 inch TV in an electrical store with surround sound, the overheard ticking buzz from headphones that you can't quite identify, the boom-boom-boom from the darkened interior of an exhaustless UV police magnet, bird song at 3am whistling out of the orange sodium glow-lit streets. Music loses its magic in London, it's just another heading in *Time Out*, another victim of the city's enormity swallowed up in the listings. We made it to posters on telegraph poles and in chip shops when we played a gig in Dover. People listened. To a certain extent, they had no choice; there wasn't anything else to do, except eat chips. Big fish in a pond or small fish in the sea?

I'm watching David stretching a string on his Gibson. He is an absolute pro. Of the six members of the band, three of us are good enough to play as session musicians; the other three are good at writing material, good at providing free rehearsal space, or just good fun. David is our lead guitar. Technically, he is unbelievable – his speed over the fret board, solid rhythm, diverse knowledge of music (he can play blues, jazz, reggae, rock, folk, even classical... and, of course, gypsy punk), but his real strength is his sensitivity to the rest of the band. Half the time you won't even notice what he's doing, because he's making everybody else sound good. He tends to avoid long guitar solos. He would, I am certain, be a sensational fuck. I imagine he masturbates rarely and probably has wet dreams frequently. He works for the river police or something as a diver, but he's not an asshole and smokes weed sometimes with the rest of the boys.

I'm the only girl in the band, which I like. I'm the lead vocalist. A lot of people say I look like Alanis Morrisette, which is fucking annoying, and we will often get asked to play 'Ironic' or 'You Oughta Know' and we sometimes have arguments about whether we should play some covers to capitalise on this fact. There's more chance of me doing a duet with Elvis than sacrificing my artistic integrity to do a cover of Alanis Morrisette. This was essentially what it always boiled down to – in my humble opinion, any idiot can play covers, but what's the point in regurgitating material that came from someone else's heart, when you can say something uniquely your own (or in our case something uniquely Kenny's own, who writes most of our songs)? At the end of the day, *if* I decide that it would be good for the band to play a cover song as part of our set – which, yes, I appreciate is what most bands do to help widen their appeal to Joe Public (as the scout for a record label that showed a temporary interest in us once pointed out) – it certainly isn't going to be an Alanis Morrisette cover.

I actually used to like that *Jagged Little Pill* album, and they were some of the first guitar tunes I learned when I was eight, but that was also round about the time my life turned to shit. The only two things I think about when people ask me to sing Alanis for them now is the line: 'And every time I scratch my nails down someone else's back I hope you feel it. Well can you feel it?' which ran on a loop through my head when, at the age of 15, I slept with my boyfriend-of-the-time's best friend, because I thought my boyfriend had cheated on me (turned out he hadn't, but he certainly felt the nails thing when I told him). The other is, Alanis doesn't know what ironic means.

We're waiting on Kenny tonight, which is unusual. Normally it's Damien, who has to drive, because most drummers are arseholes and won't share kit. When do guitarists ever refuse to lend their instruments? Guitars can cost as much as a drum kit. The usual way it's supposed to work is that one drummer will bring a full kit for the night and then the rest just bring their steels, a snare and a bass pedal but, honestly, negotiating with these assholes to get permission to use their kit is like giving an elephant a pedicure and sometimes talks break down. I am responsible for talks. "He won't thrash my toms, will he?", "He's not going to need a stool, is he?", "He's bringing his own hi-hats, isn't he?", "He's not going to pick up my bass drum and slam it over an audience member's head, is he?". Unfortunately the answer to that last one, on one particular occasion, turned out to be yes. I mean, Damien is the nicest guy you could hope to meet most of the time, and he was mortified afterwards – paid for the damage, no qualms – but when he gets behind a kit sometimes, he can get overexcited. Sometimes it's easiest to just tell him to bring his own kit.

Anyway, Damien is here and he's got his kit set up to one side of the stage where some other drums already are. Quincy (our fiddler) and Tem (bass) are outside smoking. Here's a wicked story: Tem's girlfriend Tanya, who is unbelievably hot (I mean I'm not that way or anything, but seriously...), well apparently she was at work today and getting loads of shit from her boss and she just stripped off her uniform, butt-naked in front of this woman, then put on her cycling gear and walks out of there. The whole office was watching and apparently they went crazy, clapping and singing like Munchkins in *The Wizard of Oz*. Fucking great story, but Tem is flipping about her overdraft, plus you can see he didn't much like Tanya getting naked in front of an office full of men. Got himself a handful there.

So, yeah, just waiting on Kenny.

It's a love-hate thing, this time before a gig. On the one hand there's all the nerves, like I said, but on the other, seeing the rest of the gang arriving to face the music by your side is an amazing thing. I mean, I love these guys better than my family, no question. They never probe into my private life or want to dig into my psychological background, they never let me down; we just share this common bond of music and it is as intimate and loving a bond as any I've ever had before. I love to get to a gig or rehearsal first, so I can see their faces showing up one by one, watching them interacting with each other - my family.

I leave another message for Kenny.

The other bands have all sound checked - nothing special. We get up and sound check, all half-hearted, but still sounding ten times better than the rest of them, and then head down to the main bar to get some food.

People start to show up in dribs and drabs and the apologies start pinging in by text. The promoter comes over all pleasant and makes small talk, which culminates with "Are you expecting many tonight?" Yes, plenty, blah.

Edgar (such a cool name) shows up and says he's got something for me, which can only mean one thing. A month ago I asked Edgar to do a little background digging for an exposé I'm trying to do on this bent councillor who I've got a hunch is a kiddie fiddler. Bastard. Edgar would need to have found some seriously incendiary material to consider it a) too dangerous to email and b) worthy of him getting off his fat arse and leaving his room to bring to me in person. Wow indeed! He gives me a USB and tells me that on it is a taster, which I need to handle with care, and that he will call me tomorrow to discuss his percentage, but won't divulge anything further. I ask him if he wants to chill for a bit and watch us play, but he laughs and says it's not his scene and then he waddles out. Too cool for school, is Edgar.

We're headlining tonight (damn straight) and the band before us go on and there's still no word from Kenny. David finetunes his new string and then starts warming up his fingers with stretches over the fret board. Me and Tem do some Sumo stomping to let out some of the tension. Damien and Quincy are drinking pints like drought victims.

Kenny doesn't show and we have to play without him. You can tell we all feel the gap. It's not as bad as playing pool on your own, but they live at the same tube stop. We still kick some heavyweight arse, mind. If we were only half as good at promoting ourselves as we are at playing together, we'd be rolling in dosh by now.

Well there's the promotion problem and then there's the image issue as well. David arrived wearing a fucking cardigan tonight - thankfully with a black t-shirt underneath, but still. I've got this tiny tartan skirt, stockings and suspenders, heels, pigtails and china doll make-up, and David looks like Father Ted! The image is a real issue. If only we looked half as good as we sound - well, you know the rest.

Shame the music industry has got nothing to do with music.

We're just about to launch into our final number when a long-haired suit from a table of three very drunk suits stands up and starts shouting for Alanis. His mates try to calm him down, but he thinks he's funny and persists. Finally, one of the other two suits gets him in a headlock and they get feisty and red-faced. The third pulls them apart and the long-haired suit says, "It's just a fucking skirt!" staring angrily at his co-suit. He takes his coat and leaves, talking loudly to himself as he does so. The other two make no attempt to follow him.

I look around at the guys and say, "'21st Century Schizoid Man'?" They all beam with approval.

I hate to admit it, but the cover feels great. You can sense the excitement running through the whole band, the unique enjoyment of playing music that is both intensely familiar and yet completely novel. The guys tear the song to pieces, then cement it back together with wasabi, while I plough out the lyrics, stomping round the stage almost bent double like a penitent Christian. By the end, the whole bar is jumping. They want an encore, but they don't get one.

As soon as we're done, I step out to think about what it would be like to have a cigarette now. I'm sitting on the red step (the three steps into the side entrance to the club are white, black and red), which is the only dry step, and let my head come back into focus. The rain has stopped finally and through the gaps in the orange clouds I can see stars.

"Excuse me, I just wanted to say I thought that was really great." She is plump, has ginger hair and is semi-suit with a cigarette – probably a Marlboro Light.

"OK," I say and look away.

"... And sorry about the moron at the end."

"You've got some choice friends," I say, letting it drip.

"No, no, he's not my friend – I just come here a lot and wouldn't want you to be put off from playing here again. A friend of mine runs the place and he doesn't get many good bands in, particularly gypsy punk."

"Oh." I'm starting to feel a bit uncomfortable for being so rude.

"Well anyway, thanks for the show and sorry for intruding." She walks away. I want to say something, but the deed is done.

When I go back inside, Tanya and Tem are talking to the ginger woman, so I keep my distance. No-one else feels like sticking for a drink without Kenny around (who is still not answering), so I help Damien pack up and load his drums and then hit the road. I run and knock up a number 8 as he's pulling away and the driver's a rare 'un and stops and lets me on, so I'm home watching the egg timer on my laptop with a falafel wrap and a black coffee on this side of 1am instead of after 2.

I'm thinking about the guys in the band and their happy faces when we played that cover and wondering if artistic integrity really is more important than just enjoying yourselves, when the flash drive opens itself up. As usual there's a picture of a ram's head superimposed onto the muscle bound body of a chunk with a pair of socks down his posing pouch. The ram's jaw bobs up and down as a mixture of famous sci-fi movie voices, of which I recognise Darth Vader and Morpheus, proclaim: "You were right about the councillor, Izzy, more than you know. The rabbit hole goes deep on this one. I have covered my tracks, but I want guarantees for my complete anonymity before I hand over the payload. I want five thousand cash in unmarked bills on Monday morning and in return you get the councillor's head on a platter. Do not mention any of the details from this message when I call tomorrow, just a yes for Monday and the five thousand, or a no and the story goes elsewhere. This message will self-destruct in five, four, three, two, one seconds... " This, as usual, is followed by Edgar making various self-destruct noises and then playing some Rammstein music in the background – 'Fueur Frei!' – this time, which I don't mind, so I let it roll.

Five thousand! Bloody hell, what's he found? I munch on my falafel thoughtfully. Edgar is no more a hacker than I am, but he's a good researcher when it comes to digging out the facts on industrial espionage cases. I usually pay him five hundred quid a pop for his research and maintain the artifice of his secret hacker double life, when he tells people about it at parties. Besides, I secretly enjoy the entry-level drama of his *Mission Impossible* messages. I've never asked him to dig the dirt on an individual before and to be honest hadn't had high hopes that he'd come up with anything. I mean, apart from my lack of faith in his actual ability as a hacker, what do I have to go on? I'd gone to cover a children's event at Greenwich Maritime Museum and seen the councillor picking up the kids and sitting them on his lap for the photos and I hadn't liked it. That was it. He was hardly putting his hand up the little girl's skirts.

But his face said he wanted to.

I'd seen a face like that before.

Shalwar

Elsa is on the first floor of a big house in the country and Scott is out in the garden with Ben and a girl she doesn't know. Scott's hair is all huge and dreadlocked, like it was in the photo taken in Thailand, and he's wearing the baggy beige trousers that he bought in Peshawar, when he tried to sneak into Afghanistan. They are called *shalwar* and have a blue drawstring with tassels to secure them. She is knocking on the window to say hi but they can't hear her. The three of them walk away from the house across a field and into some woods, chatting and happy and pushing each other around. After an interminable time of waiting, she sees the girl coming back out of the woods, closely followed by Ben. The girl is crying and Ben is angry and shouting at her. As they come nearer the house, she starts banging on the window again. Somehow she knows that they won't hear and when they come into the house she won't find them and Scott will be gone. They both come into the house and she's left looking at the flaking paint of the window frame and the worm-holed wood beneath.

Now Elsa's in the old bedroom. It's dark outside but the light is on, stark and unshaded, as it always is. She is lying on the bed, back tight to the wall, looking across the telescopic crimson carpet to the top of the stairs in the opposite corner of the room. To the left of her view is the doorway, with no door, through which the unseen expanse of empty, dusty attic extends over the top of the stables and coach houses that silently circle the dark courtyard below.

In her head, she traces the route across the room: past the attic doorway, squinting ahead to fool her peripheral vision into not seeing the yawning black space to her left; down the stairs, weaving through the stacks of old Greek and Latin textbooks, pans, crockery and chairs, and out of the heavy door, into the moonlight cutting under the archway; barefoot skipping under the frosty shadow of the clock tower, over the courtyard, not once looking back at that heavy door, almost humming, but then, not humming and quietly opening the door to the familial sanctity of the staff quarters, where she is embraced by the residual warmth of the fire that has merrily munched through slow, spitting cedar and easy splitting ash and, still with eyes fixed in front of her, she pulls the door, with its warped glass rectangle, shut, feels the key, twists and breathes.

Maybe if she'd broken her inertia and left when this thought process had started she'd have made it, but not now. Now she traces a different route: from the black, splintery latibulum that lies somewhere under the gargoyles, slates and gothic buttresses, through the complex reticulum of beams and wooden pillars that support the great structure of rooftops. She sees through an unnatural locomotion that darkens the skylights as it passes, until it pans round a final corner to reveal, at the end of a last stretch of attic, a doorless doorway, a stark, shadeless bulb and a crimson carpet.

She turns away from the empty doorway, agonising over the sheening sound the musty old sleeping bag, with its dislocated zips and white stuffing, makes, and faces the wall, fighting to control her breathing, hearing the glottal liquid sounds of saliva and muscle filling her head, drawing the all-too-small bedding up to bury the noise, which suddenly frees to reveal her naked legs. She freezes, suddenly silent, and catches the end of a scraping noise from the doorway. Every muscle is straining, every fibre is locked and bound in terrified focus.

The light goes out. Every rational part of her brain that was spinning threads of disbelief to persuade and cajole her into realising that her fear was just a result of an overactive imagination is severed by the dark. The fact that she heard the switch flick makes short work of any renewed hope of power cuts and spent bulbs. She can feel malevolence and anger closing in on her, a cruel, merciless intent; a promise of something more than the mechanical grinding of hungry jaws, a boundless viral agony binding and transmitting its unspeakable horror to the host.

Her legs are still exposed. They cannot be moved. She feels the cold deliberation of them closing in. Her very being is bursting to scream, but a cold constricting weight has filled her lungs.

It is next to the bed. It is slowly reaching for her legs. Her body suddenly pumps like an airless swimmer, far from the surface, but getting closer and closer and…

She's awake, gasping, sheets damp with perspiration.

Voices and warm laughter drift through from the kitchen next door. She breathes deeply, checking the room briefly, then falls back into her pillows, drawing her exposed legs up under the duvet, and listens to the distant flow of 3am conversation.

Being in the only bedroom on the ground floor can be a trial, with parties sometimes lasting for days, but she'd learned to cultivate an 'if you can't beat 'em, join 'em' attitude, which, though it hadn't exactly boosted her employability, had certainly expanded her horizons in the eight months she'd lived in the house. Besides, she secretly enjoys the proximity to her housemates, who have become like a family to her.

She thinks about a huddle of penguins in the depths of a dark Antarctic storm and luxuriates in the warmth of her nest.

After a time, she jumps down from her self-built scaffold bed to stand naked in front of the mirror and inspects herself: pulling down each eyelid (minimal red eye), inverting her lower lip to stretch the chin skin taut like a chicken's (clean), touching her cheeks, breasts, belly (all firm). She stretches, arching her back, yawning, swinging her arms over her head and down in front of her before absent-mindedly scratching her pubic hair. Satisfied with herself, she dresses quickly and enters the kitchen and is immediately assailed by a thick cloud of marijuana smoke.

Nat, Hendo and Pedro are arranged around the kitchen table in various states of activity and inactivity. Hendo has an inverted, wheel-less bicycle next to his chair and is meticulously oiling assorted cogs and components with a soft, yellow rag. Nat is assembling a shark fin in her rusty smoking tin lid; her previous assemblage is hanging from her thin lips. Pedro appears to be concentrating on sagging. Considering the number of empty wine bottles, beer cans and overflowing ashtrays, she is surprised to not be encountering more saggage.

"Oi oi!" shouts Hendo.

"*Hola bonita*," drawls Pedro, momentarily smiling through his narrow window of languishment.

"Oh darling, I'm sorry, we didn't wake you did we?" Nat appears genuinely concerned as she moves a couple of coats from the chair next to her.

"Nah, that's OK," says Elsa, "anyone else about?"

"Tanya and Tem have crashed – they're off sailing early – haven't seen Billy or Sammy and Ben and Anna are in bed," says Nat, raising an eyebrow.

"You mean... in bed, in bed?" says Elsa, looking surprised.

"That's right," says Nat again, "think that one's been brewing for a while."

Elsa hopes no-one will notice the force she is having to put behind her smile. She doesn't know whether she is more envious of Anna for getting together with Ben or for being in love with someone warm and breathing and able to return her love. A little vacuum waits for her to decide.

"Fancy a wee drop?" Hendo is holding up a quarter-full bottle of Highland Park.

"Mmmm, why not?" she says, her smile becoming a little more relaxed as she appreciates, not for the first time, the way Hendo's Scottish accent becomes fully liberated by whisky. He pours and hands, she sips, grimaces, then experiences the warm glow as the spirit runs down her throat.

"Are you OK, hun?" Nat puts a skinny arm around her shoulders.

"Yeah, I just had a horrible dream."

"Dreams are the window to the soul," states Pedro.

"I think you'll find that it's the eyes which are reputedly the window of the soul, Pedro," says Nat (Pedro is nodding as if someone has just agreed with him), "but most oneirologists would probably agree that dreams are merely random reflective responses of the brain's activity of the day, both remembered and experienced." Nat continues, as she finishes rolling the joint, talking about the transformation of things according to a Chinese philosopher called Zhuangzhi, who dreamt he was a butterfly, then woke up and didn't know whether the dream was real and he was a butterfly dreaming he was a human, or vice versa. She is glad she feels no such confusion after the dream she just had and once more experiences a deep sense of comfort and belonging amongst her housemates, the like of which she has not felt for the last three years.

Nat is still talking. "Nevertheless, this perspective raises interesting questions about the when, where and what of the soul."

"Which leads us back to what I was sayin' before about Cambodia," says Hendo. "So this wee dude takes us to The Killin' Fields, right, and yer've got a glass-sided monument with all the bones and skulls, right, and they're all riddled with bullet holes and that, but I thought, right, that I'd feel somethin' more from it, but it's jus' left us cawld, aye."

"Just a load of old bones," says Nat.

"Exactly. So anyways, o' there on the other side of the village is this church, right an' soon as I looked at it, it feels jus' wrong, like somethin's out of place, aye, so I asks this wee guy, 'What's wrong with that church there?' and he says, 'That's where they'd take the villagers and shoot 'em', and I knew it straight away. It was stark, like. It was a bad place, you could tell, like something got left there when the villagers were killed."

"Have you ever walked into an empty room," says Nat, "and found there's an obvious tension in the atmosphere as soon as you walk in, and later you find that your parents have had a blazing row, then stormed out before you got there, or some such?"

Pedro once more surfaces briefly, like a marine beast taking air. "Eh Nat, tha's bullshit baby – you don't know what you're talking about."

"Ach, just because your emotional and spiritual sensitivity abides on the same end of the spectrum as neeps and tatties, that doesn't preclude the possibility that others might be picking up on frequencies above the subterranean. I know what you mean love, aye," says Hendo.

"If the emotional release of an argument can reverberate for hours afterwards, imagine the reverberations of watching every single person you love getting shot in the head and then having your own brains blown out. It's hardly surprising that we can connect with these currents decades after the event," Nat says, as she finishes rolling.

"That's right," says Hendo.

Elsa is crunched up on her chair and looking distant, but then she starts to speak slowly:

"The house I grew up in was a huge old stable block. It had a courtyard, a clock tower, forest all around... We weren't rich, but my parents looked after the place so we were allowed to live there at an affordable rate. As a teenager, I always wanted independence and space, so I took a room as far away as I could from the rest of the family, across the courtyard and under the bell tower - it was cold and damp, but it was freedom. Rumour had it that no fewer than three people had died in tragic circumstances on the property: one man shot himself in the greenhouses in the walled garden, another girl was accidentally trampled to death by a horse in one of the stables and another man hung himself in the clock tower. In the daytime, it wasn't so bad. If you went into the bell tower, you could still feel the building's energy, its sadness, but it was during the night that this sadness turned to anger. It may sound ridiculous, but it was a very real presence that flooded through the dark empty spaces of the house. As real as the light in this room, or the smoke in the air an oppressive, palpable, malevolent force, it would find me isolated and alone, hiding in bed under my blankets."

"Aye, the best thing for that is to get up, get the lights on and face your fear," says Hendo, trying to shake the haunted looks that have crept around the table.

"I know, that's what Scott used to tell me, but sometimes I just couldn't, I just froze up..."

A moment of quiet descends. Whisky is sipped. Hendo lays aside his cloth and picks up the communal guitar and starts playing a Tom Waits song by the name of 'Trampled Rose', his voice guttural but surprisingly tender.

She's drifting as the music flows over her, her eyes looking at the grain of the table top as her fingers toy with the blue tassels of her trousers. Her grief comes to her gently now.

Sweater

Gary's eyes are watering and he can feel the nitrogen trioxide getting into his lungs. The red gas burns his eyes, so he opens the window a little further, but not before it sets him coughing – and that really hurts like a mother fucker. He lifts his sweater up and holds it over his nose and mouth. This is always the worst bit of the process and his wounded chest is not helping. He knows he should get out of the room, but the lowest heat on the stove is just a little too hot and so he needs to stand over the mixture of sulphuric acid, potassium nitrate and sodium nitrate to ensure that the nitric acid, which is running out of the retort into a beaker that is sitting on the side in an ice bath, is correctly produced. He knows very well how important it is to keep every ingredient required for the making of RDX stable.

His best and oldest friend, John, works as a cleaner at UCL and has access to every laboratory in the university. He'd given him his shopping list and told John he was experimenting in making fertilisers for his allotment and there were a few ingredients he was finding it hard to source. John had agreed to do it on the condition that he paid a small sum to the value of the chemicals that John could donate to the university and that John would be able to sample one dinner's worth of vegetables for him and his wife Barbara, once the crop was in. Gary gave him £100 and a promise on the veggies and John brought him the goods the next afternoon, each ingredient sealed in a dry glass jar as instructed.

The rest of the required ingredients and equipment he picked up from Halfords, Blacks and Boots.

Gary considered hunting down the two animals who had worked him over, but deep down he knew that they were merely instruments obeying the instructions of a higher power. He'd decided, as he'd poured neat vodka into the gaping wound in his chest, that he wanted to take matters up with whoever that higher power was. Fat lot of good it would do, he was sure, but there were principles to be maintained.

Gary was both resourceful and well connected, and he also had a considerable number of favours to call in. He'd saved several lives when he was posted in Northern Ireland and they weren't the kind of people who forgot. Barnes had provided the bolthole – a caravan near Dartford, where he was currently hiding out – and Jonesy had confirmed that the instruction to apply pressure had come via a small-time thug called James Kent, from the resolution manager of Seagull; a certain Miss Grace Evans. He'd also provided Gary with a residential address in Blackheath. Both lads had offered additional services, but he'd said no, this was personal.

His unit in Northern Ireland was specifically trained to locate and neutralise IRA bomb-making factories and his superiors made sure he had a comprehensive understanding of how the mind of a bomb-maker worked. He could manufacture a dazzling array of plastic explosives and produce pressure triggers, electronic triggers – you name it. For this particular job, he'd opted for RDX, which he intended to wire up to the target's ignition. He'd chosen RDX because, with a detonation velocity of over 8,500 metres per second, RDX was considerably more powerful than C-4. And he was pissed off.

He was also conscious of the fact that he needed to make a statement. It was only a matter of time before someone blabbed that Chris was his son and he was not prepared to expose his son to danger if he could help it.

The nitric acid is ready. He takes more ice from the freezer and adds it to the various ice baths that he has prepared and then begins to break up the hexamine that he purchased in Blacks. This will be slowly dissolved into the acid and then the RDX will be cold-filtered out. Once it's dried out, this stuff will blow under one and a half grams of pressure. It is not the sort of explosive Gary would recommend for the beginner. It is not particularly hot in the kitchen, but Gary is perspiring heavily nevertheless.

His target (always good to follow the training and emotionally disassociate yourself with the living and breathing facts of the job, even when it's personal) is located at a substantial private residence on Pond Road, just off Blackheath: pool, tennis court, sauna, the lot - clearly the business of extortion is a lucrative one. He will park on South Row, stroll down Pond Road to the target, do the necessary and then pop in to the Princess of Wales for a jar round the corner when the deed is done. It's always good to have a pint after work.

He will begin operations at the exact moment of the final whistle of the Millwall game. They are playing at home and the police will doubtless be expecting aggravation from this particular fixture. This is an old trick the IRA used to use; they would always coincide the arrival of large shipments of drugs or weapons with the Orange marches, knowing that the police would be stretched to capacity.

Once the RDX is drying, he has some time to kill. He could do with some milk for his tea and needs some more painkillers and dressings. Gary decides that some dinner would probably be a good idea as well, so he drives into Dartford. He orders a funghi pizza to take away and then goes to the supermarket while his food is being cooked. He automatically checks the price levels and general quality in the fruit and vegetables section and makes a mental note to tell Charlie to offer a couple of pallets of clementines out to the traders. The stall is overstocked and the market is clearly short. Gary puts one pint of full-fat milk in his shopping basket and then, on an impulse, puts a large carton of blueberry yoghurt on special offer in his basket. He wonders whether his actions are a result of subliminal messaging or some other advanced marketing technique, or just a hungry belly, as he wanders off in search of dressings for his wound.

Gary is walking down an aisle that is stocked with toilet paper and washing powder when he suddenly stops dead in his tracks. He begins to pick up different boxes of washing powder and smell them, until finally he finds the one that hooked him: Linda's brand. He has not thought directly of his ex-wife for a long time, but he knows that she is always there in the back of his mind, waiting for a sensory trigger to release her.

She was never the best-looking girl, but she could move so well; whenever she danced, Gary's heart would do what his two left feet never could and take the position of her partner. She dances again, across the mindscape of their relationship, as Gary stands there with the box of washing powder in one hand and the basket with the milk and yoghurt in the other. She dances towards him in a fluorescent tank top, out of the smoke and the dry ice of the club where he'd first kissed her. She dances around him in her white dress at their wedding reception. She dances in a maternity dress, in the officer's club with the other soldier's wives, in the life in Ireland that he dragged her to that she hated. She dances two backward steps in the beige lamb's wool sweater, the same sweater which he is wearing, in their kitchen; she dances two backward steps and falls on the floor, in their kitchen, where he first hit her. The only time he hit her. He saw her only once more, her hair cut short and her glasses replaced with contact lenses, and he begged her to forgive him, if only for the sake of their two-year-old son, Chris, but she didn't need to tell him, because he could see. The dance was over.

He places the box of washing powder gently back on the shelf and finishes his shopping.

Gary stands at the bar of the Princess of Wales, fingering the moth-eaten frayed edges of his sweater, having just taken his first deep draught from his pint of London Pride. Everything had gone exactly according to plan: he got back to the caravan and took a lot of painkillers, finished making the bomb, then ate his cold pizza and the yoghurt and had a cup of tea with milk. After this he undressed and cleaned all of his wounds before applying fresh antiseptic and dressings. He put clean black clothes on, but with his usual beige sweater under his lightweight black jacket. He put the bomb in a small rucksack, along with a mini Maglite, some wire cutters and crocodile clips, then got in the car and drove extremely carefully to South Row, on the edge of Blackheath. He walked silently down Pond Road, disappearing into an alcove, when a couple approached from the opposite direction. He located the drive and found, to his relief, that the gate to the property was open. He had not fancied pulling himself over walls and fences with his torso in its current condition. He located several motion sensors as he made his way up the shadowy edge of the drive, which he bypassed and then disabled with the crocodile clips and wire cutters.

When he got to the house, he made a quick, careful circuit and, having ascertained that the target was entertaining a gentleman in one of the upstairs bedrooms at the rear of the house, he made his way back to the front of the house where two cars were parked in the drive. On the one hand he felt lucky that the cars were not parked in the garage, which would have been an extra hassle, but on the other, he needed to make a decision on which one to wire up. In the end he opted for the white Audi sports car; the alarm and immobiliser were considerably more sensitive, but he just couldn't bear the thought of destroying that beautiful old Jag and, besides, it is Monday tomorrow and the Jag was surely only for weekend afternoons.

He set the bomb, slipped back down the drive and then walked back along Pond Road, turned onto South Row and made for the Princess of Wales on the corner.

Gary is thinking about that night again, fourteen years ago. After Linda had called her mother, she had gone upstairs and showered, then she had dressed, packed a bag and taken Chris in his buggy and walked out of the house. He had followed her from room to room, too drunk to really comprehend what was going on, just leaning in the doorframes saying sorry over and over. When she had left the house, he had followed her to the front door and watched his wife and his son walk off into the night. After a time he climbed back upstairs and took the bloodied sweater from the bathroom floor and washed it in the sink. He washed it over and over, with soap, bubble bath, shampoo

– anything he could find – until there was no trace of blood left, then he'd pulled off his jumper and put on the beige lamb's wool sweater, all heavy, wet and cold, and sat on the bathroom floor until he was well and truly sober.

She had refused to see him, until the day of the dissolution of their marriage when he had begged her to change her mind. He had told her he could make things better, he had cleaned up his act, he was off the drink, but to no avail; he wasn't going to be able to wash this one off.

Gary stands at the bar and twists his pint on its beer mat, first left, then right, and thinks about going back up the drive.

String Vest

Edgar twists his wine glass from left to right and back again. The waitress approaches his table and, giving him a hand towel, says delicately:

"Will Sir be dining alone?"

"Actually no, thank you. After giving it some careful consideration, I've decided to dine in tonight," he says, mopping his face. "May I have the bill please?"

"Certainly Sir, I'll bring it right over for you," she says as kindly as she can.

He looks around the restaurant; people are beginning to return their attention to their own meals. He can feel red wine running down his belly, into his underpants and collecting around his balls. Well, it had been a good run of luck, but it had to end sometime.

It had started yesterday when he was trying to dig the dirt on the councillor that Izzy was interested in. He'd tried all his usual methods for hacking into the guy's background - doing web searches and analysing the data for abnormalities - but it was considerably more challenging to try and look around in the shadows of an individual's private life than it was to poke about in a publicly limited company's dirty laundry, even one who works as hard as the councillor to maintain a high profile in the public eye. Photos of the guy's mug were literally everywhere on the council's website and in the local newspapers, but nothing in the way of shady deals - and certainly nothing to suggest that he was into kiddie fiddling.

Edgar located the councillor's email address and managed to find his way onto the council intraweb, but after a couple of random guesses in the dark about what the councillor's password might be, he gave up. Besides, what were the odds that there would be anything incriminating on his council email address? What he really needed was to get onto his private home server and email, but how could he do that?

He ran a couple of searches on the internet on how to be a hacker. A lot of the results appeared to be duds that showed you how to create a skull and crossbones screensaver and various other techniques to 'impress your friends', but he was already considerably more adept at this side of hacking than the online tutorials. Edgar had to admit that when he thought about it, the odds are probably pretty remote for a search engine to offer up links for people to learn skills that would essentially undermine the authority of the company behind the search engine.

Finally, he found what appeared to be genuine information about a hacking community and was horrified to discover that he was not only *not* a hacker, according to the general definition of the word, but he wasn't even a cracker, which was apparently someone who could break into a phone system and 'phreak' it! The article made multiple references to learning code in the manner of a Zen master and that to become a hacker was like learning any discipline – it took years of hard work and intensive study. The article went on about being prepared to make sacrifices, such as foregoing sex, money and social approval – Edgar believed that he already ticked all of these boxes – and the importance of not falling into the trap of calling yourself a 'cyber punk' or getting involved in 'flame wars on UseNet'. Edgar began to realise that he couldn't even speak the language that instructed the student in learning the language of the hacker.

The article stated that, contrary to public opinion, hackers and nerds were highly likely to make good lover or spouse material, and advised the hacker initiate to attend science fiction conventions (where hackers tend to hang out), and learn a martial art or musical instrument. At no point did the article give even one hint or tip for the beginner on how to engage in some sort of basic hackage. Specifically, it did not tell him how to access the councillor's private home server.

Edgar was essentially a very lazy man and realised quickly that investing ten years of his life in high intensity study was not going to be on the cards. He had gone way beyond the point already where he would have normally given up on this particular line of enquiry, but he had never failed Izzy before and she really believed that he was a hacker. In fact, she had inferred as much at parties, which had done no end of good to his kudos at the housing co-op where he lives. He looked at the screen and saw that the councillor's home address was shown on the council website. He could go over there and break in. Edgar instantly dismissed this thought as quickly as the ten-year hacker training plan – balaclavas and bolt cutters really wasn't his scene.

Underneath the councillor's home address was a phone number. Before Edgar had really thought about what he was doing, he picked up his mobile and dialled the number. The number rang and rang and rang, and just as Edgar was thinking better of his actions, the ringing stopped and the voice of a woman said, "Hello?"

"Hello, my name is Edgar," *stupid, stupid,* using his actual name, "and I'm writing an article on paedophiles and the danger they pose to our children. I was wondering if the councillor might be willing to talk about what local authorities are doing to address this issue."

There was a long silence.

"Hello?" he said.

"Yes, I'm still here." The voice sounded dreamy and spaced out.

Another long silence. Edgar waited. Finally, after what seemed an interminable gap, the voice said:

"What was your name again?"

"Edgar Coleridge," he said; all his instincts for self-preservation and subterfuge had evaporated.

"Well Mr Coleridge, I have a story for you."

Silence again. He waited, his heart beating hard. There was something quite unnerving about this disembodied voice at the end of the line. Edgar started to think that maybe the phone had been answered by mad Aunt Jemima or some such, but then again –

"Do you have an email address, Mr Coleridge?" said the voice.

Edgar gave it.

The voice read it back to him, then told him to check his inbox in an hour and hung up. Half an hour later, Edgar received an email. The body of the email was empty, but had several large attachments. As he opened each one, his sense of anticipation was replaced with at first astonishment, then horror, and finally the growing realisation that a) not giving this email to the police would probably be a crime in itself and b) he needed to up Izzy's rate on this one.

He put together Izzy's *Mission Impossible* file using the voice toolbox to make it sound cool and then saved it on a flash drive. He knew that Izzy was playing at Purgatory tonight and this delivery needed the personal touch.

His next stroke of unbelievable luck came the next morning. Edgar was lounging in his room, stripped down to his usual comfort wear; boxers and a string vest. He was enjoying a Ranchers burger and a large bag of prawn cocktail-flavoured snacks and was scrolling through women's profiles on a dating website. He'd never managed to facilitate a date, let alone sex, but once he managed to get a girl to talk to him on a webcam chat and show him her boobs. Regardless of all this, he enjoyed looking for the saucy photos and having a perv at real women, which seemed more exciting to him than looking at the flawless pneumatic bimbos in porn films.

He didn't know what drew him to that one particular profile and prompted him to open a chat window, but the response was instant:

> Fancy a chat?

> Hiiii sexy

> How are you?

> I'm fucking horny darling – can u help me out?

> I'd love to

> Wat do u want to do to me?

This was the bit Edgar hated, where he usually lost the girl's interest. He paused for a moment, debating what to say, but before he got a chance to say anything another chat message came through:

> Can u meet me 2night?
> Yes
> I'll be at Gio Gios on Camden High Street at 8pm 2night. Where a red rose – my friend has a place we can go nearby
> OK
> Here's my number – 07********* my pussy will be waiting – it will be like sliding between silk sheets
> Here's mine – 07*********
> Gr8 c u later lover boy

Moments later his mobile pinged, indicating that he'd received a photo file. He opened it and his other hand automatically slid down over his string vest, following the contours of his belly to the growing tumescence in his boxer shorts.

He spent the remainder of the day umming and ahhing about whether or not to go. The arguments for going were considerable; the most prominent being that Edgar had not had sexual intercourse for over eight years. The arguments against were that Edgar had used the same photo for his profile picture that he uses for all his internet interaction -the muscular, bronzed torso of a model with a great big schlong in his posing pouch. Edgar did not look like this.

Edgar goes to the supermarket and buys a bunch of flowers, which include red roses, just in case he decides to go. When he gets back to the house, Lorenza is in the kitchen:

"Hey Eddie," she says, "who are the flowers for?"

"Oh, I've got a date tonight," he says in an offhand way as he turns the pages of the *Guardian*, which is on the kitchen table.

"Nice one – where are you going?"

"Gio Gios in Clapham, maybe…"

"That's fantastic Eddie – I hope it goes really well for you," says Lorenza enthusiastically.

"Yeah, well, it's no big deal," says Edgar, and then goes upstairs to his room and lays the flowers on the bed. He's told Lorenza now, so he's got to go, he realises. He goes back out and gets himself a haircut and some new shoes, then, returning home, he has a long soak in the bath, which annoys Frank and Tina, who both want showers and the top floor shower is broken. He shaves very carefully and then applies a generous amount of aftershave and deodorant before laying a long collared shirt, smart trousers and blazer over the top of fresh boxer shorts and string vest. He puts on his lucky socks and new shoes and then, standing in front of the mirror, he applies the final touch – a red rose in his breast pocket.

Edgar looks at himself. 'Hackers are highly likely to make good lover material'. He smiles.

He arrives in Clapham at 5.15pm. The early evening is grey, but he decides to go for a walk on Clapham Common to kill some time. A murder of crows is scattered over the grass and as he approaches they lollop away in lazy bounces, keen to avoid unnecessary flight. It starts to rain and so he turns and leaves the joggers and crows to it. Edgar waits in the Alexander pub for almost two hours, drinking diet coke for the first hour and then switching to Peroni for the second hour for some Italian courage.

He arrives at Gio Gios at 7.45pm and gets one of the last free tables by the wall near the door to the toilets. He curses himself for coming to the restaurant so late and not booking a table. He'd wanted a window seat so he could see her coming. Still, at least he has a table.

He orders a bottle of house red and some water and then tells the waitress that he'd like to wait for someone before ordering food. He pours a glass of red and water for her and then a glass of each for himself. 8pm comes and goes. At 8.15pm, Edgar starts to feel very warm, so he takes off his blazer and puts it on the back of his chair, then he realises that his string vest is clearly visible through his white shirt and thinks about putting his blazer back on. Edgar thinks that it might look odd to put his blazer back on, having just taken it off, but then he realises that the red rose is on the blazer, so he needs to be wearing it to be recognised. He half-stands and takes the blazer back off the chair and is putting it back on again when he realises he is being watched. Turning fully, he sees her stood in the middle of the restaurant, staring directly at him. She has a face like stone. He stands up straight and pulls the blazer fully on and then gives her a small wave. She walks slowly towards him like a lioness sizing up a little warthog by the watering hole. Edgar tries very hard to smile. When she reaches the table, he begins to lean forward to give her a kiss and then stops himself as he registers her backwards movement in time with his.

"Chloe, I presume," he says, extending his hand instead, "I'm Ed." She does not offer her hand. She does not look at him in the face. She is staring at his belly with undisguised disgust. Edgar withdraws his hand and self-consciously pulls his blazer closed over his belly and then just stands there with a mortified expression on his face. Finally she says:

"Wow, you look quite different from your profile picture. Did they use a fish eye lens for it or sumfink?" She is still staring at his belly.

"Ha," he says, sitting down slowly and indicating with his hand for her to do so too. "Yeah, sorry about that – my friend set up my profile and he said I'd get a better response if I used that photo. I got us some wine – I hope you like red," he says trying to sound casual.

"Your friend," she says slowly, as she sits on the edge of her seat, with her legs tightly together and pointing to the side, clutching her coat around her and now staring vacantly at the table. "He give you any 'ints and tips on what to do when you actually went to meet someone?"

"Ha ha, well, it's funny you should say that, but, well, no."

"Right, gotcha." She looks him in the eye at last and her face suddenly transforms as she says, "You 'orrible, fat, lyin' deceitful barstard! You fink you can just go aroun' connin' girls into gettin' into bed with you and slobberin' your big fat ox tongue all over 'em and they won't mind when it comes to meetin you that you're not the tanned, fit stud from your photo? They won't mind when they see that you're a flabby, pale, ugly bloke?"

"I'm really sorry. Look, now that you're here, surely we could –"

"We could what? Being as I'm 'ere, I might as well fuck ya?" she shouts, standing up.

"Please," he says, "I'm so sorry. Won't you just stay for a drink? I've got us a bottle of red..."

"Yeah, go on then luv," she says, suddenly sickly sweet. "I'll have a drink." She picks up her water. "I'll have a drink on you," and pours her water over his head. He feels the weight of the restaurant's eyes on him and just sits there. He just sits there and takes it. "Oooh, nice vest," she says, and starts laughing at his string vest, which is now highly visible through his wet shirt. "'Ere y'are sexy, have another drink," and she pours her red wine over his head. She is laughing hard now and without saying anything else, she picks up his water in one hand and his red wine in the other and tips them both over his head at the same time as well. She is convulsed in silent hysterics now, gripping the back of her chair to stop herself from falling over and pointing at him with the other.

He just sits there and takes it.

There is a loud clattering in the kitchen which seems to break the spell over the rest of the customers in the restaurant and the low intermittent hum of hesitant conversation begins again. She finally gets control of herself and says:

"Ooooh my gawd, phew, I needed that! Well thanks Ed, I've had a wonderful time. Word of advice, luv - in future, I'd recommend looking like your profile picture if you intend to actually meet girls. They like it better that way. Oh, and ditch the string vests, sweetie. Byeee." And with that, she walks away.

Edgar pays the bill and leaves. He takes two buses home, leaving purple footprints in both. When he gets back to the street, there is a large fire burning down by house 10, surrounded by silhouettes and the sound of voices, guitars and djembes. He quietly enters his house and is relieved to be able to get upstairs to his room unseen. He closes his door behind him and for a moment stands there leaning on the door, with his head on the frame and his eyes shut.

"Never again," he says quietly under his breath.

He turns and walks to the mirror and looks at himself. He undresses in front of the mirror, down to his boxer shorts and string vest. Then, after a moment, he pulls off the soggy, purple-stained vest and drops it into his waste bin, then he sits on the floor of his room, puts his feet under his bed and his hands behind his head and slowly, painfully, he does a sit up.

He puffs heavily, but he doesn't stop. He has decided not to stop until he looks like his profile picture.

Sarong

Lorenza steps into her room and closes the door. She puts her economics textbooks on her desk and switches on her laptop, then goes downstairs to make tea. She has to borrow a teabag and a little bit of milk. She looks in her section of fridge and cupboard, but they are empty. She has a cursory glance in her housemates' sections of fridges and cupboards, but there is nothing that she can take that won't be obviously noticed. She gets back to her room and opens her emails. There is an email from her mother and her sister. She opens her mother's email first. She talks about the weather in Lima; grey as usual. She talks about how expensive food is getting, even if you go to the local markets, and that their rent has been increased again. Her mother tells her that her grandfather's small amount of savings are all but used up and that it is likely that he will have to come and live with her, but she doesn't know where she will be able to get additional money to pay for his upkeep and his medicine – the cost of drugs these days! Anyway, she mustn't complain; at least she has the thought that her two beautiful daughters are happy, to comfort her through these difficult times. Rosella is doing so well up in Mexico, with Guillermo and the two babies, and her dear Lorenza is over in London studying so hard.

Her dear Lorenza. She finds it very difficult to ask about this, but she feels she can speak to her beautiful Lorenza, because Lorenza has always been so understanding. She can't possibly speak to Rosella about it; Rosella doesn't understand the position she is in and it would break her heart to know that her mother is having such difficulties and with the two new babies to contend with, she already has so much on her plate. She hates to ask, but she knows the university's grant had been generous – could she possibly see her way to wiring just a few hundred dollars for grandfather's medicine and to help them get enough to eat, just until the situation improves?

Her mother then talks a little more about the usual topics and asks her when she'll be doing the right thing and finding herself an honest man to settle down with, like her sister. She finishes by saying that if Lorenza can send six hundred dollars, she thinks that they can get through the next few months.

Lorenza is beginning to regret telling her mother that she was getting a generous grant from the university. The truth is, she isn't getting any grant at all and is working as a cleaner in the mornings before her lectures and doing various temporary evening jobs, whenever she can, just to pay her tuition fees. She had told her mother about the grant so that her mother wouldn't worry. She still feels glad that her mother can talk to her at all about these things – she knows that she would die before telling Rosella – but what can she do? She is barely surviving as it is.

Things hadn't always been this way. In 1997, her father had been declared a hero for his involvement in Operation Chavin de Huantar, the operation that brought military resolution to the Japanese Embassy hostage crisis. In December 1996, fourteen terrorists raided the Japanese Embassy in Lima and took hundreds of diplomats and foreign dignitaries hostage. The Peruvian president of the time, Alberto Fujimori, himself of Japanese descent, took a hard line when it came to dealing with terrorists. Whilst negotiators engaged in talks with the Tupac Amaru Revolutionary Movement, plans were made in secret to find a military solution to the problem. By using tank processions out in the street and the playing of loud music to act as a cover for the noise, military forces were able to tunnel beneath the embassy. Supplies for the hostages were littered with miniature microphones and bugs and fresh clothes that were sent in were light in colour, in stark contrast to the guerrilla's dark camouflaged gear.

After 126 days of siege, a coordinated attack was carried out whilst most of the terrorists were engaged in a game of football on the first floor. Her father was one of the commandos that stormed up from the tunnels as others burst in through the windows upstairs, freeing the hostages. One hostage, two commandoes and all fourteen of the terrorists were killed in the raid. Her father had always alleged – as he drank Pisco sours at the bar, or Cesquena beer, which he preferred when playing chess – that the hostage that was killed died because he hadn't obeyed the instructions that had been secretly circulated around all of the captives to lie flat on the floor when the raid began. He instead hid himself in a cupboard when the room was sprayed with bullets, which offered insufficient protection.

President Fujimori's popularity had rocketed after the raid was hailed as a success by much of the international community, and her father – along with the other commandoes involved – had basked in the subsequent afterglow of the operation with an abundance of awards and decorations pinned to their chests. Her father had always enjoyed his status as a raconteur in the local bars near their home and suddenly he had become an icon of Peru's perceived strength and subsequent economic growth, and would have his drinks bought for him every night of the week. People loved to hear about the tension in the tunnels before the raid and the gruesome end to the terrorist ringleader, Roli Rojas, whose head was blown off in the attack. Even the death of the hostage was felt to have some moral meaning, giving the whole tale an epic timeless quality.

For three short years, her parents had lived a privileged existence. They had even gone on holiday to Bali in 1999, which made her the envy of her friends.

In the year 2000, President Fujimori fled to Japan amidst a corruption scandal and was subsequently impeached. Charges of corruption and human rights abuses were made, including accusations that several of the terrorists involved in the Japanese Embassy crisis, including Roli Rojas, were summarily executed after the attack was successfully concluded. Her father had been devastated by the news and after he himself had been interviewed and cross-examined on his version of events, he seemed to lose something vital that had been within him. He had to buy his own drinks in the bars now, and when people questioned him about the event, they listened carefully to his answers and watched his face, wishing to ascertain the truth in his words. After a while, her father stopped going to the bars and began to drink at home. He began to drink more than ever.

Her father eventually passed away from liver failure in December 2007, three months after Fujimori was extradited back to Peru, and on the very day the once-heroic president was convicted and sent to prison.

Her mother had always maintained that he died from a broken heart.

Lorenza opens the email from her sister, which briefly outlines her plans to take the kids and Ophelia, her wet nurse-cum-maid, down to the house in Acapulco to try and get some respite from the intense summer heat. Guillermo has to stay in Mexico City for work. Will Lorenza be flying back to Peru for Christmas? She hasn't thought that far ahead yet, but she supposes she ought to start planning it soon - it is no walk in the park, travelling with two young babies. She'd seen on the news that England was having the wettest summer on record - poor Lorenza, it must be absolutely abhorrent. Why doesn't she go on Skype once in a while? Rosella misses her baby sister.

Lorenza is only too aware that she doesn't miss Rosella, her older sister, for whom everything in life seems to come on a platter. Lorenza had watched her sister squander the gifts that were given to her - gifts that she would have cherished. Rosella's university education had been paid for. She had partied hard for two and a half years and then dropped out just before her finals. Lorenza had had to work as a secretary in a law firm and save her money for three years in order to afford the opportunity to study economics at Goldsmiths College in London. Rosella, with her stunning good looks and hourglass body, had fallen in love with Guillermo a year after leaving university. He was successful and they were happy with each other, yet Rosella had told Lorenza of at least three affairs which she had had since her marriage to Guillermo. Lorenza had never been in love. And now her children were palmed off on a wet nurse – children that Lorenza would have loved and cared for as if her life depended upon it.

Lorenza knew that, even as a child, she had coveted all that Rosella was blessed with. During their holiday to Bali, her father, who at the time was in receipt of a great many free things, accepted a free lift from a tuk tuk driver that ended up including a complimentary tour of a textiles factory. The sting was taken out of the hard sell at the end of the tour because the factory manager was highly enamoured with 16-year-old Rosella. By the time they left, not only had they not been forced into buying anything, but Rosella had been gifted a free sarong. Lorenza did not think she had ever seen anything more beautiful. Lorenza knew that it would do no good to ask her sister if they could share it – Rosella never shared anything with her sister as a matter of principle, and if she knew Lorenza wanted what she had, it would make her flaunt it all the more.

But Rosella knew, she always knew, and she could see when Lorenza had it bad. Lorenza could see that Rosella's behaviour was highly affected for her benefit, but there was still nothing she could do about it, and she watched as Rosella wallowed in the beauty of her gift. Lorenza begged her parents to buy her a sarong as well, but Bali had been more expensive than they had expected and the budget had been tightened to just the essentials of accommodation, food and booze for her father. A sarong was out of the question.

The whole family were sitting on the beach one evening, watching a glorious sunset, as some local fishermen barbecued freshly-caught fish over an open fire nearby. Rosella was talking to a local boy and her father was doing his best to explain to the fishermen that cooking fresh fish on a fire was a crime when you could be making lovely ceviche instead, much to his wife's amusement. Rosella had taken off the sarong and she and the boy had gone down to the sea to swim. Lorenza was captivated by the deep violet and clementine sunset, but her eyes kept straying to her sister's clothes, with the sarong lying on top. Her mother had gone over to help her father demonstrate the making of ceviche. No sooner had she walked away than Lorenza stood up and walked over to her sister's clothes, picked up the sarong, took it to the fire and, without hesitating for a moment, dropped it on the smouldering embers. She clearly remembers watching the smoke spiralling out of the material thicker and faster until finally the blackening blue and white material was engulfed in flames.

She had smiled to watch her sister's instrument of control and torture burn. She had made no attempt to conceal her crime and was beaten soundly afterwards.

Lorenza is shaken from her memories by loud sounds of grunting and groaning next door. What on earth was Edgar doing?! Maybe he really had got lucky last night and someone was in there with him enjoying the benefits of his exertions. Dear old Edgar; he really is a very strange man. She hears distant chanting from the Millwall stadium and thinks of Pedro, another strange but lovable man. She cannot help but feel a deep sense of kinship with these people who she has shared her life with now for two years, but however enjoyable she feels that they are to spend time with, she also understands by their very nature that they are transient, fluid, nomadic people, physically to an extent, but emotionally to the core. They share each other's light, but conceal their own darkness from each other.

Lorenza sits down at her desk and opens her books. The words flow over her and she realises after an hour that she has absorbed nothing. She is tired and hungry. She can hear sirens in the distance and she worries for Pedro and his two friends, who went to the game. She tries to refocus on the pages. She thinks of her mother and the six hundred dollars that she has asked her for and she wonders how she will find the money. She thinks of her father and remembers what he had said to her after he had spanked her for burning her sister's sarong. He had held her and wiped her tears and then spoken to her, so closely that she could smell the gin on his breath, and in his rich, deep timbre – a voice that could hold small groups of people bewitched for hours – he'd said:

"Lorenza, you are not like Rosella. These things that you desire, you only think that you desire them, but you do not really need them. Rosella wants you to think that you need them because she wants you to be like her, down here." He held his hand near the ground. "But you have soul, Lorenza; you have more spirit than you know and when you understand this, these material things will no longer have importance to you. When you understand that your gift is the greatest of all, my beautiful Lorenza, you will learn to fly and even your body will no longer matter." He had held his fingers pinched together like a cage and, looking her in the eye with his big, dark, brown eyes, he had slowly opened them until his hand was a smooth trembling canvas.

Lorenza turns off her light and lies on her front on her bed. She wishes she could just lie like this forever, not needing to move, without hunger, responsibility or sadness.

She thinks about her father's words and wonders if her body already no longer matters.

Slippers

Barbara opens the fridge and looks inside at the shelves, packed with a vast array of delicious items, and says: "Honestly, the things that man said to me, it was awful – and do you know what Andy did about it? Nothing, not a bloody thing! I really don't feel like going in there tomorrow."

"They need to look after you, my love, and if they're not going to do it, you need to look after yourself. Without you to keep those temps on the straight and narrow, I don't think they'd even have a business." John flicks his ash out of the kitchen door.

"Well, I don't know, I'll see how I feel in the morning." Barbara reaches into the fridge and takes out some skimmed milk and, with one last rueful look inside, closes the door. "Do you want a tea, John?"

"No love, I'm just going to finish this fag and I'd better get to bed. I'm going to try a different route in in the morning."

"Alright, I'll be up in a bit." With her tea, Barbara goes through to the living room. She sits on the couch and switches on the box with the remote. She puts on her TV glasses and then flicks through the channels rapidly, stopping every once in a while and whispering the name of the programme at the bottom of the screen to herself. On one channel there's a cycling race, and she thinks of the girl on Friday who had caused all the trouble at ISIS. She'd stripped off in front of everybody and then, cool as a cucumber, put her cycling gear on and, helmet in hand, walked out. All the temps had clapped like she was some kind of hero. Well, the real heroes of this world are the ones who stick around to clean up the mess afterwards. The customer, Mr Kent, had obviously been beside himself but still, that was no excuse for the things that he'd said. He'd called her the c-word a number of times and been very threatening – a right little muck-spreader, as her mother would have said. She didn't know what she would have done if Donnie hadn't been there to get the rest of the staff in order – she thought there might be a riot at one point. Finally, she'd managed to get in enough words between his ranting to promise him that his unit would be returned to him first thing Monday morning and he'd hung up.

"*The Black Swan*," she mutters under her breath. This was the one about the ballet dancer who went mad. Barbara's mother had taken her to see the ballet once when she was a little girl and she'd been entranced by the graceful magic of the dancers. She'd started taking lessons and she was good. She was flexible and surprisingly light on her feet for her size – she'd always been a big girl for her age. They'd had to order special ballet slippers for her, but Miss Beauvoir had been very encouraging and, even though some of the girls had made fun of her and called her the 'Giant Carrot', she stuck at it. When the class came to putting on a production of *Swan Lake*, she was amazed to be given the lead role. She'd practiced for that show as if her life had depended on it and she still remembered waking in the night with aching cramps all over her body. They were worst in her feet, which she'd grab with an "Ah, ah, ah, ah," as she massaged the spasms out of them.

On the night of the performance, Charlie Oliver had told her he wasn't going to be able to hold the lifts as he'd put his back out, and suddenly she'd felt gargantuan and certain that she would be a laughing stock. Miss Beauvoir had dried her tears and told her that people would remember her for what she had done, not what others hadn't, and so she'd gone on and given the performance of her life. At the end of the show, the crowd had roared their approval and when she and her friends were leaving the venue, John Letz (who, though two years ahead of her in school, was already four inches shorter than her) had approached her and taken her to one side and offered her his commiserations on the performance. She was taken aback and asked what he thought he meant. He said to her that he thought it was a shame that such a fine dancer as herself wasn't able to find a real man strong enough to partner her on stage. Barbara had said, "And you think that you'd be strong enough to manage those lifts?" with more than just a hint of disparagement in her voice. No sooner had she said the words than his hands were round her waist and she was off the floor. "I reckon I could," he said, without a hint of a wobble in his voice or his arms. There'd never been another man for her.

Yesterday had been their twenty-fifth wedding anniversary and he'd taken her out to Gio Gios in Clapham. The evening had been hilarious; there'd been a scene at a nearby table where a young man had clearly bitten off more than he could chew with his date, a dynamite blond who had lost her rag with him and proceeded to pour every drink in reach over his head. Poor bloke, but she and John had had to laugh after they'd gone. John was driving, so he only drank water, but Barbara had a nice bottle of Pinot Grigio to herself and both of their complimentary glasses of grappa after the meal. Even so, it was John who said he was feeling a bit tipsy as they walked out of the restaurant. She loved him dearly and he was the kindest man she knew, but he was soft in the head sometimes – drunk on water!

The film cuts to the second set of adverts since she had turned it on. Which channel was this? It seemed to be five minutes of film and five minutes of adverts. First an advert for pizza comes on, thick and juicy and covered in peppers and pepperoni, with stringy mozzarella stretching away from a slice as it is pulled away from the golden brown body of the main event, yellow cheesy goo oozing from the hollowed-out crusts. This is followed by an advert for a burger chain: plenty of nice close-ups of the meat pattie, sizzling away on a barbecue grill, and then the cheese is shown melting atop the thick meaty burger, relish is squeezed from between the bap and the meat as the soft floury bun is pushed down, sealing the deal. Barbara's belly rumbles. This is all she needs on the first day of her diet! Next is an advert for indigestion tablets and this is immediately followed by an advert for fried chicken: chicken legs coated with a golden, crispy, seasoned coating, delivered in a bucket complete with tubs of creamy coleslaw, baked beans and French fries – at the mention of French fries, a camera shot of some French fries being tossed into the air is shown; it is a happy, vigorous image of fries taking flight. The chicken advert is followed by an advert for a product that helps relieve the pain of constipation; at the end of the advert, a sad-looking girl is released from a cage and then shown spinning happily in green fields with her arms in the air. *No doubt having just done an enormous pooh,* thinks Barbara to herself. "Go girl," she mutters under her breath. Following an advert for a company that sells foot-long sandwiches, packed to the gunnels with juicy fillings, there is an advert for an artificial saliva solution for use in the treatment of dry mouth and, finally, the film comes back on.

It's all too much for Barbara – she gets up and walks through to the kitchen and opens the fridge. She gazes longingly at the cheese drawer, then pulls it open and beholds the ultra-mature vintage cheddar, blue veins threaded across a wedge of stilton; an orange cheese speckled with tiny chopped pieces of jalapeno pepper; the soft compliant creaminess of camembert. She picks up all four cheeses and, holding them gently to her breast, takes a plate from the crockery cupboard and puts them on it, then goes to the biscuit cupboard to get some digestives. In the cupboard in front of the biscuits, she is surprised to see an apple with a small sharp knife next to it. Under the apple is a piece of paper and written on the paper in John's writing it says, 'A journey of a thousand miles must begin with a single step'. She sighs, puts the cheese back in the fridge and puts the apple and the knife on the plate instead, walks back through to the living room and sits back down.

The apple is disappointing and by the time she has finished quartering, peeling, coring and eating it, the film has cut to adverts again, so she switches off the TV, puts the plate and knife back in the kitchen, checks the back door, turns off the lights and goes upstairs. Barbara brushes her teeth, takes off her dressing gown and warm, furry pink slippers and gets into her side of the bed. She turns off her bedside light and lies in the darkness, listening to John's steady breathing next to her. John has never snored, but there is a slight rasping to his breathing. They had only ever had words about his smoking once and it had been their only real argument in twenty-five years of marriage. She lies in the dark and imagines what life would be like without him, that warm, breathing, loving body that is so close to her it has become a part of her. She cannot imagine it and it brings a lump to her throat to even try. Silly to think like this, anyway; John is like her little power pack – she can't remember the last time he'd even had a cold. He cycled twenty miles a day and when she didn't have him redecorating their home at weekends, he'd be off walking in Scotland or Wales or night fishing down in Devon. John was as strong, if not stronger, as the day she'd first met him.

Barbara snuggles up to John's back and goes to sleep listening to that quiet rasping.

John is shaking her awake:

"Come on love, let's get you back to bed. Don't worry, I'll tidy this lot up."

She is standing in front of the fridge. The door is open and lying at her feet is the empty plastic triangular shell from a packet of stilton and a circular wooden box that had once contained a large camembert cheese.

"Oh dear," she says as she allows herself to be steered away from the fridge and back towards the stairs. The stone floor is cold under her bare feet.

Silk Sheets

Chloe drops Karl off at his football game and then opts to use the back roads through Dartford, Erith and Thamesmead, instead of the A2 – whether it's quicker or not, she doesn't know, but she loves to drive past her old haunts and see what has changed and what has stayed the same.

As she passes the huge new young offenders institute off Western Way, she remembers that Janice and Peter will be arriving back from Thailand tomorrow evening, so tonight is her last opportunity to use the flat in Clapham – unbelievable; she'd had the place available for two whole weeks and not yet had the chance to use it once. Last night was the worst – she'd really thought she was in business with that young guy, who'd called himself the Arctic Donkey, and she'd actually been in the car and well on her way when he texted back with a lame excuse to say he wouldn't be able to make it after all and some other time and so on. Yeah, right! Well, Jim was tied up with work all weekend, just to make a change, and Karl was planning a sleepover with his pals tonight, so this was it, her last opportunity, possibly for some time. All she needed was a man!

She pulls into Belmarsh and drives to the far end of the car park where the visitors' spaces are located. It's busy today and she ends up having to block in a Clio that is blatantly taking up more space than it should. She thinks that maybe if all else fails and she can't get a date off the dating website, she'll just go to Inferno's, which is the main meat market on Clapham High Street. If she can't snare a man in there, then she really will be losing her touch. Still, she'd prefer to have one in the bag, so to speak. Going out clubbing on her own seems a bit desperate for a woman of her age.

Chloe walks into the visitor's reception and hands over her ID for checking. As she's standing there, a tall, well-built black man is buzzed through the security doors and stands next to her at the reception. *Wow*, thinks Chloe, *that would do nicely*. Her body seems to go slightly loose as she angles herself a little more in the man's direction. Her hand subconsciously goes up to her hair and she begins to fiddle with her hairclip.

"All done, Akwasi?" says the lady behind reception.

"I hope so," says the man. "I'd like to see my wife at some point this weekend." Chloe straightens up and looks out of the glass towards the car park.

"Here you go," she says, handing him his personal items. "Hopefully we won't be seeing you till Monday then."

"Fingers crossed," he says with an enormous smile. "Have a good one," he says as he walks out of the door.

"Here we are, Mrs Kent," says the woman, handing Chloe a visitor's security pass. "That's all fine. If you'd like to wait in the waiting area, we'll let you know when he's ready."

She waits patiently scratching varnish from her nails – which will need sorting out if she's going anywhere tonight – until finally she is taken through to one of the visiting booths. There, on the other side of the glass, is a grey-haired man, wearing a pair of thick-lensed glasses that have copious amounts of tape at both corners, holding the arms to the frame.

"Hello, Dad," says Chloe into the phone mouthpiece, as she smiles at her father.

"Hello, sweetheart," says her father. "How's my darling girl?"

"I'm fine Dad, just fine. How have they been treating you, Dad?"

"Can't complain, love. What about young Karl? How's he doing?"

"Great, he's got a match today, so he couldn't come along, but he said to say hi. They're doing really well – second in the league and playing the leaders today, so if they win they'll go top."

"Oh, good lad." There is a momentary pause as her father skips asking about Jim. "Listen Chloe, have you thought any more about what I said last time about getting yourself a job?"

"Dad, there really isn't any need – Jim's work is doing very well and I'm not sure I could find the time anyway, what with looking after the house and ferrying Karl around and so on; I can barely find a minute to myself anyway."

"I know love, all I'm saying is, you never know what's round the corner and I just like to think that you're strong enough to make it on your own, if you ever have to. I know you're sleeping between silk sheets right now and, when you're comfortable, it's hard to imagine that anything bad could happen, that circumstances could change. You know Chloe, I won't be around for ever and I just want you to know that..." He looks around the insides of the booth, as if seeking the right words to say.

"'Ere Dad, what's that on your neck?" says Chloe, sounding suddenly concerned.

"Oh it's nothing, love," says her father, holding the back of his neck with his hand and smiling at her. "Just some of the lads messing around, you know how it is in here."

"Well it looks nasty Dad, have you had it looked at?"

"No honestly love, it's just a scratch. I'm fine. Hey, so have you got any holiday plans?"

"Oh, I don't know Dad. Are you sure you're alright?"

"I'm really fine. Oh, by the way, Seamus asked me to say hi to you."

"That was nice of him – is he alright?"

"He's fine –" says her father.

"Excuse me, Mrs Kent?" One of the prison guards has put his head around the door behind her.

"Yes?" says Chloe.

"Are you the owner of the green Range Rover in the visitors' car park?"

"Oh yes, sorry, do you need me to move it?"

"Yes please, you've blocked someone in."

"Right, coming now – Dad, I'm really sorry, I'll be back –"

"No don't worry love, we won't have any time by the time you're back through security. You go and enjoy the rest of your day. Send my love to Karl. It was lovely to see you. Think about what I said, OK?"

Her father seems about to stand up and then holds himself and says:

"Chloe?"

"Yes, Dad."

"I love you." Her father is looking at her in a funny way.

"I love you too, Dad."

"OK, well... You take care of yourself."

"You too, Dad; I'll see you in two weeks."

"Goodbye sweetheart."

She gets back out through security and, after picking up her personal possessions, she walks back towards her car. She switches her phone on and logs on to the dating website. She gets a chat request immediately and responds straight back. She looks at the profile as she waits for him to take the next step, glancing up occasionally to navigate her way through the parked cars. "How are you?" he asks – not exactly the smoothest operator she's ever come across, but she'd be willing to forgive a lot with a physique like that. She replies, then looks up – there's a young couple stood by the blocked-in Clio.

"Sorry," she says, as she opens her car, "you were taking up quite a bit of room though."

She gets in and glances at the chat – another message. She needs to keep the momentum going so she asks the guy to tell her what he wants to do to her and then switches on the ignition and reverses the car. The Clio reverses out and drives away, the passenger waves out of the window. She looks down at the chat window; no reply. Shit, she doesn't want to lose this. She asks if he can meet her tonight and straight away gets a "Yes" back. Oh, look at that six-pack! She tells him where to go and to wear a red rose, gives him her mobile number and, once she has his number back, she goes to her photo files and finds the one she uses for such occasions and buzzes it through to him.

On the way home, Chloe stops at the supermarket to pick up some salad ingredients for lunch. She pauses in front of the fresh herbs, holding a pot of coriander and a pot of parsley; she likes the taste of the coriander better, but the parsley looks like a more robust plant. After a moment's indecision, she puts the parsley in her trolley, then, as she puts the coriander pot back on the shelf, she puts her hand into the cellophane and tears off a bunch of the flimsy herb and shoves it into her parsley pot. She picks up condoms on the way to the checkout.

Shift

Ben unlocks and locks each door as he and Kate make their way out of the prison. They always knock off early because it takes about half an hour to get from the library to the staff exit. They wait in front of the cameras at the security barrier, to be cleared, before the automatic doors open. They pass by the X-ray machines and into the final vestibule made of bulletproof glass and wait patiently as the door behind them slowly closes. After a pause, the door in front slowly opens. They collect their personal belongings and finally, as they walk out of the front of the building, the shift ends and they can relax.

"Any plans for the rest of the weekend?" says Kate.

"Yeah, I think there's probably going to be a bit of a gathering on the street tonight," says Ben.

"Does that equate to an enormous party by most people's standards?"

"No – honestly, it'll only be a few hundred at most. You want to come?" says Ben, smiling.

"No chance. Once was enough. That place is crazy."

"And then on Sunday we're going to watch a football game."

"What, really?" says Kate shocked.

"Yes, really – you remember Pedro?"

"How could I forget!"

"He loves Millwall and he's been badgering us to go to a game for months. Their ground is only round the corner. So we finally decided to go along – 'we' as in the rest of the boys from the house. It'll be like a school trip."

"Well, be careful – the crowd can get pretty nasty at Millwall games…"

"Yeah, sure. I'd say the biggest danger is for someone else in the house to actually start liking football, then we'll really struggle to keep it off the box. What about you – any plans?"

"Oh, I'm exhausted – TV and a takeaway for me, I reckon. Would you look at this?" says Kate suddenly. Ben looks up and sees that a huge Range Rover has blocked in Kate's Clio.

"Nice one – some people are such morons," says Ben. "Don't worry, they'll have everyone's number plate on the visitor list. I'll ask them to send the idiot out." Ben takes a photo of the vehicle with his phone.

Ten minutes later and a woman is walking towards them, clad in heels, leopard print leggings, sunglasses and a furry coat. She says something to them about it being their own fault, which they both ignore, as they are already immersed in their phones and their evenings and the people they choose to spend their time with. The woman moves the Range Rover, Kate reverses out and as they pull away Ben waves to the lady with one hand as he lights a spliff with the other.

"Not in the prison car park," says Kate.

"Oh come on. It is but a lightly aromatic Moroccan squidgy black blend that I rolled specifically for leaving the prison car park. I shall roll up the window until we are clear. Oh, listen to this tune!" Ben turns up the radio on which 'Little Fluffy Clouds' by The Orb has just started.

"It is a great tune," says Kate. "Wow, that really takes me back. Give me a toke, you man of evil influence."

Kate gives Ben a lift back to Sanford, and as they roll through Greenwich, they reminisce about legendary Glastonburys, Womads and Whirl-y-gigs they have been to. As Kate pulls up the car outside the gates of the housing co-op, it is clear that the 'bit of a gathering' is gathering momentum. An enormous rig is being unloaded from the back of a rainbow-coloured van and further down the street there are already dozens of people milling about, juggling fire, slack rope walking, or standing about drinking and smoking and tapping their feet to the music, which is currently thumping out of the windows of the houses. The rain has momentarily stopped.

"Kate, why don't you stick around? It looks like it's going to be a good one," says Ben.

"OK, I'm in. Where can I dump the car?"

They meander slowly down the street, past the orchard-topped bicycle shed, the raised beds and wildflower gardens, stopping at every heavily laden bench and table to tip the hat and pass the bat, until they reach Ben's house, where the party is already well under way. Even though Kate has only been there once and it was some considerable time ago, she is remembered and warmly absorbed into the mayhem. Apart from Tanya, who has gone away for the weekend with Tem, and Pete, who rarely surfaces for long at such gatherings, the whole house is in the kitchen, along with a considerable array of usual suspects arranged around the dinner table, laughing and shouting with each other to be heard over the music and their own racket. Sammy is pouring Kate and Ben absinthe while shouting something at Kate about farmers having sex with their animals; Hendo and Elsa are arguing over the desktop in the corner about which music to put on next, an argument that appears to have gone feral and is being resolved with tickling and punches in the arm; Nat is rolling joints on the table and nodding periodically to Pedro, who is talking loudly into her ear, his eyes like dinner plates; Billy is sat opposite Pedro, talking to a couple of girls that Ben thinks he recognises from House 6; and, over in the far corner of the kitchen, is Anna, talking to Quincy from House 2. Ben takes one moment just to drink her in and, as if she feels his eyes on her, she turns and for a second the room around them disappears.

The general rule of the street is, don't date other people from the street, never mind the same house: a rule that is frequently broken. Ben and Anna have been seeing each other for about a month, but have been taking great pains to keep their relationship from the rest of their housemates. Still, it's only a matter of time before someone notices their stolen glances or one of them sneaking from the other's room in the morning. As if they are both thinking the same thing, they pull their eyes away from each other. Ben turns to Kate and Sammy, who is holding a burning spoon with a sugar cube in it above the aqua blue glass of absinthe.

"... And apparently the suction pulled his guts out of the end of his penis," concludes Sammy.

"Fascinating," says Kate. Sammy hands Kate a flaming glass. "Bottoms up!" Then, turning to Ben, he says:

"Tough day, mate? Peds has got something for you, should take the edge off..."

Ben squeezes through the tangle of bodies to Pedro.

"Hey Benjamin, they le' you out of the prison? We shou' celebrate, huh? Excuse us for a moment, Natalie. Hey Elsa, may we use your room?"

"Door's open sweetheart," says Elsa, who is kneeling on Hendo's chest and punching him in the legs.

Pedro leads Ben out of the kitchen and into the quiet of Elsa's room at the back of the house.

"You had a good day brother?" says Pedro.

"Not bad mate," says Ben.

"Hold onto your socks, man - it about to get a whole lot better." Pedro pulls a cellophane bag out of his pocket that is full of brownish white crystals. "Man, this MDMA is a fucking madman! Fill your boots brother, fill your boots."

Ben takes out his credit card, pulls a CD case from Elsa's tower and tips out a little mountain of crystals onto the case.

"Is that enough?" says Ben to Pedro.

"Man, you take as much as you like," replies Pedro, staring at the crystals, rubbing his stubbly chin and gurning as he does so. "If it too much, Pedro tidy up for you." Then he looks at Ben and smiles like a maniac.

"OK, you got a rizla?"

"Sure, but maybe you like better up the hooter." Pedro takes a crisp tenner from his wallet and rolls it up into a tube, then hands it to Ben. Taking Ben's credit card and the CD from him, he sits on Elsa's only chair and begins to chop and crush the crystals into a fine powder.

"Hey, so what's going on with you and Anna?" says Pedro.

"What do you mean?" says Ben, suddenly showing a keen interest in Elsa's CDs. Pedro turns from his duties for a moment and waits silently, motionless, for Ben to meet his eye. When he finally does, he says:

"Man, you think Pedro don't notice when people in love? Everyone in the house they notice. We just have to wait until we are full of drugs before we can talk about it."

Ben smiles in resignation.

"I think I'm in love," he says, relieved to be able to talk about his feelings with someone at last.

"I know it," says Pedro.

"Peds, I've never felt like this with anyone before. She's brave, she's generous, she's unbelievably attractive –"

"Eh, make a joint while you're talking – if we doing this, let's do it proper," says Pedro, handing Ben his tin, "and put this up your nose first."

"Oh sure," says Ben and, taking the offered tubular tenner, he snorts half of the thick line of MDMA powder up his right nostril and then the rest up his left. "Oh holy shit, that stuff is disgusting!"

"'E like Satan piss in the back of your throat, huh? But the angels will come and chase he away soon enough. Hey, I make another line for me – you make the joint. And please continue – you think Anna, she attractive…"

"But it's more than the usual stuff when you get together with someone. It's like we know what the other one is thinking half of the time, but then, just when I think I know her, she does something amazing and unexpected. It's like she's half soul mate and half mystery."

"Man, it sound like a healthy combination, but you know I got to say it – you living in the same house, you spending all your spare time with each other. Go slow man, tread carefully. When things come together so good, so fast, sometimes they can go right back in the opposite direction at the same speed."

"I know Peds, we both know it and we're trying to be sensible. We're both trying really hard to stay independent of each other, to keep doing the things that we were doing before this happened, but it's difficult – we want to be together all the time."

"Well that's good," says Pedro, looking at Ben, and then he bends his head down to the CD case and snorts an enormous line up his right nostril.

"You only use one nostril?" asks Ben.

"The other one already full," says Pedro, smiling. "Hey, you going to roll that joint or not? You been holding those two rizlas for five hours. Give it to Pedro."

"Oh OK, what was I saying? Jesus, that stuff is strong – I'm off my chops already!"

"'E nice be off the chops, eh?"

"Sure is," Ben is taking deep breaths. "Mate, I think I might've overcooked the goblin."

"The goblin?"

"I mean the goose, or something. Do you know what I mean? I mean, I feel a bit sick, or I'm coming up too much, or, I mean, what was I saying?" Ben is puffing away and rubbing his legs.

"Don't worry Benjamin," says Pedro calmly as he rolls the joint. "Pedro, he look after you. I finish making this nice joint while you tell me how happy you are at the moment with the wonderful Anna and then we go back out to the party and have a good time. OK?"

"Yes mate, that's right. Hey, thanks Peds, you know you're one hell of a mate. You know I hate the fact that we have to wait until we're off our chops before we tell each other how much we love each other, but I do – I mean, I love you Peds, you know not in a gay way, I mean you're like family to me, all of you are."

"I hope how you behave with Anna is not how you hoping to interact with the rest of the family."

"You know what I mean."

"Of course. Hey, listen to Pedro for a second. Be very careful with Elsa."

"What d'you mean?" says Ben.

"I mean, she like you a lot. I think she have a crush on you a leedle bit, so for sure you and Anna is out of the bag, but just don't be too blatant in her face – you understand?"

"Sure, Peds – I didn't realise."

"This is why you need a Pedro to tell you these things."

Pedro glances at Ben, who is looking a little crestfallen.

"Hey, don't worry, Elsa's gonna be fine. She still sad about her ex who fell off the motorbike, but she coming out from under the cloud. She find a man soon enough. You don't got to be worrying about that. What you got to be worrying about right now is this." Pedro holds up the completed spliff.

The door to the kitchen opens and the room is flooded with smoke and sound.

"What's going on?" says Elsa as she walks in, closely followed by Sammy.

"Speak of the devil," says Pedro.

"Damn, my timing is good," says Sammy as he eyes up the joint in Pedro's hand.

"What have you two being saying about me?" says Elsa.

"Benjamin was just saying, how can a person live in such a dirty room? *Es muy guaro!*" says Pedro as he lights the joint.

"How dare you say disparaging things about my love nest!" says Elsa and hits Ben on the arm.

"Love nest?" says Sammy. "And how exactly do you plan to lure men into your love nest?"

"For your information Sammy, I have joined a dating website."

"Do you guys want a line?" says Pedro.

"Yes," they both say in stereo, before Sammy continues, "which one?"

"Never you mind," she says.

"And how are you getting on?" says Sammy.

"Good," says Elsa.

"Been on any dates?" says Sammy.

"I'm biding my time," says Elsa.

"Hmmm, I don't know about the whole idea," says Sammy, taking the joint as Elsa bends to the CD cover. "Have you ever thought about the fact that contemporary western civilisation sometimes frowns on the idea of arranged marriages, as it seems like we're surrendering our freedom of choice, but then we spend years failing to make a choice and then surrender that freedom to a computer instead? I mean, do you really think that a computer is better qualified to guide you in your love life, than your own family who have nurtured you throughout your life?"

Elsa is staring at Sammy with her mouth open.

"And one for Sammy," says Pedro. "Eh, Elsa, you want to give Sammy the tube?" Elsa shakes herself and passes over the rolled-up tenner. Sammy puts it to his nose and bends down to the CD case.

"It is strange," says Elsa, staring at Sammy again. Her mouth is still open. She tips her head back for a moment and then looks back at Sammy again and says, "Don't you think the hardware is so alien? I mean, how weird is a mouse as a sexual appendage?"

Sammy finishes his line and sits upright, eyes and mouth wide open, staring at Elsa, with one finger still holding his nose. Ben and Pedro both look from Sammy to Elsa and back again, before Pedro says, smiling:

"'E's good gear is 'e?" Both Sammy and Elsa are not saying anything. Ben and Pedro look at each other.

"Eh, maybe we see you guys in a bit," says Pedro, before looking at Ben and tipping his head towards the door. They both head back into the kitchen.

"What was that all about?" says Ben.

"You got me," says Pedro. "Let's get a drink."

Suddenly, Anna is by Ben's side.

"There you are," she says, pressing herself against him surreptitiously and pushing him away from the general chaos.

"Hello gorgeous," says Ben.

"Oh my goodness, has somebody been giving you obscene amounts of drugs?"

Ben smiles sheepishly.

"Listen to me, my little space cadet, I've got a surprise for you, but I can see I might have to postpone it for another time."

"Ooh, I like surprises," says Ben. "Please can I have it?"

"Maybe," says Anna. "You'll need to seriously moderate your intake of intoxicants for the rest of the evening."

"Sweetie, I've had enough to last me a month."

"Oh dear, then it may already be too late."

"No, no, it's never too late. I'll go have myself a boogie and in a few hours I'll be right as rain."

"OK, you do that. I've promised to help Quincy with the sound engineering, so I'll catch you later."

"Hey," Ben grabs her arm and pulls her back. "I didn't tell you how beautiful you look."

"Why thank you - you don't look so bad yourself, handsome."

"I love the dress - you look like Audrey Hepburn."

"It's called a shift and it used to be my grandmother's."

"Give me a kiss," says Ben, leaning forward.

"Whoa, not very discrete!"

"The cat is out - Pedro just told me that everyone has known for weeks."

"Oh, well in that case..." Anna gives him a quick kiss and squeezes his bum. "I'll see you later." With a wink, she's out of the kitchen door.

Ben's perception is shifting and suddenly he feels like instead of looking through one door of reality, he is looking through several, and each fragmentary window that he is watching contains a picture that he loves. Time is passing quickly and he knows he is only in one window at a time and acutely aware of the present, but everything he experiences adds another window to the mosaic and builds onto the huge mountain of happiness that he is creating. Kate is in one window and she is dressed in red, as she was before, but he knows she is dressed in a deep and meaningful red now and her eyes are huge. She says that Pedro dosed her and holy shit is it strong and she's so glad she came and thanks Ben and she's so glad that they work together and they're mates as well, because sometimes you just work with people that don't matter, but he matters and they hug and it feels good. In another window he is smoking with Hendo in the trees by the ponds and they are watching as, one after another, inebriated and spaced party goers, who have clearly never been to Sanford before, accidentally step into the black water and then haul themselves back out, much to his and Hendo's utter amusement. One particularly short girl on her mobile phone disappears completely under, but for her mobile phone, which she manages to hold above water level. So impressed are they that they fetch her a towel. In another window he is dancing with Anna and the music is so good and for one brief moment, the tunes hit a break, and then, as they start to build again, a breeze blows across the huge crowd of dancers and his whole head and back ignite into spirals of tingles as he breathes in that fresh magic to fuel his fire and then the beat pounds back in and every flex of every muscle commands joy out of him and Anna's hot skin right there next to him. A window where he and Billy are bouncing on the trampoline and their timing is so perfect that they must be higher than the trees. Then another window where he sits around the huge fire pit next to Sammy and Elsa, who eventually came out of her room after many hours, arm in arm, and have not let each other go since, and he feels almost unparalleled happiness that Elsa is not thinking of him any more, or feeling hurt, and they are all three of them talking happily and comfortably and smoking joints and drinking beer and looking at the flames. More and more windows are opening and connecting with the last and there are too many of them to see and he knows that some are disappearing. But he can't feel sad, because each one is replaced by a new window, with guitars and drums and rain and lights and colour and heat and smoke and movements that linger like orgasms in his head.

And then, as suddenly as it took hold of him, it is letting him go. The cold wet dawn has long cast its grey light upon them and long heavy rain showers have driven the party back into the houses and he finds himself with a guitar in hand singing with Hendo. He's thinking about whether he should ask Pedro for some more when Anna takes the guitar from him, gives it to Hendo, pulls him up the stairs and into her room. She undresses him and puts him in her bed and then undresses and climbs in next to him and Ben tells her that he loves her so much and she says it's just the drugs talking and he says he'll prove it to her and she says how and he says he'll run now to Covent Garden Flower Market and bring her back the most beautiful flowers in the world and she says that that would be nice, but maybe he can leave it till after they've had a sleep and he promises he'll do it after they've had a sleep and then he knows she is asleep.

Ben lies in Anna's bed with Anna in his arms and grinds his teeth. He looks at the daylight pushing through the sides of the curtains and grinds his teeth. He listens to the sounds of the ongoing party downstairs over the sound of his teeth in his head. He looks around the room at Anna's things: the little fish tank, her huge canvas juggling bag and other circus things, her toothbrush and paste next to her spare brush which he uses, her shift dress on the floor. He grinds his teeth. He feels Anna's warmth next to him and he feels the tension easing out of him. He relaxes, closes his eyes and imagines that even a plane crash bursting into their room could not disturb his happiness.

Ben thinks of explosions and the floor collapsing beneath their warm, happy nest and he grinds his teeth and smiles.

Part 3

Sneakers

I love my Asics sneakers. I don't think they's as cool as the Adidas or Nike sneakers but, for comfort, man, they are the kings. I am also crazy about running and these two go hand-in-hand, or foot-in-foot: Asics and running. I feel like one of those paraplegic guys with the blades on when I put my Asics on. I don't mean I feel like I've lost my legs; I mean, I feel like I've got springs on the end of my feet. You know what I'm sayin'? I had this beat-up old pair once and I knew the time had come to get some new runners, but I opted for some Adidas instead, because they were a) cheaper and b) cooler. First couple of runs I kinda figured that I just needed to break 'em in or summin', but a week after buying 'em, I was back in the beat-up old pair of Asics.

My current pair, I just bought 'em last week and so I know I'm still precious 'bout 'em. I love it when they're fresh out the box and they got that smell and that spotlessness. These pups are white and got the blue and yellow stripes on the side, like in a weird shape, (which is like they tried to mix the Adidas and Nike brands, which are cool and ended up with this shit mess, which is less than cool, like I said). I have to make myself wear 'em when they're new, because no matter how much the absolute pure colours of a new pair of sneakers please me on an aesthetic level, I am conscious of the fact that these puppies are built for a purpose and must serve that purpose. I wear the new ones reluctantly. If someone kicks dirt on 'em, I have to hold back from dropping a John-o on their nose, have to stand there and tell myself that this is a necessary part of the process; that all sneakers must eventually become unclean, that all beauty must die.

This kid I knew in school used to put his sneakers through the laundry, said they come out shining good as new. I've done this a couple times and, sure, the results are pretty impressive in terms of getting the sneaker clean, but the wash cycle weathers the sneakers and the stitching comes out; they grow old before their time. It's a tough trade-off and most the time I prefer to let nature take its course, even if it is vexing when some pretzel grinds their shitty Clarks on my toe on the tube, or a double decker red flings an oily puddle onto your feet.

Mr Kent is not a fan of the sneakers. The first and only time he saw me wearing sneakers, he told me that appearances are important in our line of work. I replied that I thought the practical benefits of a good pair of sneakers in 'our line of work' could also have benefits, and he said that *if* it was me that was expected to think then I would be paying him. I said that just in terms of running after people or getting away from people, you'd have additional speed. He said that if I ever found myself running away from or after anyone whilst under his employment, then I'd best keep running, as, if he caught up with me he'd shoot me hisself, as I would have 'failed to generate the necessary respect which we need from our customers, our competition and the forces of law and order in this town'. He said that a shortcut to finding myself in this scenario would be to continue wearing trainers (Brits call 'em trainers). He also said that if I questioned his authority again without his express permission, I would find myself picking up my bloody teeth with my broken fingers. I love Mr Kent. He's an absolute don (this is Mr Kent's phrase – an absolute don – he uses it for football players and snooker players that's smokin'. "Ronnie O'Sullivan is an absolute Don").

I keep a pair of G-Stars in the car for whenever I need to see Mr Kent.

Of course Mr Kent ain't never gonna knock out my teeth and bust my fingers. He'd get Bernard to do it and, I'll be honest, I wouldn't like to watch him try. Bernard, he's a big unit. I look at him now in the passenger seat, face flashing in and out of darkness as we pass beneath the orange streetlights. He still goan' on 'bout the Scottish dude who weren't Scottish: one minute he's sayin' it's all a big accident and goan' on 'bout the wrath of God and how he's goan' get punished, how we're all goan' get punished, and the next he's laughin' and sayin' fuck the guy, he should've chosen his friends more wisely. He sounds like he's crackin'. Maybe I should just pop him now before he becomes even more of a liability and throw him in the trunk with the other dude. I finger my piece speculatively. Not a very big trunk on these Brit cars, though, and as I say, Bernard, he's a big unit. I don't think Mr Kent would approve either. He loves the guy – calls him his *arseshloch*. Bernard, he's good as gold in front of Mr Kent, a con-sume-ate professional; saves all his wrath of God and manic depression shit for me. I keep steering us down the A2, back towards London.

Bernard goes on.

Wrath of God! I mean, Jesus, what the fuck! As far as I'm concerned, God is just humanity's way of filling in the gaps. Example: you understand the jungle, where to collect clean water, where to get honey from the bees, how to shoot a monkey with poison darts you made from scratching a frog's ass, which vines to boil up and drink to get your freak on, but there's this great yellow ball of fire swinging across the sky some days and other days the ball ain't there and it's pissing it. You got yourself a gap in your meteorological understanding and you're not feeling too comfortable about that. It's making you feel stupid and you been the lord of the jungle and all, can scratch a frog's ass and shoot monkeys. What you need is a sun god. Hell, why not have yourself a rain god too? You can even join up the little white dots in the night sky and have yourself a goddamn polygodrous religion or whatever you wanna call it.

Alright, now fast forward a few thousand years, or a few thousand miles if you prefer, into the moronic head of the man to my left. Now look at you, come a long way from scratching ass and eating monkey, right? Got yourself some shiny ass satellites up in space so you can figure what the weather goin' be and phone your momma in Lichtenstein or wherever on the cheap tariff and tell her you're changing your pants regular whilst you're working as a big man criminal in London town, selling Colombian grade A and extorting money and signatures from honest tax-paying citizens for shady businessmen. You got an idea from your schooling days that the earth ain't flat and you don't need to rip your neighbour's heart out to pacify your sun god and get yourself some rain once in a while. Still got a problem, though; you see, when your boss tells you to rough up some guy a little and you accidentally break his neck, it makes you feel bad and you can't figure out why. I mean, you know your momma in Lichtenstein would be pissed if she sees you killing guys, but this ain't enough for you. You can't have the buck stopping with you like this. If Mr Kent had told you to whack the guy, no problem, you're just following orders, but this was your doing and you can't figure out why. What you got here is a gap in your moral fibre and it's making you cry like a baby and you been a big man criminal in London town, extorting good folks and all. If only there was somebody could listen to your dumbass sins and tell you to repent and that it was all gonna be OK. What you need for yourself is a wrathful god, some nasty old testament mo' fo' who's gonna rip your big old arms off and shove 'em up your ass, every minute of your afterlife, until you is well and truly sorry and paid your dues. You need yourself a god who gonna balance the books after you die and restore justice to the universe or some shit.

Man, I heard that Stephen Hawking dude who know just about everything there is to know about everything, even he found gaps in his understanding and decided to plug the hole with God. And him being the smartest human in the universe. Damn, everyone at it, making up gods and using 'em like Polyfilla. What the hell wrong with saying, 'I don't know? I don't know why the yellow ball's going across the sky, I don't know why the man had to die today when I gave him a John-o on his nose, I don't know what's at the bottom of a black hole or living inside an electron.'

Religion all about not feelin' stupid, cos we too dumb to admit we is stupid.

Ole 'wrath of God' Bernard's gone quiet on me. I look across and the mutha fucker is staring right at me; not real friendly, either. My hand drops to my automatic, as I say:

"'S'up Count Burn-you-la?"

"Stop the car. I need to piss."

"Oh yeah, sure thing," I say and put the flips on. We pull up on the side of the A2 on some underpass near Eltham. Bernard gets out and just starts pissing straight away and groanin' like he's finalising business with a *senora*. Man, he just keeps on pissing like a goddamn Niagara by the car. Every time the flow slows and I think, *That's it, time to wind things up*, it turns out he is just taking a breather and then he pushes back to it with extra groanin' and it keeps coming out like a fire hose.

"C'mon man, let's go. You pissing for Britain, man?" Man, he is pissing for goddamn Lichtenstein!

"Quiet, I must concentrate," says Bernard.

I'm getting' the heebie jeebies listening to this goddamn supernatural pissing.

"Burnula, this is not the time. We've got a goddamn body in the back of the car to dispose of and this is not a fucking john, man. This is not what I'd call discreet. If the cops come, we're fucked. Shut the tap, let's hit the mac, man!"

"Quiet, it will take longer with your talking." No end to the gushing. I look down at his feet and see he's standing in a puddle of his own piss.

"Shit! Burns, listen up man, if you ain't back in this car in five seconds, me and the corpse is departing with or without you, hear me? Shit, you's standin' in your own piss man!"

"You will wait. Be quiet, I must concentrate."

"Hey, fuck you Burns, I'm outta here." I hit the gas hard enough to close the passenger door and watch Count Burnula out the rear mirror as I push her up to 50. Sum bitch don't move a muscle – he just standin' there by the side of the road, pissing like he's in the you-rine-al. That's when I hear a noise from the trunk. Shit, that's all I need. I swing the car off the freeway and follow the A2 up onto the

Blackheath, then take her off the main vein and onto a quiet stretch running along the wall of the south side of Greenwich Park. I park her, get out and open the trunk.

"Help." Shit, this poor bastard ain't just alive, he's talking. "I can't feel anything."

"Tha's right bro'. I'm sorry to have to report to you that my dumbass colleague done gone and accidentally busted yo' neck."

"Oh, I see. Well, that explains why I can't feel anything I guess. Listen mate, please can you take me to a hospital? Just leave me outside." Man, this guy talkin' to me like he askin' a cabbie to get him to the theatre on time, not like he talkin' to a gangsta who 'bout to dump his sorry ass in the river.

I put on my best plantation slave accent for this here white man talking head. "Why I wish I could help you, sah, I surely do Mr Talkin' Head, but my boss, well he insist that I drop yo pa-ral-ized body, along with your talkin' head, in that there River Thames tonight, no question. I so sorry, sah. My boss tell me that if I fail to carry out his orders, then I ain't gone get no cotton pickin' candy and nice time with Mary-Lou this weekend. Plus, he also maybe gone kill my sorry ass and throw it in that there River Thames after he thrown you in hisself."

"Bugger, seems like we have a problem then." Damn, he cool! What the fuck is this English stiff upper lips, huh? If that be my sorry ass in the back of this trunk with my neck all busted and being told I got to die, I ain't able to guarantee I be lookin' so cool!

"But don't think for one moment that I ain't awful sorry to have to do this to ya and if you'll accept my apologies on behalf of my colleague and the company, that'd be mighty decent of you."

"Apology accepted." He swallowing now and blinking some and his head looking around like he thinking. I lean back on the car and look out across the heath. Moon's rising. I come running up here at night. Even in the winter sometimes, with gloves and a scarf, bout a dozen sweaters and some heavy-duty socks (them Asics is not built for warmth). It snowed one time and when I stopped running the whole town had gone so quiet you could hear the flakes landing, I swear;

never seen or heard anything like it before or since. The sound of snow falling. When I got home I needed to tell someone, so I called my sis, but she just started straight in with, "Where you been, Ignatius? Are you back in New Orleans? Why ain't you called your momma? When you gonna stop being a bad man and take some responsibility in your life, Ignatius? Why you calling? You still takin' drugs? You need money from me again? When you gonna get a proper job?" On and on, until I hung up. That was eight months ago and I ain't called her since. Never did tell her 'bout the snow.

"Excuse me?" says the head.

"Oh sorry, my mind wanders. Did you say something?"

"No, that's fine – I was just wondering, well, d'you need to throw me in the river immediately?"

"Well... I guess not. Might be best to leave it a while, let the streets quieten down."

"I wondered if you might be prepared to grant a dying man a last wish?"

"Such as?"

"I've always wanted to visit New Covent Garden Flower Market. It's meant to be spectacular and, well, if I had one night left on Earth in London, I'd go there."

"Shit man, I'd like to aye-com-mo-date you, but what's to say you ain't gone start screamin' blue murder soon as we get in there? Then where's poor ole' Ig goan' be? This ain't the Duck Tours, man!"

"Listen, Ig – is that your name? Ig?"

"Ignatius."

"Ignatius – good name. Ignatius, from the sound and feel of things, I'm in a bad way."

"No question."

"There's a tribe in the South Pacific called the Trobrianders and it is rumoured that when the Trobriand Chief of a tribe reaches an age where he no longer deems himself fit to rule his people, he takes his canoe and paddles out into the open sea, returning his soul to the spirits that created him."

"I can respect that."

"Now I don't know about you, but for me a life where my loved ones have to spoonfeed me and wipe my arse morning, noon and night, where I'm unable to dance, make love, or bowl a Yorker, just doesn't seem like a life at all."

"What's a Yorker?"

"Cricket swerve ball."

"I hear ya."

"My problem is that I've got a girl, right, an amazing girl who I've not known for long, but for sure it's going to break her heart when she finds out I'm gone. The last time I saw her, I promised I'd get her flowers from the market in the middle of the night and if I could just do this one thing, before I go, she'd know I was thinking of her at the end and that might give her some comfort. Make it easier on her. I'd feel a lot better about going if I got my last wish. I'm not gonna make a fuss in the market, I'm as good as gone. I don't want Anna to see me like this. And I don't want my sister to come look after me - she'd waste her life to look after me, even if I begged her not to. I can't have that. You know it's not easy to find someone to kill you in this country, even if it's the only thing you want. Don't get me wrong, I'm not saying I'm delighted about my predicament, but if I'm going to go, I want to do it right."

"What's your name, man?"

"Ben."

"Well damn Ben, I never heard no talking head could produce such compelling arguments before in my life. Let's just say, for the continuation of this argument's sake, that I agree to grant you your last dying wish, what's in it for Ig?"

"Firstly, like you said, it'd make more sense for you to drop me in the river later on when there're less people around, so you've got the hassle of having to while away time and, with me in the boot, you've got the risk of being caught - with my cooperation, the element of risk is removed."

"'Pends if you prove to be trustworthy."

"Ignatius, I am a Trobriander at heart."

"OK, what else?"

"Secondly, the flower market is meant to be an amazing place to visit. I'm told that flowers are flown in from around the globe on a daily basis to supply shops, smaller markets, garages, even the guys who stand at the central reservation at busy junctions and throw themselves at your window at red lights, desperately clutching roses – even they go there. Imagine the smell of the place: flowers for every lover, every birth, every wedding and funeral in the country in one building. It would be an experience." I'm thinking about the sound of snow again: could I be on the verge of another profound sensory experience?

"That it?"

"Well, finally, you get the warm feeling from having done a good deed though, as a hardened criminal, I appreciate this may be lower on your list of priorities."

"Woah there, I may be a cold hard professional when it comes to carrying out my duties, but that don't mean I don't got feelings. OK, so in summary, you's telling me that if I take you to the flower show, you'll play good talking head and I get's to smell the roses and feel all cosy on the inside." I pull my unimpressed Ig face.

"Well, yes."

"Man, I was goan' to say yes, but now I feel like you insulted me, telling me I'm a cold heartless killer an all."

"Ignatius, I'm very sorry about that, it was an honest mistake."

"OK, well, bad head."

"Yes, bad head... So does this mean we can go?"

"I don't know..."

"It's right by the river..."

"OK, OK!"

"You mean it?"

"Yeah, what the hell."

"Mate thanks, I really appreciate it..."

"Alright, alright, this don't make us best buds or nuttin'."

"So how are we going to get me out of the trunk?"

"What?"

"Well if you're pulled over and I'm found lying in the trunk, that's still going to be kind of hard to explain. Now what we need to do is brace the neck – have you got some clothes to wrap around my neck for moving me?"

"Hmmm, well shit, I didn't know that this was goan' be so complicated – I ain't got any spare clothes..."

"What about that coat you've got on there?"

"Shit, it's cold bro' – I need this!"

"C'mon Ig, it won't be for long."

"Shit, goddamn!"

I can't believe the talking head is giving me orders, but nevertheless I'm still taking off my coat. I wrap it round his head and secure it by tying the arms round the front, real gentle the whole time so's I don't hurt him any more than he already has been, but he still blinks like crazy when I do it.

"OK, good. Now the easiest thing will probably be to drop one of the rear seats and pull me through onto the other rear passenger seat."

I've given up complaining now – seems like I might as well just get on with it – so after a whole heap of tugging and pulling, I manage to get his lordship strapped into the rear passenger seat.

"Perfect, thanks."

"OK, well if everything is to Sir's satisfaction, I think it's 'bout time we hit the road."

I drive. He aks me if I know the way and I tap the GPS for answer, but I guess he cain't see it from the angle of his neck, so I tells him. I look in the mirror once in a while but the talking head's done talking for a while. I guess he's got things on his mind.

We's approaching the Elephant and Castle roundabout, when the head pipes up:

"Go straight over."

"The GPS say it ain't that way."

"But we need a wheelchair."

"What in the hell?!"

"If we go to St Thomas' you can pick up one from there."

"They's just handing out wheelchairs for the needy, huh?"

"Come on Ig, you can do sneaky. Besides, how were you planning to get me to the river?"

"Man, I was jus' gonna throw your ass off a bridge until your head started talking. Now I guess I'm goan' have to build you some goddamn funeral pyre and shoot you with flaming arrows with a goddamn gospel choir an' all!"

This cracks up the talking head.

"That won't be necessary – just the wheelchair and the flowers. That's all I ask."

"*All* you ask?! Man!"

I park on Royal Street opposite the Accident and Emergency drop-off.

"Now listen here, Mr Talking Head – I's goan' go in there and secure us a wheelchair, but I's goan be watchin' you and if I see you callin' out for help or any shit like that, I's goan come out here and shoot you and whoever you done talkin' to and then your lady friend ain't gonna get no flowers and know that you love her. We understand each other?"

"100%. Thank you, Ignatius."

"Alright. Sit tight."

I gets out the car and slip my piece down the back of my pants. I prefer it in my coat, but his lordship got my damn coat. I cross over at the pedestrian crossing and walk up the ambulance ramp. There's an ambulance out front and some dude is being helped out the back, but there's no wheelchair in sight, so I step through into the lobby. There's a fat security guy, not looking too sharp, half a dozen sicks in the waiting area and two young women behind the reception. I'm scanning the area for a wheelchair when one of the women says:

"May I help you, Sir?"

"Yes ma'am," I say and limp over to her. "I do believe my leg might be busted and I think I'm goan' have to use a wheelchair for a while until it's fixed."

"OK Sir, would you like to take a ticket and fill in these forms and we'll get a doctor to have a look at your leg as soon as possible."

"Why thank you ma'am." I still cain't believe that you can get fixed up in this country for free. It's a damn fine thing. I sit down next to an Indian dude in a football shirt, who look like he got into a fight with a train, his nose is so busted. I make a show of studying the forms, while all the while I'm looking over the top and casin' the joint. I see a sign for the restrooms, an' they's out of sight of the security dude, so I make a painful display of getting to my feet and hobble off down the corridor. No-one says shit. Soon as I'm outta sight of the reception, I drop the limp and start checking doors. I find a cleaner's storeroom, where I pick up a mop an' bucket an' a plastic apron, an empty room, looks like it's been refurbished, but most doors are locked. I keep movin' along, keepin' casual an' hummin' like a happy cleaner boy, wheelin' along my mop an' bucket. I see a couple of nurses running here and there, but they is all looking harassed and ain't paying me no mind.

I think I must be somewhere in the south wing when I finally see an old dude rolling along in a wheelchair wearing a dressing gown. Fuckin' A! I roll up behind him.

"Excuse me sah, allow me to introduce myself." He turns his fat glasses roun' to me and squints out of some real cloudy eyeballs. "I represent St Thomas' (I say this like the old momma from the Tom and Jerry cartoons) wheelchair cleaning service and your wheelchair has been specially selected for a complete overhaul and facelift. If you'd be kind enough to vacate your chair temporarily, this will enable me to take your chair and apply the necessary cleansing fluids and a replacement chair will be brought along to you directly."

He squints at me a while and rolls his chops. He ain't got no teeth for sure.

"What the devil are you talking about, young man?"

"I'm jacking your wheels ole man!" I tip him out and watch him sprawling on the polished floor and then he starts hollering and balling and I'm running like crazy down the corridors, pushin' this damn wheelchair for the head. Damn, why didn't I put the Asics on when I got back in the car? I'm just running, with no clue as to which direction I should be goin' in, but I figure if I just keep cutting and running in the same zig-zag direction I'll get out eventually, but this damn hospital seems to go on for ever. I round a bend and see a nurse up ahead and I call out and stop her and say:

"Which way to the Accident and Emergency entrance please, Miss?"

"Straight down," she says, pointing, and then I see 'em, the restrooms that I passed on my way out. I practically sprint down the corridor, slowing as I approach reception, but there ain't no sneaking through, the word's clearly gone out that there's a wheelchair thief on the loose and the security guard is walking towards me with a serious fat man face on him. As he gets nearer, I put my hands in the air and says:

"Oh thank goodness, Sir," moving round the chair, which is still rolling forward. "That man's insane," I say, and he drops his serious fat attention for just a second, which is plenty long enough for me to butt him in the nose, square and hard, and feel a light spray of blood as he reels backwards away from me. I'm back behind the chair and running without having missed a beat, passing the faces behind reception, a phone at one ear, two mouths hanging open, sicks on the left, and I can hear fat man up and behind me running – more to fatty than I'd thought – and bang, I'm out the door and I turn the wheelchair to face down the ramp and I jump my legs over the top and push off rolling down the ramp, and fatty's breathing down my neck and I feel my piece slip at the back of my pants and from the right corner of my eye I see a double decker red heading for a collision path with me on the chair at the bottom of the ramp and, as I'm calculating whether or not the bus is gonna hit me, or the fat man's gonna grab me, or my shooter's gonna fall out my pants, I hear what my sister said on the phone and wonder whether it is time to think about a career change.

Strides

"Where's that fat-handed twat with my peonies?!"

I can hear Ken going ape again, but I know he's too busy to hunt me down and, anyway, I'm dealing with a potential sale here.

"I'd say your boss is requiring you roun' the front," says the tall lanky black geezer standing behind the wheelchair. He's got a proper yank accent and sounds like he belongs in the movies or from that series *The Wire*. He's got veins in his neck, is wearing shades and looks cold.

"Don't worry about him," I say. "He's old enough to find his peonies himself." Not even a flicker of a smile from the yank. The fella in the wheelchair smiles. He's blinking like crazy, like he's got a nervous twitch.

"Hey, whassup with these tulips, huh? My man here is looking for some serious premium ass foliage and he ain't wantin' none of them cheap ole' flowers, been lying roun' for three weeks, that are goan' turn brown by the time his special lady friend receives them, you know 'm sayin'?"

"Patience, patience, Rome was not built in a day," I say as I roll a smoke. "The trouble with the world these days, my friend, is that folks don't have a sense of the time and effort that goes into the turning of the wheels behind the scenes. Take, for example, the Underground. Now I bet if I asked you whether an Underground ticket represents good value for money for the average London commuter, you'd probably say no, am I right?"

"What you talkin' 'bout the Underground fo'? I'm sayin' my man needs the best tulips available in the whole of Great Britain and he need 'em now. I ain't goan' try to explain how important it is that these flowers leave a lastin' impression, but take my word, they got's to be the mutts," he says impatiently.

"Easy Ig," says Wheels. He is not looking like a picture of health. "Agreed; the Underground is a rip-off."

"There you go," I continue. "What most people assume is that the whole show is practically automated." I pause to light my rollie. "But what they don't realise is the sheer volume of effort going on behind the scenes, to make the whole system roll. Did you ever watch *Doctor Who*?"

"What the hell has *Doctor Who* got to do with the Unnergroun'?" says the yank.

"Well d'you remember all those gay midgets that operated the Daleks?"

"Rings a bell," says Wheels.

"And what about the little guv'nors from *Time Bandits*?" I continue.

"I 'member that one. Terry Gilliam film," says the yank.

"Well does it not seem unusual to you that you don't see these little folks around the place any more?"

They both look at me with a did-you-just-pull-a-parsnip-out-of-my-arse face.

"Who else is small enough to fit in those ticket barrier machines? That's where they all are, badgering away behind the scenes, making the whole transport system move like a well-oiled machine." I do a nice little performance here of crunching myself up in a ticket machine like a nice gay little midget, taking the ticket, checking the date all camp-like, then operating the turnstyle and handing the ticket back out the other side. It's a nice little show and even the yank is smiling. Time to press home the advantage:

"What about the tube trains themselves?" I say.

"He summin' else, huh?" says Yank, looking at Wheels. "Goan', tell us bout the trains."

"I guess you're old enough to remember the old school wrestlers Martin Ruane and Shirley Crabtree, better known as 'Giant Haystacks' and 'Big Daddy'?"

"How could I forget? *World of Sport* on ITV." Wheels is smiling at the memory.

"And what about Andre the Giant?"

"Oh yeah, I 'member that dude – he's one big unit for sho'", the yank is getting in the swing now.

"Well, these lads hadn't finished growing, I mean they weren't even half done when you saw them on ITV. They'd all got acromegaly. You must've heard of that?"

Two parsnip faces lookin' at me again.

"You got a lot to learn, you kids. It's a rare genetic defect that means the pituitary gland keeps producing growth hormones until you end up literally with a man mountain – real life giants. And what the hell happened to these gargantuans? Explain to me, if you will, how comes we don't see these absolute mahoosive specimens wandering the streets anymore? It's not like they'd be the kind of thing you wouldn't notice if it strolled by you."

"That true," says Yank.

"Slung 'em under the trains, didn't they..."

"Killed them!" exclaims Wheels, half smiling.

"No, they strap these giants under the trains and, using their superhuman strength, they haul the tubes from one stop to the next, hence the great roaring sound that precedes the trains as they come into a station. It's a huge effort, you see."

"Whoa there, just one second bro', I get the distinct impression I knowing where this be headed." The Yank has got a rather smug look on his face. "Let's suppose for an instant that this is all true an' that the reason why tube tickets are so 'spensive is due to the fact that the whole system is run by thousands of dwarves and giants."

"Midgets," I say. "They prefer the term midgets."

"Well OK, so the Tube's bin run by giants and midgets. The point is, now you're goan' tell us that the whole process of growing tulips is conducted by doped-up leprechauns in Amsterdam, who is transportin' the flowers over the North Sea, strapped to the back o' home-o-sex-you-al dolphins, in a complex process that, though costly, be ensurin' the rights and behavioural freedoms of aquatic animals and goddamn magical midgets the world over and therefore we should be happy to pay three pounds sterling for a bunch of yo' tulips instead of two pounds a bunch, which is what they's prob'ly axing roun' the corner."

"Nah, my friend, the point is..." I pause to drop and step my smoke. "Is that if I have the ability to convince you, even temporarily, that London Underground is run by giants and homosexual midgets, then do you really think I'm going to have any difficulty whatsoever in convincing you that the finest tulips available to purchase in the UK are worth a miserable quid more than the sad, drab, ready-to-wilt offerings round the corner on Chunky's stall?" I looked a second too long at Wheels when I said half-dead, but the yank's laughing his socks off and reaching for his money, ready to pay whatever I ask. *It's OK, I think, everyone's smiling.*

This is why the market is better than school – because my big mouth earns respect and money here instead of detention. Plus, I'm taking home five hundred clear some weeks and that is having a decent impact on the lifestyle, I can assure you. I am getting all the toys – the latest iPhone, a funky little Vespa – and buying some nice threads too. These strides for example – three hundred and twenty nicker and when I told Bella she nearly died. Here's the thing; Bella tells her girly friends that my jeans cost three hundred and twenty quid and she gets kudos too. Life couldn't be simpler really – you've got money, you've got respect.

Gary (I refuse to call him Dad) is always going on about putting some away and how you never know what's round the corner, because I don't want to end up like him, working the markets in his old age, but he doesn't understand that I was made for this. I know it doesn't matter about saving; all that counts is your ability to borrow. As soon as you've got a little cashflow, the banks will offer you some money, you take it and then pay it back and then they offer you a lot more, then you can start borrowing from other banks and do the same with them and pretty soon you've got enough to buy your first business, then you can *really* start moving money around and borrowing big time. It's how all the entrepreneurs do it: keep borrowing as fast as you can until you're so big, the banks can't afford to watch you sink, then you're set for life.

"Ha, ha, ha, whoooo-weeee! That's nice, that's nice. What's your name bro'?"

"Chris."

"Well, pleasure to meet you Chris, my name's..." he pauses a moment, "... Bernard, an' this here is my man the Talkin' Head."

"Pleasure to make the acquaintance of such fine folks at such an ungodly hour," I say. I take another look at the Talking Head to make sure I didn't cause offence, but he's still laughing and blinking in a way that looks less feeble than the rest of him. He starts coughing and the laughing stops.

The Yank, whose name is clearly not Bernard, is just grabbing bunches of tulips randomly out of the pallet I was in the middle of unloading and pushing notes into my hand. The coughing sounds bad, like you don't know if each slow wheeze will be followed by another. The Yank has heard the coughing, his face changes immediately and he drops everything he's doing, literally, and walks to the side of the wheelchair and squats next to the Talking Head. There's something terrible about that cough. I realise I'm just standing there, with a handful of notes, staring at the tulips on the floor: Flaming Parrot, Kingsblood, Queen of the Night, Blushing Apeldoorn, Blueberry Ripple and Humbugs.

Suddenly the Head starts breathing again and we all start breathing again too. I bend down and pick up the flowers. The Yank is talking:

"I need you to tell me the address, Ben."

The Head reacts strongly to this. His eyes are wide and blinking like crazy. He's looking round like he's lost something.

The Yank says, "It's OK bro', you need to trust me. I'm goan' write down the address and give it straight to Chris and axe him to get those flowers sent first class, special delivery. You know a'm sorry bout this situation, but a'm goan' do the best I can to get yo' final wishes carried out."

The Head is crying, but he starts telling the Yank the address, who writes it down. When he's done, he stands and walks to me.

"Chris, my man - we's goan' need one enormous bunch of tulips for a lady to be delivered to this here address," he hands me the slip of paper. "And another smaller bunch for a funeral." Then he takes out his wallet, peels off a ton and gives it to me. "These'll be fine," he says, taking three bunches of Queen of the Night - they are velvety black and purple. "This way to the river, right?" he says, indicating with his head.

"That's it - just go straight back over Nine Elms Lane and you're there."

"Thanks man," he says, and I see there are tears running down from under his shades, though the rest of his face stays exactly the same. He walks back to the wheelchair, puts the flowers on the Head's lap and begins to walk slowly away. As soon as they get round the corner, I follow them.

I keep my distance and, once they've crossed to the other side of Nine Elms Lane, I follow them across and then slip left into the car park of Riverside Court. There's no one around at this time. I move quietly through the hedges to where the wall around the car park is replaced by a spiked fence. The Yank and the Head have stopped in front of the wall that marks the edge of the path. They're both looking across the river at the dawn. 'Bernard' is stood behind the wheelchair and has his hand on the Head's shoulder. I feel like I want to roll another cigarette or something but then something weird happens and everything goes still and quiet, like someone just turned London's volume down for a second. The first rays of morning sunshine cut through the cloud and ignite a shower of fine rain falling over Parliament, generating a solid double rainbow onto the dark grey background. The sunlight isn't shining directly onto us, but we're lit up in a strange half-light as it comes off the clouds, a bit like in a photo's negative.

The moment passes and the rain begins to fall in earnest. The Yank crouches down beside the wheelchair and I can see him speaking to the Head, but I can't hear what, and then he puts his hands up to the Head's neck. They stay like that for a while, with the Yank looking round from time to time. Next he takes the flowers and, pulling a plastic bag from his pocket, he puts them inside, then pushes them inside the Head's coat. Then he lifts him out of the wheelchair and onto the wall and pushes him over.

I can hear my heart beating in my head.

The Yank is looking out over the river again. For a moment, I feel like nothing will stop him from turning round and looking directly at me. I see it happen in my head, the shades turning to stop on me, the face impassive. Then he seems to shake himself and looks down briefly before turning and walking back to Nine Elms Lane, crossing over and jogging away east, rounding the corner in seconds.

I breathe. My hands are shaking and my hair is dripping. I look down at my strides and see they are dirty and torn at the knee.

Stab Jacket

Michelle can see I'm bothered about the guy with the flowers and asks me if I'd like to come round to her place for dinner later. I tell her I've got a gig (I haven't) but maybe if I finish up early I'll pop around and say hello. I have no idea what I want to do.

I go home and automatically take out my gear for a smoke, but then I can't stop thinking about that guy in the river, with the broken neck and the tulips, and I know something needs to change. I phone Michelle, tell her the gig's been cancelled, say I'll be there in an hour. Then I roll, smoke, go to the shower block to clear my head, lock up the boat and walk.

Little Angus is still awake when I get there, so we mess around fighting with pillows, then I show him some guitar and we play a board game where you have to answer questions about dinosaurs to win the plastic toys and get to the end. We don't really figure the rules but we have great fun and fight over the Styracosaurus with the yellow horns at the end as if it was the last chocolate in the box. Michelle watches us quietly as she makes dinner, smiling from time to time but saying nothing.

She leaves me with a glass of Malbec and takes a reluctant Angus to bed. The extractor fan has been turned off and the music suddenly permeates through me with some force. Once again I experience the blind moment of first contact as my fingers grope along the silty bottom of the Thames and encounter the dead man's hand, recoiling instantly at the familiar shape, oddly inert. That moment again and the sight of the flowers in the plastic bag stuffed into his coat. Kev had flung the bag of flowers in my stab jacket and I'd shouted at him. It was a clumsy thing to do but I shouldn't have shouted at him. He knows what it's like. I hope he knows what it's like.

I hope he doesn't know what it's like.

The wine is rich and warm in my mouth and seems to emanate waves of comfort as it flows down my throat.

Michelle returns to the living room with the dinner: chicken roasted in chilli jam, with garlic and rosemary roasted potatoes and steamed mangetout. We eat.

I ask about her day. She talks animatedly about one of the groups of lads she teaches, illiterate no-hopers from difficult backgrounds who are completely incompatible with any kind of conventional education. She describes them in detail, with real fondness, identifying their physical abilities, their strength at social interaction, balancing this against their academic frailty, their resistance to authority. We discuss the limitations of an education system that must cater for everyone and she stresses that the limitations are within us as individuals and it is we who determine the parameters of the system. I encourage her to talk about these things. I nod with interest and smile when she confides in me that she can't help having a soft spot for the bad boys.

We've finished eating and are well into our second bottle. She asks me if I want to talk about it. I drain my glass and say yes, it's fine, but can we open another bottle? I don't think she's really drinking much.

I tell her everything in detail: I talk about the split in my mask and the constant mask clearing. I talk about the gloom and the sound of propellers rotating now closer, now further away. I talk about the dryness in my mouth and the disorientation. I talk to Michelle about touching someone's hand, how we touch each other's hands every day, shaking, stroking, holding, squeezing. How the expected sensations, the associated warmth and pressure, have become ingrained in our minds and to find that cold dead hand in the blackness at the bottom of the river touched me in a way I had not been prepared for. I see Michelle look at my hand, which is resting on the table, so I lift it, rub my face with it, then run it through my hair and leave it at the back of my head with the other. I tell Michelle that I have located and retrieved more bodies than I'd care to admit from the bottom of rivers and lakes and thought nothing more of it than the small satisfaction of doing my job well, but this was different.

I tell her that the man had a broken neck and probably did not drown, but this in itself is not something. I tell her about the flowers; tulips, these are. I tell her about Kev and about him accidentally leaving the bag of tulips in my stab jacket. I describe my anger, my out-of-character outburst and subsequent guilt and confusion. I try to talk about the bag of flowers in my stab jacket again, I try to explain about the boundaries I work so hard to maintain in order to do my job and to live the way I do, but Michelle begins to ask what I mean about how I live and I digress and make no sense.

I am suddenly drunk and emotional and frustrated. Michelle senses me pulling away and moves around the table to take me in her arms and give me comfort. I push her away. Michelle looks hurt. I am like a child and I hate myself. I stand and grab the back of my chair to steady myself. Michelle tells me I can stay, there is a spare room, or at the very least she can call me a taxi. I say no, the walk will do me good, I apologise for my behaviour, thank her for dinner and leave.

I walk for a long time. I get off the main arteries and London becomes quiet; not silent, but the background noise diminishes, so that nearby sounds become stark: a dog barking, a black cab snoring over sleeping policemen, the click clack of high-heeled shoes on paving slabs. I am walking beside the black iron railings of a darkened park when I see her. I don't know where I am. She slows down as I approach and asks me if I'm looking for something. She has clear eyes. I automatically say no thanks and she says OK and walks on.

I stand still. I hear birdsong from the park. It is nighttime and birds are singing in the park.

I turn and jog back to the girl and tell her I am looking for company. She tells me company costs £50 for 30 minutes or £500 for the evening, cash up front; she doesn't take cards. I tell her I have £220 cash on me, and will that do for a start? She smiles and says yes. I take the money from my wallet and give it to her, making sure she can see there is no more cash in there. I ask her if she'd like to go for a drink somewhere and she says yes, she knows a place. We go to the bar and she orders a Corona with lime. I take the same. I pay with my card. She asks me what I do for a living and I tell her, then reciprocate, before immediately apologising, but she says it's OK: she is only doing the 'company' work to help pay for her studies. She is studying economics and says she wants to be a lecturer one day and wear tweed and smoke a pipe. She seems pleased when I laugh.

She asks me more about my job and I tell her about the guy with the flowers. I tell her in the same level of detail as before with Michelle, but when I reach the part about the bag of flowers being left in my stab jacket and about my anger, guilt and confusion, they sound like natural emotions in front of this girl. When I finish speaking, she says there must be a sad story behind it all. I buy more drinks.

She asks me if I'm single, where I live and, when I tell her on a boat, she asks me if I'm rich. I tell her most people with a boat will never be rich and she says her father always used to say the second best day of a boat owner's life is the day he buys his boat. The best is the day he sells it, I complete.

We talk about childhood, the sea, zombie economics, nitrogen narcosis, ecstasy, great pie crusts we have known, and with every passing moment something sad grows inside me as my £220 ticks down. She says she'd like to see my boat. I point out that my time is nearly up and she says that I look like a nice guy and she'll put it on my tab. I ask her if she likes nice guys and she says who wouldn't? I say doesn't she prefer the thrill and excitement of bad guys? She says she's seen enough bad guys to last her ten lifetimes. We take a taxi.

She is astonishingly attractive. Despite my initial desire for simple company, I am aware as we ride across Dulwich towards Bermondsey that in the bar I had already imagined her naked several times, had considered the sensation of unhooking her bra and kissing her shoulder as my hand runs under her small breasts. I feel like there are certain protocols I should be observing in this situation, which I am unaware of: unwritten rules of conduct between a call girl and a punter, such as not kissing on the mouth.

We get to the boat and I fix us mojitos while she looks around. She asks me about the guitars and then asks me to play her something. I ask her if she's heard of Skip James and she says no, so I tell her a little about the man. I describe his life as a bootlegger and how, when he was 28, his friends convinced him to enter a music competition that he subsequently won, earning him a record contract with Paramount Records. He recorded 18 songs on both piano and guitar in two days and was offered a flat fee or a percentage of profits from sales of the record in payment and Skip, believing people were going to love his music, opted for the percentage. He took the train back to Mississippi with a light in his heart. The trouble was, it was 1931 and America was caught in the Great Depression. People didn't have money for food, never mind records, and pretty soon after Skip did his recordings Paramount Records went bust and Skip's songs were forgotten about. Some say that Skip took his broken dreams to the bottom of a whisky bottle and others say he found solace in religion, but no-one knows for sure.

Thirty years later, Skip's records were found in a dusty old basement and caused something of a sensation. The word went out to find this legend. Skip was found in 1964 in a hospital in Washington, suffering from life-threatening cancer, and was hauled out to play at the Newport Folk Festival. He blew the crowd away. Young Eric Clapton was a huge fan of Skip's and Cream recorded a cover of one of his tunes, the proceeds of which were sufficient to pay for life-saving surgery for Skip, who went on to make many more recordings and play gigs to a wider audience until his eventual death in 1969.

I pick up my beat up old Tanglewood, drop into the D-tuning and begin to play 'Devil Got My Woman'. I watch my fingers as they work the fret board, hanging and holding the long swing notes and lingering through the licks, just like Skip. When my voice starts, it comes from an ache so deep it almost catches on the way out, but I cradle those words and offer them up to this girl, and within every moment of every note I am utterly lost and I show her this without shame.

When the last note has finished, she leans over and gently kisses me long and slowly on the mouth and when I reach up to the back of her neck and squeeze her hair and neck she moans softly. She pulls away for a moment and reaches over to her handbag, opens up her purse and takes out the £220 I had given her earlier and puts it on the table. She tells me that she doesn't want a flat fee; she wants a percentage.

She tells me her name is Lorenza.

Slacks

I get back in the van and make myself look like I'm doing some paperwork. 'Fat Bottomed Girls' by Queen comes on the radio and I hum along in approval as I look at the signature on the receipt. It's clearly a 'J. Kent' underneath all the squiggles. I'm still not going to let myself believe it was the same bloke, but the coincidences are mounting up: the name and address fit the profile; the property couldn't look any more like a drug baron's tasteless demonstration of ill-gained wealth, boasting ridiculous pseudo-Roman pillars juxtaposed with thatch and black and white timber frame among other horrors; and now the man himself – unquestionably shifty, and lounging around in a football shirt after 9am on a Monday morning.

"So what?" I say to no-one in particular. *Even if this is the infamous, drug-dealing, murdering James Kent, what do you intend to do about it, Annabel? Pop in the back of the van for a torque wrench, ring the bell again and then beat him to death on his doorstep to avenge the murder of your lover's brother, which he may or may not be responsible for? Since when did you become Charles Bronson? And, if you didn't need reminding, you have a family to provide for, a bank that is threatening to repossess your house, three more deliveries to make before 1pm – all of which are long swingers – and a boss with a very short fuse. A boss who would love an excuse to fire your arse, cute though it is in those pink 1970s action slacks with the rainbow stitching down the side, which she hates and wants to use as an excuse for your dismissal, and would have if Dorian hadn't told her it would have been discrimination (in what way discriminatory, Mrs Birch can't tell, but the word is a scary one). Either way, regardless of the context of the action slacks, beating a customer to death with a torque wrench is not going to win you employee of the month.*

I must admit I can be pretty convincing at times.

I put the Merc in gear, turn up 'Fat Bottomed Girls' and swing around the immaculately-kept lawned roundabout with a small Japanese Maple tree in the middle and start the journey down the long wooded drive. But I'm still mulling. There was just something about his face – he looked scared. I pull the van to the side of the drive, next to a thick rhododendron, stop the engine and open the catch on the bonnet. I turn off Queen and then radio HQ and tell Dorian that I've got an engine problem and that I'm just going to have a quick look – might be that oil leak again. All our vehicles have trackers and if Mrs Birch sees a blip on her screen sitting still for more than five minutes, she will expect an explanation. I get out of the van, release the hood fully and then start checking the oil.

Petra took me there once. Her brother's body had washed up on an artificial beach, next to a holiday park overlooking the estuarine Thames, and we had walked along there at low tide, stepping over the groynes and round the bladdery weeds and watching the gulls swoop and cry over the mirror-flat slack water. Petra is the most giving, generous person I have ever met, but it took a long time for her to tell me about her past; there were a lot of painful things that she preferred not to raise of her own accord. We sat on the cold damp beach under a clear bitter February sky and with my arm around her shoulders, she told me the whole story about Christos.

When their parents had separated, Christos had taken it hard. He'd always been something of a mummy's boy, happy to wallow around in the house, being waited on hand and foot by their tireless mother, just like his father, but when their mother had tired of the life of a slave and ran off with a milky tea-drinking builder that had come to fix their neighbour's wall, when it had fallen into their garden during a storm, Christos lost his taste for home comforts and began to seek his pleasures elsewhere. Petra had already left home by this point, but she would receive anxious calls from her father now and again, asking her if Christos was with her. The answer was always no.

Petra had gone back to the house one weekend and found the place empty and in a state - clearly her father and Christos had not yet managed to fill the domestic void left by her mother's departure. She found an old pair of Marigolds under the sink and started to clear the empty beer cans and ashtrays. There'd been a hard knock on the door. Petra had described the man in detail, so he'd clearly made quite an impact: sharp, dark tattoos snaking out of his V-neck and ending under his jaw, small piggy eyes, piercingly blue in colour, an almost vertically flattened nose and small incongruous looking rosebud lips. The man had said "Christos," to which Petra had replied that he was not home, and then the man had just looked at her for what felt like a very long time. He hadn't asked when Christos would be home, or where he was; he'd just looked at her. Petra had felt analysed, threatened and violated all at once by that long, cold stare and then a car horn had sounded and the man had turned without another word and walked away.

No sooner had Petra seen the car disappear at the end of the road than she'd locked the house and gone looking for Christos. She'd tried all of his old friends' houses that she could remember. Most of them said they didn't see much of Christos any more, but eventually one told her that he was usually knocking about at Dee-Dee's place, over on the Pembroke Estate - not a very salubrious location, to say the least. After pounding on the door for a few minutes, it was eventually answered by a chubby Caucasian girl with dark bags under her eyes and a sluggishness to her movements. The sound of a baby screaming came from somewhere within the dingy confines of the flat. Eventually Christos was summoned from the darkness, bare-chested and rubbing the sleep from his eyes. She described the man who was looking for him and he'd told her to calm down - 'Teenth' was an associate of his. He was a businessman now, didn't she know, and both he and Teenth and Jim - she must remember Jim Kent from school - had gone into business together.

Petra had found it very hard to describe her brother on what would be the last time she had seen him alive. She said it was like he had been partially erased: when he spoke to her, his voice was devoid of emotion; the pigmentation of his skin had been taken away, leaving a paleness where olive brown had been before; the vitality had gone from his physicality and even when she battered her fists on his chest to try and get a response, like a medic administering CPR, he had remained unresponsive, not bothering to even raise his arms in protest.

Petra had cried and begged him to come home, she'd said she was sorry that their mother had left, but that if he only came home, she'd come back home too, and they could be a family again and things could be right, but he'd slowly, gently taken her hands from his too-thin upper arms and put them by her side and, with his empty eyes looking at an indeterminate point behind her, he'd wordlessly closed the door.

The police had been unable to contact either of her parents six months later and so she was the one who had been taken to identify his body. She never described it, but I know that the body had been in the water for a couple of days before it washed up, so I can only imagine that it must have been incredibly traumatic for her. Christos had been shot in the back of the head, from close range, execution-style. Petra had given the police a statement and Jim Kent had been interviewed in connection to the murder, but he said that he knew Christos only as a friend of Dee-Dee's really and he certainly didn't have any business dealings with him. Dee-Dee told the police she had not seen Christos for six months. The police did some background checks on Mr Kent, who had a small number of properties that he let out, but everything seemed legitimate. The police were unable to track down the man called Teenth that Petra had described to them. With no murder weapon and no witnesses that could claim to have even seen her brother since she had, the murder investigation had not gotten much further and remained unresolved.

It begins to rain heavily. I have no idea what I'm doing here. I have checked the dipstick, taken a bottle of oil and a funnel from the back of the van and topped it up. I have replaced everything and now I'm stood at the back of the van as the rain starts to pour. I have no reason to stay here. I look around at the damp woodland around me: tall, thick ash trees, with little in the way of ground cover in between each great trunk. I shake my head. I look again, harder this time. I could've sworn I'd seen a figure moving between the trees, somewhere near the boundary wall, which is just visible in places 150 metres directly to my right. I squat down and scuttle to the edge of the rhododendron. Yes, there is definitely a person moving very quickly, light in build and dressed in dark clothes. Again, they are moving towards the house in incredibly swift, fluid bursts. Whoever it is, they don't wish to be seen. I cannot believe that I haven't been seen, but then I realise that although my van is bright yellow, with red lettering all over it, it is also obscured from the person in the wood's trajectory by the big rhododendron bush. Is this why Jim Kent looked freaked out? Was he expecting a visitor – the kind of visitor that climbs over your wall and sneaks through your woods when they pop round?

I've lost them. Suddenly I feel very exposed. What if Mr Kent's guest does a circuit of the grounds before they drop in for a cuppa? What the hell am I doing squatting behind this bush? I need to get back in the van and drive away immediately and quickly. I have a strong sense that I am in danger here. I can smell the sweet dank cloying smell of rotting hummus. Great fat globules of rain drip through the forest from the treetops.

I have heard gunshots many times before, as I grew up on a farm, but I am used to the sound of shotgun blasts, bold and brash, echoing away down the valley. This sounds different, quieter and muffled and considerably more frightening. I get up and quickly walk to the van door, then stand still and quiet again, listening. The wind blows the tops of the trees, releasing a cascade of droplets onto the leaf litter below.

I am amazed at what I am doing, even as I am doing it. "This is clearly not the most prudent course of action," I say to myself as I turn and begin to walk back up the drive towards the house from which I have just heard gunfire. I mean, Mrs Birch may believe me to be a woman who lives life on the edge because I wear pink and rainbow action slacks to work, instead of the standard black uniform trousers, but those trousers are my one act of rebellion, they are my one single comment to the system, whose rules I otherwise adhere to like a Velcro teddy bear. Petra loves me because I am not adventurous, I do not do stupid, crazy, unpredictable things; she thinks I am rational and wise and dependable.

I find myself walking up the drive like a Zen master who has let go of the mental reins for too long and found, when they drifted back down from meditation, that someone else has taken command of her body; a stranger, a demented stranger. I am rounding the bend in the drive and am in full view of the house and my heart is beating so hard my head hurts. The gravel crunches like atom bombs going off under my feet. The rain falls heavily, but certainly not loud enough to disguise the explosive crunching of my feet carrying me noisily up the drive. I reach the little roundabout, listening for the sound of another gunshot, looking for the flash from a window that will give me the split second to get my affairs in order before I die. I do not hesitate and walk right over the grass, past the Japanese maple, and over the gravel once again and up to the house. I stop. I look down at the large stone doorstep, dry beneath the pillared, Romanesque porch. I wonder whether my feet were dry when I stood there before, or if my wet footprints dried. I cannot go further. I feel that if I go one step nearer to the door, it will be the end of me. Rain drips from the prow of my baseball cap. I feel the Zen master gently taking back the reins from the demented stranger and suddenly all my boldness has gone and I am terrified. I lurch on tiptoes around the porch and, as I squat down in some thick shrubbery to the left of the front door, I hear the sound of the door handle turning. She is a middle-aged woman, wearing a brown, tight-fitting jacket and black trousers, and I am less than five metres away from her. I do not breathe. I assume that if I can see this woman, if she were to turn and look in my direction, she would see me. The woman takes out a silver case from her pocket, puts a cigarette in her mouth and, holding a protective hand up to shield her lighter from the wind, she tilts her head towards me and flicks the flame to life. The flame is directly between her eyes and me. I do not move a muscle. I can see the flickering light in her eyes. She shuts the lighter off and turns her head away, taking a deep inhalation and then blowing evenly out. She puts her lighter back in her pocket and steps into the rain, quietly crunching across the gravel, directly past my hiding place and then onto the lawn, moving back in the direction she had approached the house from.

I breathe finally, deep and quiet. Her cigarette smoke hangs in the air.

I remain hidden like that for a long time, the rain falling on my crouching back and soaking me through. I know I should stand up, walk back down that drive, get in the van and drive away, but I can't stop wondering what is behind that door. I imagine Mr Kent shot and dying. I imagine going to him and saying, "Did you kill Christos?" and him nodding sorrowfully as he coughs up blood and then saying, "Tell Petra I'm sorry." At the same time that I am telling myself that this scenario is utterly cuckoo, I am standing and slowly moving back round the porch. The front door is ajar. I untie my laces and step out of my shoes, onto the dry stone step, and push open the door. Beyond the door is a wide hallway with a sideboard on the right and coats hung up on the left. I step silently in. At the end of the hallway, a flight of carpeted stairs on my right lead upstairs, whilst an open door on my left leads into a large kitchen. I can smell coffee in the kitchen, but when I poke my head in the room is empty. There is a door at the far end of the kitchen but this appears to lead to the garden. I turn slowly back around and look up the stairs. It is darker up there. I see a light switch at the bottom of the stairs and pulling my sleeve over my finger I flick the switch. A trail of little spotlights illuminate the stairs and disappear along the landing. I walk quietly up the stairs. They do not creak. The landing has several doors, all of which are shut, apart from the one at the end of the landing, which is open slightly, with daylight showing around the edges and through an odd-shaped hole in the upper left panel of the door at about head height. I walk along the corridor, past the closed doors, and stand before the door with the hole in it. I can smell cordite and wood dust. Splinters of wood are splayed out from the hole in the door and looking at the wall of the landing I see a neat hole where a bullet finished its journey.

I nudge open the door. Mr Kent is lying on his bedroom floor in his boxer shorts, with a shirt half done up. His arms are spread out wide and his right leg is bent at the knee and thus raised off the ground. He would look like he was sunbathing, were it not for the pencil stub sticking out of his bloody eye socket. There is a gun in his hand. I can smell aftershave. I feel sick.

OK, so no last minute confession from the late repentant. I need to get out of here now. Too late; I'm going to be sick. There is a door leading into an en suite that I barge my way through and then I'm on my knees, throwing up the veggie burger I had for breakfast. I take some deep breaths, calming myself down, and realise I actually feel a lot better now that I've been sick. I pull my sleeves over my hands again and wipe down the toilet seat and outer bowl, flush the toilet and turn to wipe down the door.

My heart stops for a moment. Behind the bathroom door is a very large, wide open safe in the wall and in the safe I can see thick bundles of what looks like money. I take a closer look. No question. Thick bundles of crisp fifty-pound notes, little jewellery boxes and a gold bar, all sitting on top of a Pink Floyd *Dark Side of the Moon* album in vinyl.

I turn my attention back to the bathroom door, wiping it down carefully. I take off my red and yellow fleece and take hold of the sleeves, the neck and the lower edge all in one hand to make a basic bag, and then I put all the bundles of cash, the jewellery boxes and the gold bar in. The bag is full. I step back out of the en suite and, taking care not to look at the customer who I had delivered a laptop to not half an hour ago, I walk out of the bedroom. I pad carefully down the landing and down the stairs and quickly make my way back out of the house. I put my makeshift bag down briefly, whilst I put my shoes back on, and then walk quickly and quietly down the drive.

Once I'm back at the van, I call the police and tell them that I need to report a murder. The man quickly and efficiently takes down my location, then, once he has ascertained my safety, he tells me to wait where I am and that a patrol car will be with me within five minutes. I get in the back of the van, put together one of the spare heavy-duty packing boxes and place the money, jewellery and the gold bar securely inside. I write Petra's name and our address on one of the labels and use the hand stamp to officiate the delivery. I put the box with the rest and then close the back door of the van. I climb back into the cab of the van and call up Dorian on the radio. I do not find it difficult to sound shaken up. Dorian tells me she will let Mrs Birch know and that they will get a replacement driver organised and over to me as soon as possible to finish off my deliveries. I tell her it's OK, I'm fine, and that I can get the rest done, but she says that there is no way I should be driving after what I've been through – it must've been a hell of a shock – and that the police will probably need me to make a statement anyway, so I might be tied up for a while. I tell her I hadn't thought of that and thank her. She asks me if I want her to stay on the line and chat with me till the police come, but I say no, I'm fine.

I'm cold and damp and the van windows are misting up, so I turn the engine on and put the blowers on. I rub my hands between my thighs.

I can only hope that the killer was professional enough to disable or check for CCTV. Her exposed face suggested this wouldn't be an issue.

I rub my hands between my pink thighs and wait for the police as the hot blowers clear the mist from my windscreen.

Sauna Suit

Billy's up at 5am and immediately begins his stretches and warm-up exercises. The movements are so hardwired into him that he is only conscious of the routine in its absence. Out on the street he can still hear a handful of party diehards loitering around the fire pit, clinging to whatever social embers they can find after the weekend-long party. They are the unsung champions of their class, the enduring detritus that will not go home.

Once Billy has warmed up, he takes his Swelter Sauna Suit from the wardrobe and, with a look of distaste on his face, he puts it on. The sauna suit is a black, two-piece tracksuit made of coated nylon, with rubberised seals round the neck, waist, wrists and ankles, which are designed to help retain heat and moisture within the garment, thus maximising calorie burn and weight loss during a workout. Billy does not enjoy wearing it. He grabs his keys and heads downstairs.

The multi-seed batch loaf he bought on Friday has gone, but there is a value loaf of thin-sliced white bread on Pedro's shelf, so he takes a couple of slices and drops them in the toaster. He can hear Pedro talking in the living room, so he puts his head round the door. Pedro and Hendo are slouched on the couches in front of the television. Pedro holds a still-lit joint in his hand and is talking some sort of incomprehensible monotone gibberish, whilst Hendo is staring blankly ahead, ignoring him – his nose is swollen and bloodied and his eyes are bloodshot and red-rimmed in a way that doesn't look solely weed-induced. Suddenly Pedro's monologue switches from Spanish to English and changes pitch with his mounting excitement:

"*Hijo de puta.* 'Ere 'e comes, the fuckin' cun' – look a' that big fuckin' whale man. Look a' him."

On the screen, a large barnacle-encrusted whale is emerging from a green sea beneath a white roof of pack ice.

"'Ey Billy, wha' happen to you? You look clean as a baby man. Look a' that big fuckin' whale."

"Hey Peds, he's a nice one for sure." Billy looks seriously at the disappearing flukes. "You OK, Hendo?"

"Aye, Billy, am alright mate."

"Looks like the match was lively."

Hendo makes an attempt at a smile and then just says "Aye" again.

"Hey Peds, I've taken some of your bread."

"*Mi casa, tu casa* man. Smell like you're burning some of my bread though, brother."

"Ah shit, we've got to get a new toaster." Billy goes back into the kitchen and takes the two black slices out of the toaster and puts them in the compost bin.

"I'll speak with Tanya. Maybe she can ask a' the next meeting," comes Pedro's voice from the other room.

"Lads, I gotta bust, I'll catch you later," says Billy.

"Later man."

"Seeya Billy."

Billy has got specific measured routes depending on where he is in his training calendar, but he often finishes on Blackheath; the gradient up onto the heath is good for hill sprints and he likes to catch up with Petra, an old friend of the family, who works the early shift at the all-night burger shack.

He gets his breathing under control as he jogs the final stretch across the wet grass to the 'Blackheath Tea Hut'. Petra is, as she always is when she doesn't have a customer, cleaning:

"Alright darlin'?"

"Oh hey Billy. How are you, love?"

"Good. What's new?"

"Billy, I'm in a spot – Sue's not due in for another twenty minutes and I've just remembered I've signed up for a pottery class today and I've got to go home first and get the car. Would you be a darling and keep an eye on things here until Sue gets in?" Petra is making ready to leave.

"Ummm, what if someone wants something? I can't even make toast!"

"Don't worry, you'll be fine. Here, it's easy." Petra steps out of the back of the hut and walks around to where Billy is standing. She takes off her apron and pops it over Billy's head like a noose, reaching under his arms and around his back to fasten the tie. She still has an unbelievable body for a fifty-something and her huge breasts rolling over Billy's stomach cause an instant stir in his trousers, which he desperately hopes she won't notice. Petra puts her arm around Billy's shoulder and steers him around the back and into the hut.

"There's plenty of coffee in the pot, bread here, bacon in the fridge and eggs under the microwave. It's all anybody wants this time of day anyway. Thanks Billy, you're a superstar."

Petra grabs her handbag and her coat and steps out of the door, then, turning, she puts her head back in and says:

"Hey Billy, listen to me, you need to find yourself a girlfriend. You can't go round poking old ladies with that thing, someone's going to get the wrong impression." She winks at him.

"Get out of here." He flicks a tea towel at her, but the door is already closing.

"See you soon Billy, thanks."

Billy stands in his wet, cooling sauna suit and apron, with his hands on his hips, and looks at the steadily increasing traffic outside. He turns and looks at the confusing array of utensils and appliances, the tubs and packets of uncooked things to eat, the enormous list of possible things to order on the black menu board.

"Shit," he says.

"Morning," says a voice from behind him that makes Billy jump. "Can I get a black coffee and a veggie burger with cheese, please?" The woman looks early thirties, slim, with a DHL uniform, complete with cap and ponytail.

"Oh hey, sure, yes, let me see, let me see..." Billy starts opening cupboards and looking purposefully in each for answers to questions which he is not really yet processing.

"Petra not about?" says the woman.

"You just missed her." A *veggie burger*, thinks Billy to himself. *Do we do veggie burgers? Is that a beef burger with onions? If a cheeseburger is a beef burger with cheese and an eggburger is a beef burger with an egg, then a veggie burger must be a beef burger with veggies. Why's a beef burger called a hamburger?* That's irrelevant. He needs to focus. *Why doesn't a chicken burger come with a beef burger and some chicken? Why doesn't a cheeseburger come with a chicken burger instead of a beef burger?* OK, he must try to stay calm. So far he's established that burgers do not follow any logical patterns. A burger can refer to the pattie that goes in the bun, or the combined fillings inclusive of the bun. Maybe a veggie burger is just veggies in a roll? Do the vegetables go on the griddle? Where are the vegetables? Maybe it's a salad roll? He can see salad ingredients under the counter in ice cream tubs. He needs to buy some time - make the coffee. He takes a Styrofoam cup and pours coffee from the glass jug, adds milk and hands it to the woman.

"Here we go. How would you like that veggie burger?"

"With all the salad, onions and cheese please. And I ordered a black coffee."

"You did? Course you did, this one's for me," he smiles winningly at the woman. "And yours is coming right up." The woman is looking at him as if he has an alien hanging out of his nostril. Billy is sweating again. He gets the woman her black coffee. So the veggie burger comes with all the salad, onions and cheese, therefore the veggie burger is something in addition to those ingredients. He doesn't think it's a beef burger - veggie burgers are for vegetarians. Maybe it's an egg, but an egg is not a vegetable. What about an eggplant? He looks around for an aubergine - nothing. What the fuck!

"Just need that griddle to warm up - shouldn't take long." The woman is busy looking at her phone and drinking her coffee. Good; at least he's not been watched now. He looks in the fridge again – beef burgers, chicken burgers, bacon and processed cheese slices on the top shelf. OK, well that's a start. He takes out the cheese and turns back to the salad containers. What's the difference between salad and vegetables on your dinner table? Salad is cold, right? And vegetables are served hot. He takes a handful of iceberg lettuce and chucks it on the griddle, where it begins sizzling away, which he quickly follows with red cabbage, slices of tomato and cucumber. He takes the bun and pops it on the griddle as well to toast and then grabs an egg. He knows that the veggie burger may not be exactly what the customer wants, but if he throws in an egg it might sweeten the deal sufficiently for her to swallow it. The bun is done, he takes it and puts it on the chopping board in front of the salad tubs and puts cold iceberg lettuce, red cabbage, cucumber and tomato on the lower section.

"Any sauces, love?" Now that a decision has been made, Billy is relaxing into the mould. It may not have been the right decision, but it has now been made and Billy can focus on the action phase and implement the plan to the best of his ability.

"Chilli and garlic mayo," says the woman. Billy turns and gives the griddling salad a quick flip over, before bringing it together again in the approximate shape of a burger. It's browning up nicely. He cracks the egg next door on the griddle, which immediately begins to bubble and spit. He brings the sides in and seasons.

"Chilli, chilli, chilli, aha." He draws a spiral of chilli sauce on the top bun half. There are two bottles of white sauce, both unlabelled, so he drizzles a little of each on the cold salad, assuming that some garlic will have found its way in one way or the other. He puts a slice of processed cheese on the top and the bottom halves of the bap and then, picking up the bottom half, he turns back to the griddle. He scoops up the 'veggie burger' and deposits it carefully on top of the cold salad, then slips his spatula under the egg and pops it on top. He turns and completes the burger with the upper bap. Smiling his biggest, shit-eating grin, he passes the woman her order between two serviettes.

"Great, thanks, oh..." The woman has passed Billy a ten-pound note and taken receipt of her order. Billy busies himself with getting her change.

"Here you go - £6.50 change." The woman is looking at him. She is not eating her burger. She is looking at her burger with a furrowed brow, but she is not eating her burger.

"What is this?"

"Veggie burger," says Billy enthusiastically.

"OK, look: you've done a good job with the bap - that's well toasted; excellent work with the two slices of cheese - I feel like a special customer in respect to the double cheese; sauces - fine; salad - here's where things start to go awry, you seem to have fried half of the salad; but it's the burger that's the main issue - it appears to be an egg."

"Yes."

"You're Billy aren't you?"

"Yes."

"Petra's told me about you."

"She has?"

"Yes - you're the boxer."

"Yes."

"OK. Listen, I don't have mountains of time and I'm fairly ravenous, so why don't I come round there for five minutes and knock up a veggie burger for myself? In the meantime, you come round here and eat your 'veggie burger' and drink your coffee. You look like you need it."

"Might make sense..."

"It might."

The woman walks to the back of the van and opens the door. Billy is compliantly removing the apron. He hands it over and walks out of the van. Once he's round the front, he says:

"What's your name?"

"I'm Annabel." She is washing her hands in the little sink. Billy feels a hint of shame for not having done this before he started operations. She then goes to the little freezer compartment at the top of the fridge and pulls out an open box and says, "And these are veggie burgers."

"You're vegetarian then, Annabel?"

"Bingo."

"Why, if you don't mind me asking?"

"Well, there're all sorts of reasons. It's healthy, as long as you make sure you get your full complement of vitamins. It's better for the environment; you need a tenth of the land to fulfil a human's nutritional needs using vegetables than if you were to use meat. But, deep down, the real reason is that I like animals."

"I like animals too."

"Do you? You know, I grew up in the countryside in East Anglia and I was a proper farmer's daughter. I loved it, looking after the cattle, driving round in tractors, throwing around bales of hay. I loved the outdoors, being out in every kind of weather. You know when you wake up in the morning and you look out of your window and it makes a difference if the sun's shining or not? I loved that, the fact that it mattered. Anyway, my father used to take me hunting and it was something I always found difficult. How is that?"

Billy is chewing a mouthful of his veggie burger.

"Unusual. The fried cucumber is particularly unusual."

"So, there was one occasion when our dog had caught a pheasant in a hedge and as the dog came out of the hedge, I took the pheasant from it. My dad was on the other side of the hedge and he had to run down the hill to get through the gate and back up the other side to get to me and the pheasant. I can still see him now running in his wellies and his underpants – Dad was always running around with next to nothing on when the sun came out – and he was shouting "Pull its head off, pull its head off!" and I looked at the pheasant and the pheasant looked at me and I couldn't do it. I couldn't take that life, so I let him go. Well, Dad went ape shit as you can imagine, said to me, "If you can't kill it, you shouldn't eat it," words he instantly regretted, knowing what I was like. I said "OK, that makes sense," and

I've lived by his accidental rule ever since. So, technically, I'm not vegetarian – if I kill something, I'll eat it, but that totals one chicken and two fish in the last forty-two years, since I made the switch."

Forty-two years! *Jesus*, Billy thinks, *how old is she?* Must be in her fifties – she looks amazing.

"What I do find interesting," Annabel continues, "is the number of people out there who eat meat, who are horrified at even the thought of the killing, skinning and gutting of an animal, despite the fact that these are all absolutely necessary stages in every single bit of meat's journey to their mouths."

Billy thinks about killing a cow. How would he do it? Shoot it? Dynamite it? Hack into it like they do in *Apocalypse Now*? That's a distressing scene to watch; maybe he wouldn't find it so easy to kill a cow either, let alone skinning and gutting the thing. Maybe he should be vegetarian? He looks at his veggie burger – maybe not.

"Anyway, I'm done." Annabel is taking off the apron. On the counter is what appears to be a picture-perfect cheeseburger (as in one made with a hamburger/beef burger).

"That looks good," says Billy.

"Morning, sorry I'm late," Sue is stepping into the hut. "Oh, has Petra gone? Oh hey Annabel, oh you know I thought for a minute we were starting a burger delivery service! Ah ha ha ha. Proper fast food! Ah ha ha ha. You know, with the DHL outfit, ah ha."

"Hi Sue," says Annabel, handing Sue the apron.

"You covering for Petra, Annabel?" says Sue.

"Technically, I'm covering for Billy and he's covering for Petra, but either way, we're both glad you're here."

"Well, thank you both. Would you like a bacon sandwich, Billy?"

"No thanks Sue, I need to get cracking."

"What about one for later?"

"No honestly Sue, I'm fine. I'm thinking of lowering my meat intake." Billy looks at Annabel, who is stood to the side of the van, looking across the mist on the heath and smiling as she drinks her coffee.

"Very nice to meet you Annabel, thanks for your help," says Billy.

"You too Billy, thanks for the coffee."

They look at each other a moment and then Billy offers his hand. She shakes it.

"Right, I've gotta go, cheers. Seeya Sue."

He heads back to the house. Pedro is sound asleep in front of a shopping channel in the living room, but Hendo must have gone up to bed. He lays a blanket on Pedro and turns off the TV. He showers, drinks a protein shake, then makes coffee and eggs. Once that's down, he spends the rest of the morning helping a fuzzy-headed contingent clean up the after-party mess from the street. At 1pm he puts together his gym kit, gets his tracksuit on, goes up to Pete's room and knocks. A moment later Pete opens the door, as always wearing his cowboy hat. Black curtains leave the room in almost total darkness and even though Billy cringes slightly in anticipation of the animal smells he expects to come from Pete's room, none are forthcoming. In fact, the room seems oddly odourless.

"Ready?" says Billy.

"Of course, how are you feeling?" answers Pete.

"Good."

"How many miles this morning?"

"Four and a half, including hill sprints."

"Hmmm, we might want to ease off on the running over the next few weeks and shift the emphasis to Tabata workouts and 10 by 10 drills. Shame we can't get some shark tanking into the regime, but I'll think of something to fill the gap. Where's your sauna suit?" Pete has picked up his bag and coat and is locking his room.

"Oh c'mon Pete, I've had that thing on all morning."

"Well, no problem; if you were your own trainer, you wouldn't have to wear it, would you?"

"OK, look, the thing is dripping and it stinks. I'll wear it next time."

"What are you, deaf? No problem, next time you wear it if you feel like it, because I'm not gonna be there to keep you in line." Pete is turning to go back into his room.

"I'm putting it on – two minutes." Billy goes back to his room and takes the sauna suit from his wash basket. He takes off his comfortable fleece-lined tracksuit and puts on the cold, wet sauna suit. It smells. Pete is waiting outside his door.

"OK. Listen Billy, this guy's meant to be a really big bastard and he knows what he's doing."

"Sure."

"No, I'm serious this time. He sparred with Bobby the Bento a fortnight ago and Bobby is still in hospital."

"Yeah well, Bobby's slow," says Billy. They head down the stairs.

"Bobby is a good fighter, Billy. He's strong as an ox. He's fit too – I've seen him knocked down three times and still win a fight. And he ain't all that slow. I'm telling you, he'd give you a good run for your money."

"No, he wouldn't," says Billy.

"You sound pretty sure of yourself."

"I should do – I fought him five years ago before you started managing my affairs."

"Is that right? And?"

"He was slow."

"Well OK, look Billy, all I'm saying is this guy doesn't hold anything back and he's vicious. There's something about him – his mechanism's gone. He's not a proper boxer. I've got a couple of contacts who know some good fighters, who might be willing to spar with you, so all I'm saying is let's just stick to the training programme and wait till we get someone who you can properly spar with." They get to the bike shed and Pete climbs aboard his ladies-style folding bicycle and they set off for the boxing club off Old Kent Road, with Billy running along beside him.

"Pete, you know training hard is not going to get me match fit. I need someone who's going to challenge me. This guy – what's his name?"

"Bernard, and you can always train harder, in fact you *need* to train harder," says Pete.

"Bernard – he sounds perfect. You know I respect your opinion and you're in charge, so whatever you say goes, but I haven't had a sparring partner for three months. Pete, if you feel like it's getting out of hand, just call it."

"OK, I just don't want to see you end up like Bento."

"What'd he do to him?"

"Four broken ribs, a punctured lung, fractured and dislocated jaw. Get those legs up, Billy."

They get to the club, Billy gratefully changes out of the dripping sauna suit and, once Pete has strapped up his hands and got the gloves and head protection on, they head to the main ring. As Billy starts his warm-ups, a blood-curdling howl echoes out of the changing rooms. Billy has long ago learned to filter out any kind of external influences when he's building himself up to fight; it's one reason why he's been so successful at the sport up until now. That, and the fact that he's good at reading his opponents, is built like a brick shit house and has incredibly fast hands. But there is something inhuman about the noise that gets through to his head. There are two voices in the changing room now, both shouting in a language he doesn't understand – Russian, maybe. One is obviously trying to calm the other down, the other sounds like he's just been told his family has been slaughtered or is having his foot removed without anaesthetic. The sound is monstrous. Insane.

Billy suddenly imagines that there are a wide variety of things that he should be doing with his life and this isn't one of them.

As suddenly as it started, the pandemonium stops. At the end of the long corridor, where the hollering has been coming from, is a glass brick wall. A door opens on the right-hand side of the corridor and a figure steps out and begins to walk towards them, presenting a short and slender, dark outline against the day-lit brickwork. The figure is wearing a head guard and gloves. Billy breathes a deep sigh of relief. The figure nears the end of the corridor and then opens a door in the left-hand side of the corridor and disappears. At the same time, another figure steps out at the far end of the corridor again and blocks out most of the light. Holy fucking shit!

Billy looks at Pete. Pete is staring wide-eyed down the corridor. "Pete. Pete." Pete finally turns his attention back to Billy and says: "I'll go get you a sledgehammer."

Billy turns back round. Bernard has reached the end of the corridor and is walking slowly and deliberately into the gym, staring at Billy all the while, whilst his trainer emerges from behind him, a relatively tiny Chinese man in a dirty brown suit, fitting onto Bernard's side like a remora on a shark. Bernard has no protective headgear on. He steps into the ring, walks directly up to Billy and swings at his head. Billy is caught by considerable surprise, but manages to duck awkwardly out of the way of the blow and back steps clumsily out of reach of the next swipe coming his way.

Billy recovers from the surprise attack quickly and begins bouncing on the balls of his feet, moving quick and seeing the swings early. He can hear Pete and the Chinese guy shouting at each other but he filters it out, focusing on the enormous man who seems very difficult to evade in a ring that he seems to half fill.

"Quiet bell they're using today," says Billy jovially as he bounces away from another huge gloved right hand. Then he cuts in fast, his left catching Bernard's right eye socket and his right coming over and hammering him square on his left temple, before pulling back and then - what the fuck! He's scrambling off the floor, his head is ringing, he turns and Bernard is there with another right fist, this time into his chest. He feels a rib break with certainty as he falls backwards towards the ropes. *Fuck, don't let him get you on the ropes*, his head screams. He runs out the way, not bouncing, but literally running like a child dodging in a game of tic.

He has never been hit so hard in his life.

Billy is bouncing again. He keeps the monster at arm's length. He takes no risks now, keeping out of the corners, watching the man called Bernard. The man's eyes seem vacant. He cannot see anything behind them. All boxers keep their cards close to their chest, and he's an expert at spotting the human hiding behind the wall and exploiting what he finds, but there's no human here; just wall. He keeps taking cheap shots, moving from side to side and jabbing where he can, but he's desperate, because there are no patterns to follow or break. Sometimes Bernard seems clumsy and Billy is able to get in some big shots, but the next moment he's right there again, breathing down his neck and seemingly only angered by Billy's punches.

Considering the fact that there was no bell to start with, Billy doubts the likelihood that they'll be adhering to the usual boxing practices of rounds, bells and ceasing to box when one's opponent is unconscious. Billy is tiring and his broken rib is affecting his breathing. He's been chased around for over five minutes now, but Bernard doesn't appear to be short of breath in the least. The man is like a character out of *Street Fighter* or something, with unlimited stamina that just keeps reaching and swinging as long as you can be bothered to wiggle the joystick. Billy realises that he needs to try and incapacitate the man or he's going to be in for some serious physical damage. Billy waits for an opportunity again; it's easy enough to step inside and deliver the goods, not so easy to get back out in one piece if the bombs don't have the desired effect.

Bernard overextends himself slightly, swinging a huge haymaker with his right, growling angrily as he misses. Billy steps around to the side of Bernard and batters him quickly with three extremely hard left punches to the man's unprotected head and then swings the right upper cut beneath his still flailing right arm and catches him full cock square on the chin. Bernard doesn't fall over. Bernard turns his head and smiles at Billy, who realises too late that he's worked himself into the corner to make his move.

Everything seems to slow down for Billy. He watches as Bernard turns smoothly, his left swinging through and thumping up under his protective elbows and bouldering into his abdomen, ramming up into his diaphragm. The right is following up and he moves his glove and head to try and minimise the damage, but he's reacting too slowly now, still reeling from the last blow, and the huge arm batters his glove out of the way and sends his head spinning on his neck like a speedball. He has a moment to wonder what happened to Pete and the Chinese guy and anyone else in the fucking building, before the bombardment commences. He tries to keep his arms up and protect himself; tries to stay on his feet as he doesn't believe there'll be any mercy on the floor. He keeps spinning and staggering along, clinging to the ropes, and suddenly he can see the cow in *Apocalypse Now*, machetes slicing slabs out of its neck and back as it drops to its knees, and now the huge whelk-encrusted whale comes emerging from the green gloom underneath the pack ice and he can hear crying. He must be crying. But it's not him crying and suddenly the blows are erratic and he sees through his swollen, battered face that Bernard is sobbing like a baby, swinging randomly as if he's fending off an unseen enemy and then, suddenly, with a clang, he drops to his knees and falls flat on his face. Through his puffy eyes, Billy can see a blurry man wearing a cowboy hat standing where the huge blubbering figure of Bernard had been moments before, with what appears to be a fire extinguisher in his hands.

"What took you so long?" dribbles Billy through his bleeding split lips.

"Couldn't find a sledgehammer," says Pete, helping Billy to his feet.

"I feel like a Bento box."

"I told you, you need to train harder." He holds the ropes open for Billy, who steps through gingerly. The small Chinese man is lying unconscious on his back, next to the ring.

"Woah, and the winner by two knockouts..." says Billy, laughing and grimacing at the same time.

"Ah, he was being unhelpful."

"Remind me to be more helpful to you in the future." Pete helps Billy back to the changing room. They both look at the sauna suit hanging on his peg. A moment passes.

"I'd best get that back on then," says Billy.

"I think we can make an exception this one time."

"No, no, I should put it on; like you said, I need to train harder."

"Well no problem Billy, if you want to be your own trainer, you can wear that thing all day if you want. Hell, sleep in it if you like."

"I'm just trying to be helpful here, Pete. I don't want you to think I'm being unhelpful. I should put it on."

"What are you, deaf? Give it to me." Pete takes the sauna suit and puts it under one arm, then, with Billy draped over his other shoulder, they walk out of the gym.

Smutter

Frank and Gunderson follow me into the gym. Teenth is already there with a couple of heavyweights - I'm guessing they were tight outside, because none of them bother to check the other's composure. None of 'em moves a muscle. I'm pleased to find that my heart doesn't skip a beat - it never has in these situations, but then I'm old and people change.

I've told Frank and Gunderson that we're here just to talk, but they're both old enough and ugly enough to know that a man like Teenth isn't the talking type and they've both made sure to put their affairs in order - as much as that's possible to do from the inside - before they came. There's only two ways for this to end: Teenth goes down or Frank does. You may be able to tell from the fact that I'm stood at Frank's end of the pitch that I'm not a fan of the latter being the final result.

Teenth's been in two weeks and he wants to be a big fish. Now there's all manner of ways of proving yourself to be a big fish (one being to take out another big fish, which is how I did it), but not in all my forty-four years in prison has one of them been to watch a man knock your tray of dinner all over you and let it go unpunished. Wiping off the sauce and saying, "That's OK, I don't think bolognaise stains," is not really the big fish way. But, to be sure, my man Frank can be a clumsy one. Teenth had grabbed Frank rough round the neck and shaken his glasses off, but no real damage was done before the screws intervened. Teenth still requires satisfaction.

I size up Teenth; he must be in his fifties, but he's in very good shape. He clearly spends plenty of time in rooms like this, but he doesn't have a bodybuilder's physique – his muscular arrangement has been cultivated for more practical application. He looks like a cage fighter. From the angle of his wrist, I can see he's tooled up as well, which is impressive – it's damned hard to get yourself a weapon in Belmarsh, and he's been here only two weeks. The man must be resourceful, I'll give him that. Well, all the better I suppose.

I must admit that considering what's about to happen, I am feeling in particularly fine spirits, stood here in my smutter with my two greatest friends at my side, at the end of what has to be the best twenty-four hours I have had since they locked me up. The lads were feeling pretty tense yesterday afternoon, after I sent word to Teenth that we should meet tomorrow in the gym at 3pm to iron out the problem, but then we all got visitors: Frank's daughter Chloe came to see him and give him the family news; Gunderson's partner (as in business) had visited to update him on his company's growth (Gunderson was an architect on the outside, believe it or not); and I had my first visitor in over twenty years.

I don't know how she managed to get a visit with me with such short notice and I don't much care. What I care about is that she showed me the truth, and I cried like a baby when I heard it after all these years of darkness. They say the truth will set you free, and in my case this may literally be the case.

We reconvened later in the library. Apart from the staff and Le Tran, the medical orderly, who is reading Vietnamese books, it's just us in there. Ben, the library assistant, has managed to get hold of a copy of *Roger's Profanisaurus* for us, and while the boys quietly read out various crudities and their definitions, I allow myself to think of the outside for just a little while.

I imagine what it would be like to lie in a park and look up at the trees, with no screws to tell you your time's up, but then I think that maybe I'd feel lonely, laid out there on the grass on my own. I think about how it would feel to lean on a bar and drink a skinful, but then I think alcohol might make me sick after all this time, and then I imagine someone might recognise me, even now, and suddenly I'd be running down the street, getting chased by an angry mob. I consider how it would be to try and track down Jed's family – I'm sure my brother had children before he died, but they might be in Canada or New Zealand and, even if I did find them, would they be happy to see their child-murdering uncle? I think about how it would feel to have a woman in my arms, but I think I have even lost the taste for that.

I am sixty-three years old. I have no-one on the outside. Freedom is a terrifying thought: the horror of a silent, private bedroom; the desperation of sitting on a bus just to be near people; the emptiness of being woken up alone in a cinema, the film over.

I look around me. This is my family, this is my home. I have been here since 1991, when they opened Belmarsh, after twenty years in Scrubs. I have protected the weak, I have guided the curious and I have punished the cruel. I am respected here, by the inmates, the staff, even by the screws. I am known, I am understood.

I cannot leave now. I will not leave now. Teenth will be my ticket to stay.

That night when Gunderson climbed down to my bunk, I told him I wasn't in the mood, but he stayed anyway and we held each other. He traced his fingers over the imperial eagle tattooed on my chest and finally went to sleep. I stayed awake, listening to the sounds of the night: men breathing, snoring and crying out in their sleep; radiators rattling and pinging; the distant echoes of the screws chatting, making tea and watching TV; and every once in a while, the sound of birdsong somewhere on the outside. Tiny thudding little souls that will not even be held by daylight. I drifted off as grey dawn filled the gaps between the bars of my window.

We are early. I need to buy some time. I nod to Frank and Gunderson, indicating for them to stay put, and take a few steps towards Teenth. He does the same, without bothering to look at his deputies. I begin to mutter under my breath.

"Summink to say?" says Teenth.

"You ever hear the word 'smutter'?"

Teenth says nothing; he just looks at me intensely, with his piggy eyes, waiting for it to begin. He is not interested in the talk element.

"I first heard it when I arrived in Wormwood Scrubs in 1968. American fella was one of the big fish in there at the time and he used the word to describe your kit, your prison clothes. *Your* smutter is what Frank inadvertently spilled his spaghetti on the other day. Angie, his name was, the yank I mean – girl's name – and he took a real shine to me. Unfortunately, the feeling was not mutual and I had to break open his head in the end to get the message through his thick skull. Course, that then made me a big fish and I've been a big fish ever since. If you want to be a big fish, you might need to crack open my thick skull before the folks round here believe you've got what it takes.

"But we'll come back to that, and don't worry; I'm as eager to see what's in your hand as you are to show me, I'm sure. Smutter," I say slowly, relishing the word, "I liked the word, so I kept it. I looked it up and the dictionary had a different meaning; said a smutter was a machine used for separating out the impurities found in harvested grain and I thought that maybe that was a little bit like me, now I'd become a big fish. From then on I decided it was my duty as a big fish to police the inmates and make sure to keep those nasty elements separated out from the good grain, so to speak." I check the clock and then continue.

"That's not all though," I say, my finger in the air, as I begin to pace slowly left to right just out of Teenth's reach. "Yesterday I discovered even more meanings for the word smutter – I know, hard to believe a word that up until now you'd probably never even heard of could have so many meanings. Apparently 'to smutter' is to use profane language under one's breath, so that those nearby cannot hear you, which is exactly what I was doing only a moment ago, when you asked me whether I had 'summink' to say and – you're not going to believe this – but what I was saying also relates to another meaning of the word smutter. I know, crazy! My final meaning of the word smutter, as defined by *Roger's Profanisaurus*, is one who has sexual relations with many gentlemen." I check the clock and then check the viewing window. "And what I was smuttering was that you, Teenth, are going to be a smutter, because when I said that I didn't take a shine to Angie all those years ago, it wasn't because that wasn't my style; he just wasn't my type. But you, Teenth, you're exactly my type, and I've got a whole bunch of friends who'd be just over the moon, so to speak, about making you their smutter too."

That's enough for Teenth. He moves in fast and I see the glint of whatever it is in his right hand. I open my arms, as if welcoming a loved one home and, as a burst of blood jets into my eye, I look over Teenth's head and smile at the warden who is standing at the viewing window, staring down in horror as Teenth punctures me again and again.

You don't need to spend too many years in Belmarsh to know that the warden always looks in on the gym at 3pm on Sunday.

Smoking Jacket

It was as I was scraping the old floral wallpaper off that I realised that the plaster covering the entire internal wall of the Gallery Room would need pulling down and plastering again. Some areas would come off after a good steaming, but in others the patterns of gardenias seemed to have laid roots of their own and were inseparable from the soft crumbly plaster beneath. Initially, bits of this plaster came off in small lumps, but by the time I'd reached the end of the wall, some significant sections had fallen off and it was clear that papering over the cracks really wasn't going to be possible. In order to get the job done properly, the whole lot would need to come off.

I put up the plastic sheeting around the doors and over the few large pieces of furniture that I couldn't move out for the decorating and began to pull it down. The internal walls had clearly absorbed some dampness over the years and they came down in great dusty blasts with ease.

At the back of the lower ground floor there is nothing but the earth and rock of Royal Hill, but the front looks out over the long landscaped garden that slopes down towards the Connelly's house, before the view finally opens up north towards the Isle of Dogs and Canary Wharf. The Connelly family have owned Elm Rise for practically as long as Ted's family have owned Apple Tree House, and the gentle rivalry between the families, about whether the more elevated location is of greater merit for its views or the lower for its closer proximity to the pub, is alleged to have been debated for over a century.

In certain areas, some of the wooden slats behind the plaster are also rotten and I snap these off too, pulling out the rusty nails that were left behind by the fickle wood with the hammer claw. There are old newspapers stuffed in the cavity as insulation, ancient old copies of *The Times* from 1968 – I am fascinated to read headlines and fragments of stories from when I was 23, mainly about the assassination of Martin Luther King, but also the successful test flight of the Apollo 6 space shuttle. Underneath the newspapers, as I sweep out the deep dust drifts, I find a small green circular tin, a wooden ball about the size of a golf ball and a little hand-made wooden whistle. There appears to be a mouse hole behind the insulation cavity and I can feel a slight draught coming through, but I think that if I keep on digging, I might not stop until I get to Lewisham! I decide it is time for a cup of tea, so I take my discoveries along with some of the more interesting fragments of the newspaper through to the kitchen.

On the tin is written ;T. J. Pickering & Sons Peppermints'. It is empty. The ball is roughly made and unadorned, and the whistle was the same as the ones my father showed us how to make when I was a child. He would take his old, very sharp, immaculately kept pocket knife out of its small canvas sheath and cut a short length of willow stick, then, using the handle, he would tap the stick evenly up and down its length until the bark was loosened from the wood. Next he would slide the wood out from the bark and cut it into two lengths, one long and one short. Taking the short piece of wood, he would slice away a thin reed along its length and then insert the remaining piece of wood back into the bark casing. Finally, he would cut holes along the length of the bark and then, sliding his longer piece of wood beneath the holes and blowing through the end, he would play 'March of the Animals'. He always cleaned the blade of his knife for several minutes after use. It was extremely sharp and shiny.

Whenever I think of my father, I always imagine him in his pinstripe black and red smoking jacket, standing in the conservatory with my mother, Uncle Henry and Auntie Sarah. He always stood very erect and moved well.

I look again at the newspapers, dominated by two headlines: one terrible and one hopeful. Both would pave the way to momentous events – the passing of the civil rights act in the US, and humankind landing on the moon. There isn't much else of note – a child sex killer is jailed at Woolwich Crown Court and an elephant escapes from London Zoo, but is caught munching grass on Primrose Hill. There is a grainy black and white photo of some bemused picnickers and a nonchalant elephant.

I must zone out for a while, because I suddenly notice that my Lapsang Souchong is cold and I am still holding the tea-stained paper.

The next day Ted and I pick up our grandson, Paul, who is 10, who we are looking after for a few days. Carole and Graham have decided to go and spend a long weekend away with just the two of them to see if they can work things out. I let Paul ride in the front seat as he enjoys identifying the different makes of cars with Ted as we drive along and, besides, I like to talk to Millie, who calmly sits in her basket in the boot and watch out of the back window at the world receding behind us. Sometimes I feel the future is becoming less important to me than the past.

When we get to Blackheath, Paul takes out his kite and I help him to get it launched, while Millie scrambles around at our feet, making a general nuisance of herself. Once he has it in the air, I walk over to Ted, who is hunched over on a bench, staring intently at his Blackberry phone. I look at the screen and note the grimy edges and multitude of scratches. There are a few other kite flyers out and watching the lines against the cloudy sky seems to stir something long dormant within me. A shaft of sunlight is moving over Lewisham to the south of us and gulls are crying. So many gulls in London now.

Ted has been a councillor for most of his working life and it has always been extremely important to him. I remember when he was first elected. I had just given birth to Carole. There was a distinct moment when Ted was forced to choose between being at my side for the birth and making the final push with the election campaign. I never queried his decision, but he would often justify it afterwards by saying those final efforts had made all the difference. He never really

226

explained how exactly. Truth be told, he always kept a barrier between me and his work. I had once complained about the amount of time he put into his job and how it would be nice if he could spend more time with his family. He had responded by saying that perhaps *I* didn't care about my community, but he did and, if his work bothered me, the best he could do was try and keep it out of my hair by working more from the office. I tried to explain that this was not what I was saying, but he steam-rollered me. After this, he spent more time working than ever. I often felt that the words I spoke to him landed on angular ground and were frequently upended by the time they settled. He was, and still is, an excellent politician.

I look back at Ted: white wispy long strands of hair flail around restlessly on his large pink shiny head, strands that will be combed over for council meetings, neighbourhood regeneration events and children's club launches, which he does voluntary support work for. His long years of bad posture have given him a slightly hunched back but done nothing to conceal his large flabby belly. He licks his moist lips often and he puffs occasionally, despite the fact that he has been sat for some time now.

I do not love him. I have fought to hold this thought at bay for forty-six years; after all, we were married and our first son was on the way within six months of meeting each other, so what good was it to think of such things? But now I do not care; our children have all grown up and are busy loving and not loving people of their own. I sit there for a moment and watch Paul, our grandson, as he runs backwards, jerking his arms to try and generate lift, and I accept that I do not and never have loved my husband.

I know I should be feeling anxious, considering what I am planning to do. I do not have considerable financial resources at my disposal. Aside from annual visits to France and one family holiday in Crete, I have never left the UK. I imagine verdant green fields after the monsoon rain, with the towering Himalayas behind.

I feel a tremendous sense of relief and with it comes a burst of childlike joy and excitement.

Seemingly unbidden, an Indian Elephant lumbers across my vision – something disturbs me. Its trunk seems to have sprouted tree roots and is overlong and dragging on the floor. Its teeth are hidden, but I imagine them to be broken and bloodied. It is very dark against the azure Indian sky and its skin seems broken into huge plates that weep crimson at the boundaries. The black elephant sees me with its hollow, empty eye, turns and begins swaying towards me.

The sky has darkened and rain begins to fall on the heath. The kite is wound back in.

We get back to the house and Ted goes to his study. Paul is happy reading his book up in the spare room, i.e. playing some sort of *Warcraft* computer game, so I make tea, go to the drawing room and switch on my tablet. After a little digging, I find the story. The name of the man that was convicted at Woolwich Crown Court for the child sex killing back in 1968 was Seamus O'Hara. I knew it – this was what had been playing on my mind all day. The murder had shocked the whole community and really fired up tensions between local people and travellers. I remembered Seamus from the few times he'd come to school round about when I was 13. He was handsome and wild; too wild, in fact, for Abbey Wood School, where I'd seen him punch Mr Astley after he tried to stop him from walking out of his class because he said his brother was in trouble. Strange thing was that his brother Jed had actually been run over and rushed to hospital that afternoon. Justified or not, he'd been expelled, and the only time I heard about him after that was in the court briefs and then eventually the little Annie Reed murder, for which he was convicted. After Annie Reed's abduction, the local community searched for her for three weeks before her emaciated, tortured and sexually abused body was found on wasteland near the traveller's site. In the eyes of the law, Seamus fitted the crime so well there was no real room for other possibilities. He always maintained his innocence, but the police were doubtless happy to get Seamus off the streets by then, regardless of his guilt. Due to the nature of the crime, the judge instructed the jury to lock him up and throw away the key.

I realise I've been sat like this for a while and outside the room it's gotten dark. For a moment, the room seems menacing, as if it turned down the lights and is now watching to see how I'll respond. This house has always felt dark.

I make my way up the creaky stairs to check on Paul. His light is off and he is turned to the wall, but when I go over to tuck him in, his console on his bedside cabinet is still warm.

"Go to sleep now," I say.

"I can't sleep," he replies in a wide-awake voice.

"What's the matter?"

"The house is making noises," he says, turning to me and sitting up.

"It's just the wind, my love."

"I don't know." Funny how he says 'I don't know' when he doesn't believe you.

"Well, I do. It's just an old house and old houses make funny old noises. Would you like me to read you a story?"

"Granny, I'm 10!"

"10! Never! Come on, settle down and I'll read you the one about the hungry caterpillar –"

"Granny! OK, OK, I'm going to sleep."

"I'll be just down the hall, OK?" I give him a kiss on the forehead as he settles back under the duvet.

"Night Granny."

"Love you," I say.

I pull Paul's bedroom door shut and, moments after, I hear Ted closing a door downstairs. Millie whimpers in her basket in the kitchen. Rain is beginning to fall on the skylight above me. I go to our bedroom at the other end of the landing and find Ted is lying in bed, fast asleep, with his reading light still on. I shiver.

It's just the wind, my love.

I don't know.

Ted usually has meetings all day on Friday and the next morning Paul declares he wants to go and hang out with Adrian at the Connelly's, so I have the place to myself. Despite sleeping badly, I am determined to crack on with the Gallery Room.

I stand back to look at the job with my steaming 'World's Greatest Granny' cup of smoky Lapsang Souchong in hand. The rain increases with intensity for a moment against the thick glass wall behind me. My eye is drawn to the mouse hole. I place my tea on the stepladder and walk over and take a closer look. I squat down and put my finger into the dark hollow cautiously, not wishing to be nipped by any still-resident mice or rats: nothing. I pull away some more of the wooden slats and plaster and put my hand, then arm, into the dark: still nothing. I imagine my arm being watched from inside the darkness and quickly withdraw it. I stand slowly, my knees and back complaining after the short spell squatting, and look at the hole. The rain is so hard, it sounds like it's trying to get in.

I remember my tea, go back to the stepladder and then head upstairs, through the kitchen, across the reception hall, into Ted's study, and turn on his desktop. I take long hot swigs as I listen to the tiny components whirr and spin into life.

Password – APPLETREE
Incorrect – appletree
Incorrect – Appletree
Incorrect – APPLETREE1

Incorrect. This isn't going to work – clearly he has not used the same passcode that we use for all of our joint bank accounts and emails. I try the desk drawers but they are locked. I look around the study for inspiration, but draw a blank. I go upstairs and open Ted's wardrobe. I rummage through the first row of clothes, finding nothing of interest, then push a little deeper. In amongst the older shirts, suits and coats at the back of the wardrobe, I see the familiar black and red pinstripe of my father's old smoking jacket. I did not know that Ted had kept it. I take it out, remove the hanger and slip my hands down the silky arms, pull the jacket around me, close my eyes and there, beneath the musty smell of camphor and mothballs, is the sweet smokiness of my father's tobacco.

I frown to think of my father's smoking jacket spending all these years next to Ted's clothes, growing steadily less immaculate, as everything of Ted's does. Suddenly I'm thinking of Ted's grimy, scratched mobile phone screen and I flush at the memory. I return to Ted's study, still wearing my father's smoking jacket, and type in SEAGULL68 – the screen leaps into life.

I sit at the desk for two hours until I can stomach no more, then I return to the Gallery Room and pick up the claw hammer.

I have made a hole the size of an elephant's head when the phone starts ringing.

Scrubs

I pronounce Seamus O'Hara dead at 14.26. He had fought to hang on through the night but eventually succumbed to his injuries, which were grievous. It is a struggle for four of us to lift him from the bed in the prison ward. He is not an enormous man, but surprisingly dense, it would seem.

I inform the coroner (who, as usual, tells me to take a running jump, this time off a short pier – I have yet to adequately gauge the coroner's sense of humour) and the police, though it is all something of a formality, since the attack was witnessed by the prison warden, the chief education officer and several other prison staff. Whether or not the instigator of the violence will be transferred to high security isolation or to a mental institution is yet to be determined, but either way he will not be mixing with the general population of inmates at Belmarsh again if the warden has anything to do with it. And he has a lot to do with it.

I issue the death certificate and finally, late as usual, I change and ready myself to go home. As I pick up my jacket to leave, I notice that the bins have not been cleared out and yesterday's bloody scrubs are still looking at me from within the clear plastic bin liner. Seamus had been stabbed fifteen times before the guards managed to pull his frenzied assailant off him. One of the puncture wounds had ruptured his carotid artery, so the bleeding was profuse.

As we rushed him out of the gymnasium, helped by two of the prison officers, I kept pressure on his neck wound with one hand and held my other on his thigh, where he was also losing a lot of blood. I was blessed with a very fine medical orderly, Le Tran, who had joined my team around three years ago following a drug bust on a huge Vietnamese skunk farming operation in Woolwich. Le Tran was holding compressed pads to some of the wounds in Seamus' chest and belly. As my prognosis of the situation was not rosy, I said to Seamus quietly as we rolled along the corridor:

"God go with you, Seamus O'Hara."

"Never mind me, Doc," he'd said, spitting blood as he spoke (whether this was due to the puncture hole in his cheek or the internal bleeding, I couldn't tell). "Tell him to keep an eye on Frankie and Gunderson, will you? Oh, and Doc, could you apply a little more pressure to that hole near me thigh - I think I'm getting blood on me smutters!"

At this, Le Tran had burst out laughing and even one of the officers - Parker, I think his name is - had stifled a laugh.

"This is no laughing matter, Seamus O'Hara," I'd said. "And I do not want to see either of you two encouraging him further," I continued, looking sternly at Le Tran and Parker in turn. "This situation is very grave."

"Ah c'mon, Doc," said Seamus gently. "You need to loosen up. Life's too short," he'd choked and then taken a big swallow. "Or maybe too long, but either way, you need to let yourself go once in a while."

"Perhaps, Seamus," I replied. "But laughter will not improve my orderly's ability to concentrate on tending your wounds and the convulsions may increase your rate of bleeding."

"Ah that's OK Doc, I've had it anyway, I'm just glad this old man could do something for his boys before the end. Here, try this one Doc - did you see the one in the paper about the man who had to have five toy horses surgically removed from his arsehole?" Seamus paused for a moment for comic effect and then said: "Doctors have described his condition as stable."

All three of them had laughed at that one.

"That's enough," I'd cried, but Seamus hadn't stopped until I'd got an oxygen mask over his face.

I smile as I look at those bloody scrubs and I say another prayer for Seamus O'Hara.

I arrive home and can tell immediately that Patty is angry with me for being late once again. I know we need to mend some fences, but it will happen; we have never lost faith in each other before. I look in on Joshua, who is quietly studying, and then go for a shower. I go through my systematic cleaning, washing away the dirt of the day, using a scrubbing brush for the actual and the remembering and releasing of any impure or uncharitable thoughts I have had during the day to cleanse the metaphorical. I have missed church two weekends in a row and am currently only too conscious of the challenges that my work lays before me.

Ten days ago I was invited to sit on a panel at an evening seminar over at the University of London Union. The subject matter under scrutiny was the role of cognitive behavioural therapy in the treatment of physical injuries. Among the other panel members was a Hungarian mathematician, who had some fascinating theories on our understanding of cognition. She presented a hypothesis that until now, all fields of science, from chemistry to cosmology, were essentially understood at their most fundamental level through mathematical theory, except one: cognition. However, over the last four years, her analytical work had shown that not only could all cognitive behaviour be determined through mathematical theory, but she also claimed that through her research she had generated a workable algebraic formula that could actually reflect the mechanics of cognition. Her talk generated a heated discussion and, during the interval, I approached her and asked how I might find out more about her so called 'fifth discipline'. She said that she had some free time after the seminar and suggested that we go and discuss the matter further over a drink. We exchanged phone numbers in order to organise where to meet, as she said she had to pop back to her hotel room briefly after the seminar.

I called Patty as soon as the seminar was over and explained that I would be late and then waited for a call from Doctor Orsolya Wlodarcyzk, or Orsi as she preferred to be called. After fifteen minutes, I received a text message from Orsi suggesting we meet at the Jeremy Bentham pub on University Street. I arrived at the pub moments before Orsi and, after buying us both a drink, we took a table in the corner of the pub. Orsi then proceeded to relate a most disturbing account of how her journey to discover the truth about cognition and her concomitant ground-breaking research had turned her life upside down. The scientific community and the investment companies that fund so much of their research had quickly appreciated that if her theory became accepted knowledge, it would make many of the basic accepted *a priori* assumptions of our scientific understanding redundant and, without these foundations, huge towers of investment would collapse. Orsi said that her work had been undermined at every juncture and her life had even been threatened.

Naturally, I was horrified to hear her story and said surely the police could do something, but Orsi replied that these huge companies were far too clever to leave any evidence of their menacing tactics. She told me that she desperately needed protection and she felt that nobody could help her. She wouldn't even feel safe going back to her hotel room tonight. Of course, I offered to escort her back to her hotel, but she said it was more than that; she was terrified that these people would get into her room in the night and she would only really feel safe if someone would stay with her tonight and suddenly I felt a little foolish. I told Orsi that I was sure that nothing of the sort would happen and I thought that she'd probably just felt a bit jetlagged from her flight and she'd surely feel right as rain in the morning. I told her it was late and I should probably be getting on.

It was at this point that something about Orsi's demeanour changed and she began to talk about how she had seen three cars outside the pub as we'd walked in: one red, one blue and one grey Mazda. I said that I didn't understand the significance of this and she said yes I did. Then Doctor Orsolya Wlodarcyzk said that I knew her ex-boyfriend drove a grey Mazda and then began to talk about how her ex-boyfriend was not going to rule her life and that she was entitled to go on with her research and she was entitled to find another and be in love again and so on. She picked up her coat and finished her drink, all the while muttering venomous remarks under her breath, and walked out of the pub.

I sat on the stool for a moment, shocked and appalled at what had just happened, then I realised that Orsi was clearly experiencing some deep emotional distress and that the right course of action would be to make sure that at least she got safely back to her hotel. I put on my coat and walked out of the pub. As I did so, I received a text message from Orsi. It read:

> Fuck you you sick fucks you think you can fuck women then decide who they can or cannot fuck after you done fucking them fuck you

I could see Orsi up ahead walking towards Tottenham Court Road, but I felt it best to not chase after her to try and clear my name. Another message came through:

> Go date someone else that illuminati assigns for you

I followed about a hundred yards behind her, just to make sure that nothing bad happened to her, as I couldn't help feeling partly responsible for causing the situation. Another message:

> I told you already that I will not get in contact with anyone who has anything to do with either illuminati or my exboyfriend

Orsi reached her hotel and as soon as I had seen her walk safely inside, I headed straight to the tube station. Exiting at London Bridge Station, I composed a message back to Orsi, being as pleasant and reassuring as I could:

> Hello Orsi, I'm very sorry about the misunderstanding this

evening. I wish you well with your research and I hope you feel better in the morning after a good sleep. Please believe I am nothing to do with your ex-boyfriend or the illuminati, best wishes Akwasi

No sooner had I sent it, than another message from her came through:

Fuck you you fucks go control each others sick lives and leave me the fuck alone. My sick ex will not control my life. He can keep me as a prison and use me as a slave if that's his sick way of keeping himself fit but he will not fucking interfere with my love life. Fuck you

And then before I'd even finished reading the last, another message arrives:

Yes you are. You are just not aware

I reached home, climbed the stairs to the flat and told Patty exactly what had happened. I showed her the text messages also. Patty believed my version of the story, but she still seemed very unhappy and looked at the text messages for a long time. Later, when we'd lain in bed, I'd tried to cuddle her, but she had pushed me away. I told her that I knew that the text messages looked bad, but that she had to trust me that nothing untoward had happened, nor had I wished it to. She told me again that she believed me on that front, but she couldn't believe I had been so easily taken in by this woman and got myself into this situation in the first place. She said she thought she had married an intelligent man and that she was very disappointed in me. Then she rolled over and went to sleep. I said a silent prayer for poor paranoid Doctor Wlodarcyzk and then tried to get to sleep myself.

It's been ten nights now since Patty and I lay down together as man and wife. She is clearly thoroughly annoyed. I realise that this will not just pass by waiting. Patty's faith in me as a capable man has been shaken and I must demonstrate to her, in some new, unexpected way, that I have evolved into a better man in order to rectify my error. Patty is giving me the opportunity to grow.

This is the way it has always been and men should not ignore these opportunities lightly.

I dry myself thoroughly, dress and go down to the lower floor of our duplex for dinner. Patty has made a rather nasty carbonara, as if further evidence of my continued disapproval was required. Joshua munches silently with a vacant stare, aware of neither his parent's spat nor the bland taste of his dinner. Patty avoids my eye unless I ask her for something, to which she will respond with a perfunctory smile as she passes before returning to her avoidance. We eat in silence.

I finish my plate and, without bothering to wipe the leftover sauce with a piece of bread, I take off my glasses and as I polish the lenses, I say to no-one in particular:

"Did anyone read the article in the paper today regarding the gentleman who had surgery to remove five horses from his rectum?" Joshua is looking at me with his mouth open and a forkful of tagliatelle swaying above his plate. Patty is staring at me with a mixture of horror and confusion on her face.

"The doctor has described his condition as stable," I conclude and put my glasses back on. After a moment of silence that feels longer than it actually is, Joshua bursts out laughing. He puts down his forkful of tagliatelle and slaps his thighs and says:

"That's a good one Dad, oh that's funny."

I am looking at Patty, who is looking at me with a stern face, but then two deep dimples appear on either side of her face and she sees that I see them and finally she lowers her eyes and covers her mouth and shakes quietly in silent mirth.

Long live the king.

Thank you, Seamus.

Joshua and I wash the dishes, with me carefully scrubbing off the burnt remains on the bottom of the pans (that must have been where all the flavour went), and Joshua drying them nice and thoroughly under my peripheral scrutiny. Once we have finished, I stroll through to the TV area of our studio and, standing behind the couch on which Patty is coiled, I say as casually as I can:

"I thought I might go for a jog."

"I thought you might too," she says. This is our code for me seeking consent for sexual activity later. Patty likes me to go for a jog before lovemaking, so that I am more relaxed and less hurried with my duties as a husband. I have received a green light. I put on my tracksuit and trainers and, after a few warm-up exercises, I bounce out into the night.

I decide to do a short circuit as I splash along the puddled streets towards Tower Bridge: over the Thames along the north bank of the river to St Pauls and back over the Millennium Footbridge and home. I do not wish to be too sapped of energy and enthusiasm after almost two weeks without.

I cross over Tooley Street, past the open air theatre where they have such wonderful events, and then City Hall, before pumping up the steps onto Tower Bridge - I take the east side, as the west is frequently closed to pedestrians. I jog towards the first tower and there, where the pavement swings out around the base of the tower, I see a man climbing awkwardly up onto the safety wall. I pick up my step and, as I get nearer to him, I see that he has the movements of a man who is inebriated. I slow down, as I do not wish to surprise him, in case this will cause him to lose his footing.

"Excuse me," I say. "Would you like me to help you down from there?"

He is a very fat man, with a pink bald head, and he is puffing from the exertion of climbing onto the wall.

"No, that's OK," he slurs. "I can get down myself." He turns to look at me, swaying dangerously as he does so and almost losing his balance. "Whoops, almost got me..." he mutters something unintelligible and then fixes me with his bleary eyes and says. "My wife, she let out the little girl. She let out Annie. She knows..." He shows me a plastic carrier bag and says, "I got some flowers, but it'll do no good. She knows everything..."

I look at the clear plastic bag with the flowers inside and the red petals look like the blood on my scrubs in the rubbish bag.

"I'm sure your wife would want to talk about this with you. I'd like to talk about this with you. Perhaps if you just climbed down and we had a chat and, if you still feel the same way, then you can climb right on back up there. How would that be?"

He puts the bag of flowers next to his chest and then buttons his coat around them.

"No," he says matter of factly, and tips forward and out of sight. I run forward in time to see him hit the water below, a splash of red on the stone promontory that he hit on the way down.

I cannot follow him. I cannot swim.

I run for help.

Swimming Trunks

I don't really get back to sleep once I've brought Barbara back to bed: I lie down next to her and listen to her gentle snoring.

She sleepwalks when she's stressed. I can still remember the first time it happened. Scared the hell out of me. I'd woken up to find her standing at the end of the bed, staring at me in a manner that was none too friendly. That in itself was enough to give me a fright, but it was once I'd gotten over the initial shock and looked into her eyes and found nothing that I recognised there that I got the real deep shiver down my spine. I remember speaking to her, asking her if everything was OK, and she'd just started talking, except they weren't real words; it was just babbling that came out of her mouth, like she was speaking in tongues or something. Eventually I had to force myself to get out of bed and put my arm round her and, with words of comfort, guide her back to bed. I'd told her to go back to sleep and in an instant she had.

Right about that time was when Barb's dad was really sick and she'd been running round trying to manage her part-time job, looking after Josh, who was still only six, and trying to look after her dad as well. It hadn't lasted long; as soon as I realised what was going on, I'd given my notice to St John's Ambulance and, pretty soon, I was able to take over looking after Josh and Barb's dad and take the pressure off Barb. I had plenty of savings to see us through and soon after the sleepwalking stopped.

There had only been a couple of other occasions when Barb had suffered from somnambulism and they'd been tough times for me too. Mostly because I stopped sleeping at night, so that I could keep a watchful eye over her, grabbing power naps whenever I could during the day in order to be able to maintain the nocturnal vigils. I just couldn't bear the thought of her wandering out of the house in such a vulnerable state. Thank God nothing had ever happened, and if I've got anything to do with it, nothing ever will. Touch wood.

I think about what might be troubling Barb until the sky gets light in the east and then I decide to get up to go for a cigarette. It is as I sit up and swing my legs over the side of the bed that my head spins, and I realise that the aching in all my joints and muscles, that I've been subconsciously aware of since yesterday, was the precursor to an invasion of bacteria, or a virus, or something in between. Well, that's all I need. Maybe that's what had made me feel light-headed after our dinner the other night – I'd felt a bit worried at the time, but then when I saw it was tickling Barb so much, me thinking I was drunk after only drinking mineral water all night, I'd relaxed a bit. I'm such a dope sometimes.

I force myself out of bed, go downstairs and, after I've put the kettle on, I step outside the kitchen door for a fag, making sure the door is pulled to behind me – Barb hates being woken up by the smell of my ciggies. It's not raining, but it looks like another wet day is on its way. There's still a good while yet before the actual sun comes up, but the birds are already singing their hearts out. Mind you, a lot of them have got used to the city lights and stay up all night. Amazing that all these animals have got so close to humans, that they might not be able to do without us any more: the city birds that flit through our streets at night; the foxes that thrive on what we throw away; the cats and dogs and even the fish in our homes (though I think the fish had less say in the matter than the rest). There is a word for it. Something to do with yoghurt... Probiotnics? No? Well, it'll come to me. I stretch and it feels both better and worse than normal, due to the cold that's coming on.

Ill again. Why do I always get ill? When I was young, I used to swim almost every day, so I used to think my constantly snotty nose was caused by the chlorine in the pool water. Whenever I reached into my pockets or my bag, there'd be wet tissues or wet swimming trunks, and because I absolutely would not give up the one, I accepted the other. I was one of the youngest boys to ever swim in the national finals and probably could've swam at an international level if I hadn't given it up. Still, some things are worth more than fame and fortune, and if I did it all over again, I wouldn't change a thing.

I finish my fag, make coffee, take a quick shower and put my cycle gear on; best thing with a cold is to fight it - if you sit back for a moment, it'll hold you there for a week. I give Barb a kiss on the head, being careful not to wake her, and go down to the garage to get my bike. We can only really afford to run one car, but it's no problem, because I love to cycle. Not only does it keep me fit, it also means I get a breath of fresh air every morning (as long as I'm early enough to avoid the rush hour traffic) and it draws a natural line between work and home. Sometimes, when I've had a hard day, I can get on the bike in a right old temper, but, by the time I get home, everything has been cycled and I'm Mr Serene again.

I must admit, the cleaning job does have its challenges and there's times I long to be back in a job that pushes my brain a bit harder, but times are hard and - like I keep telling Barb - there's a lot of poor folks out there who aren't lucky enough to even have a job right now, so I've no real cause for complaint. But still, people don't treat you with a great deal of respect when you work as a cleaner. Some of the students in particular at UCL have not yet learned how to climb into another man's skin and walk around in it, as Atticus says in *To Kill a Mockingbird*. Most of them will go out of their way to avoid you at all costs; some of them throw rubbish at you, and then there's an even smaller group who make the effort to talk to you, but then these ones are generally so deeply patronising that you end up wishing that they'd thrown a Coke can at you and been on their way.

There's one particular student who has taken the time to learn my routine around the Science Faculty and he waits for me diligently every Tuesday and Thursday morning between 9am and 10am, which is when I do the lavatory cleaning. No matter which circuit I'm on, and there are five of them which Pauline and I rotate around, he will be waiting, reading the *Financial Times* in a cubicle, and no sooner does he hear me walk in and begin to scrub the toilet bowls, than he starts spouting out some nonsense like:

"Here is the goal, whence motion on his race
Starts: motionless the centre and the rest
All moved around."

He then steps out of the cubicle and calls out, "Good morning John," then he washes his hands and leaves. I never say a thing and I have no idea how he got my name. Now here's the weird bit: whenever he uses a cubicle, he will leave a small sticker on the cubicle door or the toilet lid, or wherever (it's often hid and I have to go look for it before I can scratch it off), and written on the sticker it says 'Primum mobile' and also, in the toilet bowl, there will be an immaculate, enormous turd which will require flushing. I looked up the meaning of 'primum mobile' one evening and it is a medieval astronomical term meaning 'first moved', so I guess he's just trying to say something clever about his first movement of the day. I asked Pauline about it, but she said she'd never seen him. Mind you, she generally has to make sure the men's toilets are clear before she cleans them, just as I have to with the women's, so she wouldn't have. She told me I should complain about it, or say something to him – you know, tell him to flush after he's used the toilet – but I honestly don't mind. I've seen a lot worse and I almost look forward to hearing what he's going to say each week and finding out where he will have hidden the sticker. I think I might even miss his enormous stools if I were to show up one Tuesday or Thursday and find an empty bowl after he vacated the room. I can't begin to imagine what Barbara would think if I told her about this strange little episode, which has being going on for almost a year now (including during holiday time – he is very diligent). She'd really think I'd lost my marbles, never mind me getting drunk on water!

I like to take different routes through London: I've lived here all my life, but I still find new places and things to see, even if it's just that something has changed since I last went through. The city is constantly evolving and it fascinates me to watch the people and everything that they bring ebb and flow around me: the fashions, the styles, the cultures, the businesses, the restaurants, the music, the archaeology; everything in a constant state of flux. I fancy parks today, so I opt for Queenstown Road, which will take me down to Battersea Park and then over Chelsea Bridge, up through Belgravia and between Hyde Park and St James' Park. Then I'll freestyle it up through the back streets of Chinatown and finally cut across to Gower Street, which will take me to the front door of UCL.

Even after a proper breakfast (i.e. coffee and a fag), I'm still well early after Barb's sleepwalking, but I've only been going about five minutes before things start to go awry: roadworks on the Chelsea Bridge. So I swing the old Condor onto Battersea Park Road and head up towards Vauxhall Bridge. As I'm early, I cut through to the Thames Path so I can follow the bank of the river. After a bit of weaving and a little hop up onto a pavement, which will do my aluminium rims not a bit of good, I turn onto the waterfront and face towards the sunrise, which is just coming over the horizon. The first rays of morning light are catching the clouds overhead and, for a few short moments, the reflected daylight seems to become polarised by the clouds, as if they took all the light that was there and somehow inverted it.

Symbiotic; that's the word. I knew I'd get it! The light changes back to normal grey, which has pretty much been the standard for this year. The end of my enlightenment.

Up ahead in the distance I can see a figure crouching down next to a person in a wheelchair. It looks like the crouching figure is giving the person in the wheelchair something. Suddenly it starts to rain heavily and I lean forward and then back, to put on my lights, and when I look up again at the two figures the one man has lifted the other out of the wheelchair and laid him on the wall that overlooks the river.

Then he pushes him in.

I almost fall off my bike. I have to stop because I don't think I know how to cycle all of a sudden. The figure looking at the river turns and walks away. I force myself to put down my bicycle, which has become inoperable, and make myself walk forwards. This helps and suddenly I can jog and then I am sprinting towards the spot where the wheelchair now stands alone. I glance at the river as I race along and see it is swollen and brown-beige in colour from all the sediment that has been dragged from England's fields by the floods. I hit my spot about five yards from the wheelchair and dive right over the wall.

I fall.

Then I'm under, sinking deep into the murk, my arms flailing wildly from side to side as they pull me down looking for a trace. The current is strong and I think I might be getting dragged too far. I try to turn, but this is hopeless. My lungs are burning, but I ignore them. I pull hard into the current and suddenly my arms are in silt and I'm disorientated and kicking and swinging wildly. Too long now, much too long. Suddenly I feel stone under my left hand. The wall. Far too long. A hand. I try to hold it. I try to hold it. Long. Gone.

Something about sound underwater. Like cushion. Like coming home. Safety in the arms of your mother. Safety in the womb of your mother. Regression. Like the distant sound of the television, when you lie feverish on the couch with another day off school. The sound of screeching children in the swimming baths, like Spanish whales, as you hold the steps, keeping yourself under, just a little longer, counting ninety, ninety-one, ninety-two, but two minutes is so far – how does Danny do it?! Keep counting as the Spanish whales ring around you. You stand in front of your father in your swimming trunks blubbing. He smiles, he says it's just a race. He takes out his handkerchief and wipes your nose and takes your hand.

The hand moves. I squeeze, I kick. My head screams, up, up, up...

Stetson

I have a recurring dream. It plays out over many scenarios, but the story remains the same.

In one version I am the first person to arrive in North America. How I have got there is unimportant, but what *is* important is that I am the only human. I move west, diligently surviving: hunting birds and rabbits, finding berries and mushrooms, drinking from clear mountain streams, sheltering in caves and bivouacs that I make from bracken and branches. Always alone and always moving further from humanity. Each new vista, sunset and starscape is heart-stoppingly beautiful, virgin and untouched and, as I make my way, a melancholic little tune loops beneath my hat.

"Moon River, wider than a mile,
I'm crossing you in style someday,
You dream maker, you heartbreaker,
Wherever you're going I'm going your way."

Month by month, the tune becomes sadder and sadder as the terrible truth of my situation deepens within me: I am utterly alone and will never see my own kind again. But still I press on. Still, I hope.

Then, in that godlike way of dreams, my perspective pans out and I become aware of time spinning forwards. The slow creep of days that I had been living accelerates into weeks, months, years, decades, centuries. I watch my body reclaimed by the earth, next to the riverbank where I died, the ribs turning mossy before disappearing under a flood. I see new arrivals, pioneer groups and individuals radiating out across the land, building structures and settlements of increasing size and complexity, initially fitting into the fragile mosaic of existing ecological niches before drilling them out and replacing them with carpeted, macadamised cityscapes of steel and glass. Suddenly the land is full and there is not a starlit desert road without a warm human body driving through its darkness.

It is at this precise moment in my dream, when I am linked to and aware of every human on a teeming continent, that I realise that I am truly alone, for even at this moment of complete immersion, I am still separate. And as the sad little tune plays on, I understand, more than ever, complete despair, for when I was alone I had hope, but now I am together I have none.

It is early and I am sitting in the darkness of my room, tracing the petals around the edge of my tattoo. My finger then follows the letters of the name emblazoned on the scroll that lies across the rose, as it often will. Light worms around the edges of the thick black curtains and finds its way to my ink-stained skin, seeking out the years that are hidden there. It's a hell of a thing to lose your child; to lose that which can bring you closest to togetherness. It's hard to carry on loving a world that can take away your most prized treasure and abuse it, beat it, murder it, leaving the empty shell discarded in the wasteland.

Not many people walk in Abbey Wood or Bostall Wood anymore. Years of accumulated tales about flashers, hoodies with crack pipes and rampant Dobermans are enough for people to turn their shuddery backs to their floral curtains and the woods beyond, hunching a little closer to the cold blue light of their TVs. It was not always this way. On any given Sunday afternoon in 1968, nothing but the meanest of weather would keep the good people of Abbey Wood from taking a post-roast constitutional stroll in the woods. But there was nothing mean about the weather on that particular Sunday afternoon. The warm April sunshine lit up the lazy trajectory of gadflies, as it dappled through the canopy. Annie ran ahead of us, her hair flashing gold as she jumped over logs and ducked under low branches at the edge of our sight, an ephemeral little bouncing sprite made of fragile bones and flushed capillaries. Annie at her happiest, armed with her wooden ball, the wooden whistle I made for her and a tin of peppermints. She was muddy-legged, rosy-cheeked and curious. She was ready to take on the world. Bouncing along at the back of her head, she wore the little cowgirl hat that Uncle Derek, who was over from Texas a month back, brought for her along with a *Moon River* LP, which she would play over and over. He was in London on business and brought Stetson hats for all of us. Lilly refused to wear hers out, saying they looked silly, but Annie and I wore ours proudly along and said "Howdy" to passers-by, lifting our hats respectfully.

Annie ran to us, her shoulders hunched forwards and hands cupped carefully in front of her. She didn't speak, but her excitement was palpable in her movements. She was practically vibrating with delight at her discovery. Reaching me, she looked up once and then, as I squatted down, she slowly opened her little hands. There within was a tiny frog. A frog so small it was hard to imagine a fat tadpole growing into it. I imagine that the transition from amorphous blob to detail and definition must have cost it mass, in order for the frog to end up so small.

I was waiting for her to not speak. She was almost eloquent for a five-year-old girl, but she rarely felt the need to use words. Some kind of meiotic rewiring engorged her capacity for physical expression and she was acutely aware of the impact of her behaviour on others. Words were only resorted to when she dealt with insensitive individuals or metaphysical matters.

"I think he'd like to be free," I finally whispered and she looked at me and smiled. She closed her hands carefully, stood and ran back into the trees, where I saw her squat again and release the frog, saying something quietly amphibian as it hopped from her hand.

That was when life was full. Only a few hours later, everything was empty.

My eyes look across the vast array of boxing journals and almanacs that line the book shelves on my wall as I remember the fruitless hours, crying myself hoarse, shouting her name over and over as my blurring vision searched for a trace of that golden flash in the woods once more, that little white cowgirl hat bouncing on the back of her head.

I pick up my Stetson. The inner rim is dark and smooth, with the appearance of leather, as if the hat has taken on characteristics of the living material it has contained for all these years. The rim and the pinched peak of the hat have lost their definition. The tiny buckle that can be altered to change the hat's calibre is rusted and would certainly break if meddled with. This hat has held me captive for forty-four years: a symbol of my failure as a father.

Outside on the landing, I hear movement. An early riser moving as quietly as they can up and down the stairs.

A sound like distant thunder finds my room and rumbles through my curtains.

Change is coming, the sound says. Change is here.

I walk to the curtains and, pulling them aside, I allow the daylight which I have denied my room for so many years to come flooding in. My eyes instinctively flinch before slowly widening and taking in the sight of the morning light flickering through the trees at the end of our garden, which lies shaded and waiting below. Over the fence in the communal yard, a man is unloading flowers from a van: box after box of open-topped cartons, flashing rainbows in the sunshine. In the distance, somewhere over towards Blackheath, a huge plume of black smoke is mushrooming up into the clear azure sky.

Below me, I hear the garden door open and see Tem stepping out. He is weighed down with bags and motorbike gear. He stands still for a long time as if lost in thought and, just when I wonder if there might be something wrong with him, his phone rings and the sound seemingly wakes him from his stupor. He takes out his phone, presses a button on it and then turns and re-enters the house, locking the door behind him.

Last night, when I dreamt the dream of separation, the dream didn't end as it usually does.

This time in the dream, I was a spaceman drifting into a new and unexplored sector of the universe. Once again I watched myself carefully maintaining my little bubble of life, as I drifted inexorably further from humanity, the void of space widening between myself and my own kind. As I tended the orchards and gardens that sustained me, under a star-studded glass roof, my work was accompanied by that same sad tune playing through the ship's speakers and haunting its corridors.

"Two drifters off to see the world
There's such a lot of world to see
We're after the same rainbow's end
Waiting 'round the bend
My huckleberry friend, Moon River and me."

Once again, I experienced with absolute certainty the awareness that I will never see another human again and, once more, I watched myself press on with hope in my heart despite myself.

Time accelerated and I saw myself grow old, finally lying down under an apple tree in my garden and breathing my last. Without my guidance, my ship was pulled into the atmosphere of a planet, where the overgrown jungle that held my remains burned up in a spectacular flash of a new world's sky. And then I saw more spacecraft, cruising through the void in my long cold wake, penetrating into this empty sector of space, first in pioneering little ships like my own, but soon these were followed by huge glittering city ships and geo-formers and my head became filled with the billions of voices and thoughts as my kind bred and flooded into every habitable planet. It is at that very moment, when I was connected to every soul in a galaxy and suddenly felt isolation and despair pressing in on me from all sides, pounding through my nerve endings and pressing me into a foetal ball, that everything suddenly stopped.

All the pain and sadness, the screaming sensory overload, was switched off like a light bulb and replaced with a warm darkness.

I felt safe and protected.

Light crept in gently through widening gaps in the walls around me and outside I could see two enormous faces smiling down: it was Annie and it was my younger self, with our cowboy hats on, looking down at me and smiling. A great surge of joy swept through me as I looked up at my beautiful little daughter and my younger self, so happy and contented to have found me.

After a long moment in my dream, my younger self whispered to Annie, "I think he'd like to be free," and then the walls closed in once more.

Outside I hear Tem's motorcycle starting up and then, after a couple of revs, the engine pulls away and I see him accelerate away down the road.

The doorbell rings. I place my old Stetson hat on top of my wardrobe and step out onto the landing, my head naked and open to the world.

Annie and I bounced back into the woods and there she opened her hands once more and whispered:

"Go and find your friends."

My little legs snapped like springs as I jumped to freedom.

Acknowledgements

Massive clapping hands to my cornerstones – family, friends and Lizzie – for your faith, patience and love.
Also special thanks to Hanne Busck-Nielsen and the members of the Freehand Writer's Group for all your support and encouragement.

'Green Grass'
Words & Music by Tom Waits & Kathleen Brennan
Copyright 2004 Jalma Music.
Universal Music Publishing MGB Limited.
All Rights Reserved. International Copyright Secured.
Used by permission of Music Sales Limited.

'Sins Of The Father'
Words & Music by Tom Waits & Kathleen Brennan
Copyright 2004 Jalma Music.
Universal Music Publishing MGB Limited.
All Rights Reserved. International Copyright Secured.
Used by permission of Music Sales Limited.

'Moon River'
Words & Music by Henry Mancini & Johnny Mercer
Copyright 1961 Sony/ATV Music Publishing
All Rights Reserved. International Copyright Secured.
Used by permission of Sony/ATV Music Publishing